WHO IS KILLING THE GIRLS OF BURTON CECIL?

"They think it was premeditated, that she wouldn't let him have his way with her and he was tired of her refusals. And if they're right about that, what on earth can be said in his favor? If it was a cold-blooded killing, I can't see the jury feeling much sympathy for him, can you?"

Maitland ignored the question. "But you don't believe that's how it happened?"

"No, I don't. I'll go further than that: I don't believe he did it at all. But I'd better tell you the whole story..."

"Yes," Maitland said, "I suppose that would be as well."

NOR LIVE SO LONG

Sara Woods

AVON
PUBLISHERS OF BARD, CAMELOT, DISCUS AND FLARE BOOKS

AVON BOOKS
A division of
The Hearst Corporation
105 Madison Avenue
New York, New York 10016

Copyright © 1986 by Probandi Books Limited
Published by arrangement with St. Martin's Press
Library of Congress Catalog Card Number: 86-3976
ISBN: 0-380-70478-1

First Avon Books Printing: March 1988

AVON TRADEMARK REG. U.S. PAT. OFF. AND IN OTHER COUNTRIES, MARCA
REGISTRADA, HECHO EN U.S.A.

Printed in the U.S.A.

K-R 10 9 8 7 6 5 4 3 2 1

'We that are young
shall never see so much, nor live so long.'
– *King Lear,* Act V, Scene iii

LONG VACATION, 1976

THURSDAY, 26th August

'They do say,' said Adam Shaw didactically, 'that lightning never strikes in the same place twice.'

A respectful silence followed this not entirely original thought. Adam, the landlord of the Mortal Man in Burton Cecil, was a local man, deliberate in all his ways, and so rarely given to utterance – except on the not infrequent occasions when something had happened to infuriate him – that it was probably sheer surprise that caused a hush to fall over the occupants of the bar parlour when he spoke, even though there was a pretty good attendance that evening.

It was by pure chance that Antony and Jenny Maitland were present. Antony was a barrister and they lived for most of the year in London; but they generally spent the long vacation with Bill Cleveland, a friend of very long standing, at his farm in Yorkshire. This gave them the opportunity of making shorter visits to other friends who lived not too far away, and they had come to Burton Cecil that day from Arkenshaw, where they had been staying with Chris and Star Conway. Their destination was the cottage called Farthing Lee, where they were to stay with Chris's aunt, Emma Anstey.

As the open space outside the shop was pretty well the only place in the village where one could park, Jenny, with Mrs Ryder's permission, had left the car there and had then suggested, since Mr Shaw was known to keep a supply of Miss Anstey's favourite sherry, that they should visit the pub and obtain a small offering to take to their hostess. The first person

7

they had seen on going in, however, had been Roland Beaufort, whom they had met a number of times on previous visits, sharing a table with Cyril Lansing, also an old acquaintance. It was obviously out of the question to leave again without greeting them, and the next thing they knew they too were seated and Molly – who worked for Mrs Shaw and helped out on occasion in the bar – had slammed down glasses before them with the utmost good will, and spilling rather less of the contents than might have been expected from the vigour she brought to the task.

They had scarcely had time to exchange greetings with the two men they had joined, and the other people present whom they knew less well, when Adam Shaw silenced the company with the above-mentioned remark. His wife, a small, pale woman who looked timid but was very far from that when you got to know her, gave him an admonishing look. 'They'd be wrong then, wouldn't they?' she asked rhetorically. And added, briefly, 'Least said, soonest mended.'

Jenny would have been content enough to leave the matter there, an unexplained enigma, but something in the atmosphere seemed to strike her husband as requiring explanation. 'You can't leave it there, Adam,' he protested. 'For one thing it hasn't been the sort of weather for thunderstorms. Nice enough, but not sultry.'

'I was speaking by way of metaphor,' said Adam, so portentously that the subject might easily have been closed if Cyril hadn't intervened. Cyril Lansing lived in the village, but was the Town Clerk of Rothershaw, the market town nearly five miles away. He was a widower; a prim little man at first sight, but as the Maitlands got to know him better they had discovered that he had a good deal of dry humour in his make-up.

'I believe I'm right in saying,' said Cyril, 'that until the unfortunate events seven years ago, when we first made your acquaintance, there hadn't been a murder in Burton Cecil since 1753. And what Adam means, I think, is that it's rather odd that you should turn up so fortuitously just after there's been another.'

'I don't believe it,' said Antony flatly. 'Are you telling us—?'

'I certainly am,' said Cyril. But even though he had interrupted he didn't for the moment attempt to elaborate his statement. It was Roland Beaufort who prompted him.

'You may as well tell them, Cyril. After all, Antony takes a professional interest in such things. And seven years ago . . .'

At any other time the reminder would have annoyed Maitland, but he knew well enough by now that it was unwise to take anything that Roland said too seriously. 'A *professional* interest,' he said, stressing the word. It was obvious that, come hell or high water, they were going to hear the story then and there, so they might as well make the best of it.

'It's not a very cheerful tale to greet you with,' said Cyril apologetically. 'Young Dilys Jones was strangled at Rowan Corner three days ago.'

'How horrible!' said Jenny, and became aware that Antony's left hand was feeling for her own under the table to give it a reassuring squeeze. 'Does Dilys live in the village? I don't think I know her.'

'You might not, she only came to live with the Lewises two years ago. Myfanwy Lewis is her cousin.'

'But who did it? And why?'

Cyril had opened his mouth to answer when Adam spoke again. 'You may well ask why,' he said. 'It's what comes of bringing strangers into t' village, that's what it is.'

'What on earth do you mean?' Jenny was getting more bewildered by the moment, but Antony seemed to be content to wait on events. A story like this in a village the size of Burton Cecil would be more than a nine days' wonder, and it certainly wouldn't be long before they heard ˀvery detail of what had happened.

'It's that Wainwright man he means,' said Lily Shaw. 'Mrs Anstey sold the Gillespies' cottage at last, and he's come to live there.'

Jenny was silent for a moment, digesting this, so Antony took up the questioning. 'What's wrong with him?' he asked.

The question seemed to open the floodgates, at least half the people in the room responded until there wasn't the slightest hope of disentangling what any of them was saying. Finally Cyril's voice became clear among the hubbub. He had a quiet way of speaking but also some measure of authority, so after a moment or two everyone else fell silent. 'He's a stranger,' said Cyril.

'Well, so are we,' said Antony lightly.

'That's different, you're friends of Emma's and we know all about you, where you come from and how you earn your living.' (I hope not everything, muttered Antony under his breath.) 'This Philip Wainwright is something of a mystery man. He doesn't come in here, never has a word for a dog that I've noticed.'

'Well, some people like to keep to themselves,' said Jenny weakly. 'There's nothing wrong with that.' Not a particularly good defence, but her instinct to think well of everyone lent a certain force to the words.

'That isn't all.' Bill Samuelson, the owner of one of the outlying farms, joined the conversation. 'He doesn't seem to have any job, or any friends either. And that being so, what's he doing here? Tell me that.'

It was obvious, Antony thought, that there was no use in attempting to argue the point. Wainwright might be as odd as you please, but it seemed rather hard to damn him just for being a stranger. 'You haven't answered Jenny's question about – was the name Dilys Jones?'

'Yes,' said Cyril. 'A pretty girl she was, full of life, and no more than twenty I should think.'

'And do you believe . . .?'

There was a kind of growl from around the room. 'We're saying he's odd, that's all,' said Bill Samuelson, almost as positively as Adam had spoken earlier. Then he turned directly to Antony. 'What do you think about it, Mr Maitland?'

'That the queerest thing is what Adam said just now about lightning not striking twice in the same place,' said Antony promptly. 'But I do wish,' he added, looking round the room, 'that somebody would tell us exactly what happened.'

This time it was Cyril who took it upon himself to answer, and it struck Jenny for the first time that the emotion felt by most of the others present was more anger than sorrow for what had taken place. 'Poor girl,' said Cyril perfunctorily. 'It happened on Monday night.'

'I could deduce that,' said Antony rather dryly. 'Somebody said three days ago.'

Cyril smiled at him. 'Patience,' he advised. 'I was about to tell you that she'd arranged to meet Peter Dutton at Rowan Corner.'

'They were walking out,' Lily Shaw put in.

'Yes, exactly. And as you were probably about to add, he's a serious-minded young man and he never brought her in here. They meant to go for a walk but Peter says she never turned up. The Lewises weren't used to her being late, so when it got to eleven o'clock Ivor walked down to the Duttons to see if she was there. Peter had given up waiting and had gone home by that time and all of them denied having seen her. So Ivor went on to the police station, and I gather he had a good deal of difficulty in waking up Joe Kitchener, but when he succeeded, of course, Kitchener was as helpful as he could be. He telephoned Sergeant Gilbey and they decided to have a look round themselves before trying to get up a search party. After all, unless she had wandered right out of the village there aren't too many places to look. And as it happened they found her straightaway, no more than a few yards from where Peter had been waiting for her, in the wood that's on your left as you go towards Farthing Lee.'

Jenny was silent now. Antony gave her one quick look and his hand tightened over hers. She had lost her serene look, but there was no help for it, they'd have to hear the story to the end now, because sooner or later it would be told. 'You said she'd

11

been strangled. What with?' he asked.

'A piece of cord,' said Cyril, and would have left it there, but Willie Barnes, another local farmer, chimed in from the other side of the room. 'It was knotted at both ends to make a garotte, and left in place. I'm told she wasn't a pretty sight.'

'That's enough of that,' said Cyril and turned to Antony, his manner deliberately excluding the other occupants of the room. 'And I'll answer your next question without giving Jenny the embarrassment of hearing it. She hadn't been.'

'Raped, you mean?' asked Maitland. Jenny, he knew, preferred the truth, however unpleasant, and she certainly wasn't one to boggle at a word.

'Interfered with,' said Roland Beaufort mockingly. 'You mustn't shock our bucolic sensibilities.'

'I'll try not to. What time did they find her?'

'About two o'clock, I think. Allowing for the fact that it was a warm night the doctor thought she'd been dead five or six hours.'

'How perfectly horrible!' said Jenny again, and thought suddenly that she sounded like a record, stuck in one groove.

'Yes, it was, wasn't it?' She realised now that Cyril's rather detached attitude was due to his being more interested in her reactions to the story than in the story itself.

'What time had she arranged to meet Peter Dutton?' she asked.

'At about half past eight,' said Roland. 'The family like her to wash up the dinner things before she goes out.'

'What time did she leave the Lewises' house then?'

'Just past eight o'clock.'

Antony was doing sums in his head. 'They live next door to the doctor, don't they? Fifteen minutes would surely have been enough to walk to Rowan Corner, wouldn't it?'

'Certainly it would,' Roland confirmed. 'Peter says he always tried to be earlier than she was but never quite managed it. She's one of those people – she was I mean – who always catch the train before the one they're trying to get.'

'What happened afterwards?' Antony asked.

'Oh, the detectives came over from Rothershaw, Inspector Wentworth and Constable Tankard, I think you met them once,' said Cyril. 'And it's only too obvious what they think.'

'I suppose it is,' said Maitland thoughtfully.

Adam spoke up again. 'Peter wouldn't be about to do a thing like that,' he said, 'so don't you go thinking it.'

'The police perhaps are wondering—'

'Of course they are,' said Cyril.

'Dilys would have to pass here,' said Adam, 'but no one has said as they saw her.'

'I did,' Roland volunteered suddenly. 'I was coming out of my cottage on my way here, and she'd just gone past and was walking on towards Rowan Corner. I called good night but I didn't wait and I don't think she heard me.'

The Maitlands left the pub shortly after that. They had only one small suitcase between them, which Antony fetched from the car. An old injury had left his right arm useless for things like carrying, so over the years he, and Jenny on his behalf, had become expert in travelling light. Jenny was carrying the bottles carefully. 'Emma will be wondering where on earth we've got to,' she said.

'I only told her we'd be with her for supper, and as we've already had a drink we needn't keep her waiting,' said Antony placidly. He sometimes thought that what he always called to himself Jenny's look of serenity was one of the most precious things in life, and he was anxious to restore a degree of normality after the recent revelations. 'Besides,' he added, 'you know Emma, she's probably wrestling with Mr Maltravers and has forgotten all about our coming.'

'I don't believe that for a moment,' said Jenny indignantly. 'You know how she always looks forward to seeing us. Of course,' she added thoughtfully, 'if Mr Maltravers happened to be in a great deal of trouble she might be trying to get him out of it. But that only happens occasionally.' Emma Anstey was a writer of what her nephew, Chris Conway, never having read one, called 'those lousy thrillers'. Antony contented himself with the word 'odd' to describe them and Jenny was frankly admiring, but it has to be admitted that the adventures and misadventures of Emma's chief protagonist, Lester Maltravers, were a little inclined to get in the way of everyday living.

Antony kept up a constant stream of conversation, particularly when they approached Rowan Corner and had to pass the wood where the unfortunate Dilys Jones's body had been found. Jenny kept her eyes resolutely ahead of her, while they walked across the grass to the footbridge over Farthing Gill, and then up the further track that led to Emma's gate. At this time of year the garden was a riot of colour, and the grey stone of the cottage looked mellow in the evening sunlight. Jenny paused a moment near the lilac bush by the gate, but no rattle of the typewriter greeted them. So she smiled at her husband, of whose anxiety on her behalf she was perfectly conscious, and said, 'It sounds as if Mr Maltravers has already been put to bed.'

A moment later the front door had been thrown open and Emma was greeting them, literally with open arms. She was not very tall and it couldn't be denied that her figure was inclined to dumpiness; her grey hair was untidy, and the Spanish comb that should have held it in place had slipped over one ear; her face was round and pink and almost unlined, and her eyes were a very vivid shade of blue. That evening she was wearing a summer frock in which shocking pink and orange blended unharmoniously, and in spite of the warmth of the evening she had thrown a shawl round her shoulders. Jenny recognised that shawl; it was made of silk and embroidered with purple humming birds. Extremely exotic, and very much out of place. But there was no mistaking her pleasure as she embraced them both warmly, saying, 'Come in, come in, my dears. You're just in time.' That last had a faintly ominous ring, but they knew her too well by now to be disturbed by it.

Antony took the case upstairs. He knew their room at the end of the corridor well enough. Jenny was explaining what had

14

delayed them and handed over the bottles of sherry. 'We stopped for a drink at the Mortal Man, Emma,' she explained, 'because Cyril and Roland were there and we couldn't very well cut them dead.'

'Of course you couldn't. But there's time for another drink now.' She paused there, eyeing Jenny doubtfully. 'If you've been to the Mortal Man you've heard all about our latest mystery,' she said.

'Yes, I'm afraid we did. It must have been horrible for you, Emma, having it happen practically on your doorstep.'

'Don't be silly, Jenny,' said Emma severely. 'After what happened the first time you were here you can't expect a little thing like that to trouble me. Not that it wasn't a dreadful thing,' she added more soberly, 'and I'm afraid Antony won't be awfully pleased about it because Stephen is practically sure they're going to arrest Peter Dutton and he's hoping for some advice.'

'Stephen?'

'Another of my nephews,' said Emma. 'Hugh's younger brother. You haven't met him because he only qualified last year. He's a solicitor,' she added.

Antony spoke from the bottom of the stone staircase which came down directly into the sitting-room. Neither of them had heard him, but he'd obviously been there for a moment or two and heard at least some of the conversation. 'I've a nasty idea, Emma,' he said now lightly, 'that there's some sort of conspiracy going on.'

'Conspiracy?' Emma's tone was innocence itself as she turned to lead the way down the short passage into the stone-flagged kitchen, which was really more of a living-room, with scullery and larder leading off it. 'I can't think,' she went on, waving them to armchairs while she devoted herself to pouring sherry, 'what on earth can have put such an idea into your head.'

'Chris's insistence that we stay over until today, and now the story we've just been listening to at the Mortal Man,' said Antony, accepting a glass. 'So the first thing, Emma dear, before we go into the matter any further, is for you to tell us a little more about this new nephew of yours.'

'He isn't exactly new,' said Emma. 'I've had him for quite twenty-three years.'

'You know perfectly well what I meant. We've both heard you speak of your family, and I daresay I've heard – what was his name? Stephen? – mentioned but I can't say it made much impression.'

'He's a dear boy,' said Emma, 'but not – not articulate. At least that's what he said when he decided he wanted to go in for the law and Keith – you remember my brother Keith? – naturally wanted him to aim for the senior branch of the profession. Finally Keith agreed to go along with what he wanted and he qualified a year ago, but then I'm afraid there was rather a disagreement because instead of going into a firm in London who'd have been willing to give him a partnership in a year or two he decided he simply had to live in the country.'

'Was that so very dreadful?' Antony asked, sipping his sherry.

'Oh yes, because you remember what I told you about Keith once, Jenny. Well, it isn't really his fault I suppose,' said Emma, obviously trying to view the matter dispassionately, 'it's a family tradition. Whatever profession the boys adopt they must become pre-eminent in it.'

'As your brother has done himself,' said Antony tactfully. Keith Anstey was an historian, and a very successful writer on some of the more obscure periods in his chosen field of study.

'Yes of course, and so has Richard – you haven't met Richard, have you, he's the eldest son? – who was quite willing to follow the path his father laid out for him. He's a bio-chemist and becoming successful enough to satisfy even the family's high standards. But Hugh . . . well you know all about Hugh.'

'He wanted to be a farmer so he joined the police,' said Jenny, smiling.

'Is that what I told you? Well, it's true enough, because there just wasn't the money to set him up on the scale that Keith would have thought suitable. When he married Caroline, of course, everything turned out perfectly because she'd inherited Burton Crook and she was clever enough not to tell him that until after they were engaged.'

'How are they both?' asked Jenny.

'Very well indeed, both of them, and the children too. Of course he's always busy but ... you know, Jenny, I sometimes used to wonder whether farming was really what he wanted, or whether he insisted on that just to disoblige his father. But it's quite obvious now that he really knew his own mind. Now that he's got the farmland in hand again he couldn't be happier.'

'Has that reconciled Mr Anstey to the idea?'

'Not exactly. They're very comfortable at Burton Crook but Hugh's activities are not quite on the scale Keith would have envisaged as suitable, and it isn't as if he's content just to walk round and supervise things; he will insist on mucking in, as he calls it.'

'And has Stephen's decision put him in his father's black books too?' asked Maitland, who was willing to tolerate any amount of deviation from a subject he was interested in, but always returned to it in the end.

'Well yes, Antony, I'm afraid it has. The London firm he could have gone to ... that was Keith's influence really and I can only suppose they felt the name Anstey would look well on their letterhead. But my solicitor in Rothershaw is getting on in years and hasn't been very well into the bargain, so Stephen is taking over from him. Officially at the moment he's a junior partner, but the understanding is that he'll do the work now, and take over the practice in name as well as in fact eventually.'

Antony smiled at her. 'A purely philanthropic act?' he asked, and the amusement in his voice was very evident.

'Well, I have to admit ... really the Maltravers books have been doing very well lately,' said Emma, 'so I was quite able to help him out. Only temporarily, of course, Stephen insisted on that. In fact' – she smiled in her turn – 'he drew up a very complicated document binding himself to all sorts of things that

17

I'd never have thought of in a thousand years.' She paused there, looking from one of them to the other, her blue eyes guileless. 'But I have to agree, Antony, that you were quite right in what you thought, though conspiracy is rather an unkind word to use. When it became obvious that the police suspected Peter Dutton of having killed poor little Dilys, Stephen did speak to Chris on the telephone and asked him to get you to stay on with him another couple of days so that by the time you got here we'd have seen how things were developing. And you needn't worry, Jenny, it's only a matter of advice, because Stephen is very young and quite inexperienced in things like this.'

'Of course I'll be willing to give him any advice I can,' said Antony slowly. 'It's got to the stage of Peter needing representation then?'

'It seems so. You don't mind my asking Antony to do this, do you, Jenny?'

'No, Emma, of course I don't.'

'It seems rather like making a busman's holiday for him, but it's something we all feel very strongly about. Peter couldn't have done a thing like that.'

Jenny glanced quickly at her husband, but he was fond of Emma and seemed to have taken this provoking remark in his stride. 'I'd gathered as much as far as the *habitués* of the Mortal Man were concerned,' he said. 'Is it the general feeling in the village?'

'Everyone I've spoken to is quite certain of it,' said Emma positively.

'And they fixed on a newcomer, a man called Wainwright I think. Have they any reason for that other than the fact that he's a stranger?'

'Stephen says not, and I admit I've always found Mr Wainwright quite polite, though not – not forthcoming.'

'Did he know the dead girl?'

'I don't see how he could have done. He hasn't made any friends, or even acquaintances, in the village.'

18

'Somebody said he's bought the Gillespies' old cottage, Lane's End. Has it been standing empty all this time?'

'Yes. I don't think anybody fancied it after what happened there, so Caroline was very pleased with herself for getting it off her hands.'

'Was it part of the Burton Crook estate?' Antony asked. 'I didn't know that.'

'Oh dear,' said Emma. This was a favourite expression of hers and didn't really mean anything at all. 'After a whole year there's such a lot of catching up to do. Caroline wanted something to do once the children were out of the nursery, but not a full time job, of course, like the one she had before she was married. So she dabbles in real estate – that's how Hugh puts it – it gives her something to think about and when she has to go out Mrs Dally and Elsie are quite capable between them of looking after the twins.'

'Has Elsie left you then?' asked Jenny.

'Yes, about nine months ago. I thought Caroline's need was greater than mine, and Elsie was quite happy to live in, which of course she couldn't have done here; the house is so small. And the funny thing is she loves children, and I don't suppose she'll have any of her own because she still insists she doesn't like men.' (Elsie, who was what the village referred to as only ninepence to the shilling, had worked for Emma for many years, and Jenny couldn't help feeling a little sad that the arrangement had come to an end.)

'What about you, Emma?' she asked. 'You can't possibly manage without help, all the time you spend at your type-writer.'

'It turned out to be a blessing in disguise,' Emma told her. 'I'm fond of Elsie, and I still see quite a lot of her, but Mrs Kitchener who does for me now is a wonderful cook and leaves something ready for me every day. Except weekends, of course. Which reminds me, we ought to be getting our meal, because Stephen said he'd look in afterwards.' She looked doubtfully at Jenny as she spoke, but Jenny smiled back at her reassuringly.

It was a nuisance, of course, but with Emma it was definitely a case of 'love me love my nephews', and she wouldn't have disobliged her kind hostess for the world.

The meal turned out to be as good as Emma had predicted, and over it they discussed the events of the last year in a desultory fashion. 'I must say,' said Emma, when all facets of their activities had been covered, 'that I'm a little bit worried about Maltravers at the moment.'

'What's he been up to?' asked Antony idly.

'My publisher told me that books in hard cover in the classical tradition of the nineteen thirties and even earlier, were all the rage now, so I thought it would be a change to try my hand at one . . . except that the story happens today, because I really can't desert Maltravers and his adventures have never been set in the past.'

'What's wrong with that? I should have thought you'd both have enjoyed the change.'

'I didn't have any difficulty about the beginning,' said Emma. 'I set the action in a house called Hanging Bailey, standing high on the moor. In November, naturally, with fog rolling across the bog at the bottom of the neglected driveway and pressing against the mullioned windows.'

'There is, of course,' said Antony, 'a body in the library.'

'Oh yes,' said Emma with perfect seriousness. 'And the owner of the house, Sir Jasper, is rather annoyed about it. He said, "Dash it all!" rather petulantly when he found it, and rang for his butler. "Just when I wanted to write a letter," he complained.'

'What's wrong with that?'

'I'm not quite sure where to go next.'

'That's easy. Has the butler got a name?' Maitland asked.

'I think all butlers in books of that kind were called Parker,' said Emma.

'Very well then, have him cough deferentially.'

'But—'

'I know what you're going to say. To be up-to-date you have

20

to make him a socialist, but you can explain that it wasn't really deference; the fog had affected his asthma. And he'll have to send one of the men for the police because the telephone wires have been cut again.'

'Of course!' said Emma. 'That's perfect. And I can go on with Sir Jasper saying "It always happens, I can't think why people must be so inconsiderate".'

'And they must warn the police to look out for the third bog on the left as they come out of town,' said Jenny enthusiastically. 'Unless you think Sir Jasper isn't the sort of man to feel any deep concern about that,' she added doubtfully.

'That's all right, he can be as callous as you like, Emma,' Antony told her. 'You can explain that the continued losses among the constabulary are beginning to have their effect on the rates.'

They continued to embroider on the theme while the table was cleared, and then, with the dishes stacked neatly for Mrs Kitchener's attention the next day, went back into the sitting-room. 'I don't think it's quite warm enough to sit outside,' said Emma, 'though they're talking about a heat-wave being on the way.' But before either of her visitors could reply there was a light tap on the door. Emma ran to fling it open, and Stephen Anstey stepped into the room.

Having known his older brother for seven years now Antony thought he would have had no difficulty in recognising the newcomer as one of the Anstey family, though he was not quite so tall as Hugh and much more slightly built, and had not yet acquired the same relaxed attitude to life. He was so obviously fond of Emma, who was one of their favourite people, that both Antony and Jenny took to him immediately, but it was obvious when Miss Anstey performed the introductions that he regarded Maitland at least with some awe. Jenny wasn't quite sure how Antony would take this; Stephen had obviously heard some of the more exaggerated tales about him, but he seemed in a relaxed mood that evening, and obviously his main emotion was one of extreme, though carefully hidden, amusement.

Stephen on his part took Jenny to his heart without any hesitation at all. Having decided that Antony was in no way disturbed by what promised to be merely a slight interruption to their holiday she had again her serene look, her green eyes were friendly, and though her brown curls were a little untidy the strands of gold that ran through them now that Emma had lighted the lamp were extremely attractive. Maitland he regarded more warily; a tall man – almost as tall as Hugh – with dark hair and a thin intelligent face. As Stephen got to know him better he was to discover that his new friend had a sometimes unfortunate trick of seeing the humorous side of any given situation. Some people found this disarming, but it was a source of annoyance to the more serious-minded of his acquaintances. 'Emma said you wouldn't mind my coming over the first evening you were here,' said Stephen, as soon as the introductions and greetings were completed. 'I hope she was right about that.'

'Quite right,' said Antony, and Jenny added a query.

'Had you far to come?'

'Didn't Emma tell you? I'm living with Hugh and Caroline at the moment.'

'No, she didn't tell us, I expect she thought we'd guess,' said Jenny. 'After all, it's much nearer to your work in Rothershaw than Manningbridge is.' She was perfectly well aware that his removal from the parental home was probably due to the disagreement that Emma had mentioned, but there was no need to bring that up.

'Yes, but—'

'I described your problem to Antony, Stephen,' said Emma firmly, 'and he's no objection at all to giving you his opinion. He and Jenny heard about the murder in the pub when they were buying some sherry for me on their way here, but I haven't really told them anything more yet; I thought the story would come best from you. You've met Peter Dutton, haven't you, both of you?' she added, looking from Antony to Jenny in sudden doubt.

22

'He's a friend of Roland's,' said Jenny. 'I can't say we know him well, but we've met him several times.'

'We've met the Lewises too, but I can hardly say we know them well either,' said Maitland, 'and we've neither of us met the girl who was killed, though as I understand she's lived in the village for two years we may have seen her about on one of our visits. It would help, I think, if you were to tell us something about them all, Emma. Then Stephen can tell us what's worrying him.'

It was a big room into which the front door led directly. Emma's desk was in the window with a portable typewriter and some very untidy papers, and there was still room for a circle of chairs round the huge empty fireplace which at the moment was screened by a variety of flowers. Stephen looked relieved by the suggestion, and said emphatically, 'That's a very good idea,' looking at his aunt hopefully as he spoke.

Emma obviously realised that he was grateful not to have to plunge immediately into his side of the story. 'What exactly do you want to know?' she asked.

'Meeting people isn't the same as knowing them,' said Jenny. 'All about the Lewises for one thing.'

'And if Peter Dutton didn't kill her,' Antony put in, 'who did?'

'If you heard the talk at the Mortal Man you must have realised that,' said Stephen. 'The stranger in our midst.'

'That's all very well if you want to generalise but nobody seems to be able to give me a reason for thinking it except that he *is* a stranger,' said Antony. 'I daresay that's enough for the village, but not for you, I'm sure, and certainly not for Emma.'

'You haven't met Wainwright,' said Stephen. 'When you do . . . well, he is something of an oddity.'

'That doesn't necessarily make him a murderer. But let's get back to Jenny's questions. Tell us about Dilys Jones, Emma.'

'I know a little about her,' said Emma cautiously. 'But that's not quite the same thing as being able to tell you exactly what she was like. Certainly she was a pretty girl, but not, I should have thought, the kind to drive a man to distraction. Perhaps I mean she looked nice, in the proper sense of the word.'

'I think she was,' said Stephen. 'But you see that's half the trouble. So is Peter, a very good chap.'

'How well do you know him?'

'Not too well, I haven't lived here long enough. But we're not too far off the same age and I've joined him and Roland for a pint at the Mortal Man on a number of occasions. Roland, of course, has known him all his life, and I can tell you right away he's quite certain he'd never have harmed Dilys.'

'People change,' said Maitland.

'So they do. And if you're going to suggest that Dilys may have been too proper in her ideas and Peter of a more passionate nature, I have to admit you may be right.'

'You don't really believe that,' Maitland challenged him.

'No, I don't.'

'How do you think it looks to the police?'

'I wouldn't say that Detective Inspector Wentworth is renowned for his imagination,' said Stephen slowly.

'You mean he's not likely to look any further than Peter?'

'That's what I meant, and that's what seems to be happening. But we'll come to that later, the next bit of the story is Aunt Emma's.'

'I'll tell you about Dilys first, shall I?' Emma offered.

'It doesn't really matter but you have to start somewhere. She hasn't always lived in the village?'

'Only since she left school. Her parents were killed in an accident about three years before that, but she was at boarding-school so she stayed there even during the holidays until she was eighteen. Then I think the school wouldn't keep her any longer, and that's when she came to the Lewises.'

'They didn't want her?'

'No, I don't think they did,' said Emma rather reluctantly. She had this much in common with Jenny; she was unwilling to think ill of anyone. 'And I don't think her parents left her a penny so I suppose the three years' schooling they paid for was something she had to be grateful for. She came here two years ago, I believe she's just twenty now.' She broke off there and added rather sadly, 'I keep talking as if she was still alive. I don't like thinking about it at all, you know.'

'If they didn't want her,' said Jenny, for the moment sticking to the point almost as single-mindedly as her husband might have done, 'I'm sure she could have stayed in town and got a job as a secretary or something like that.'

'I don't think that would have been quite her line. She was definitely a domesticated little thing. But however that may have been, Ivor didn't seem to see putting up the money for her training. Besides, by then the children were getting to be something of a handful, so that Myfanwy was glad enough to have a sort of unpaid mother's helper join the household.'

'Poor Dilys,' said Jenny sympathetically.

'To be fair I don't think she looked at herself that way,' said Emma hurriedly. 'That's one of the awful things about this business, she always seemed to be a happy little thing. And then about six months ago Peter Dutton started to take an interest in her, and I must say I was looking for a happy ending there.'

'What about the Lewises?' Privately Jenny thought they sounded perfectly horrible, but that was a rash judgement and she wasn't prepared to make it aloud.

Emma seemed to divine her thought. 'They're a nice couple really. A bit selfish, I suppose, though I don't know all the circumstances. No more selfish than the rest of us, I dare say.'

'You're the last person to talk about being selfish,' said Stephen warmly.

'I'll say Amen to that,' said Maitland, 'but Emma hasn't finished her part of the story yet.'

'The Lewises came here about ten years ago as far as I remember,' said Emma, and the Spanish comb that had been hanging drunkenly over her left ear decided that this was the moment to give up its duty altogether. 'I imagine the estate agent that Caroline took over from could look it up if you really want to know, because I expect he sold them their house.

Anyway, both the boys – David and Llewellyn – have been born since then.'

'If they're so determinedly Welsh,' said Antony, 'I don't see why they came here at all. Does she do any work? Is that why she liked having some help from Dilys?'

'If you want to know what I think,' said Stephen, 'at the risk of being uncharitable I should say she's one of those women with a rather cow-like disposition quite content to do nothing at all. But I don't know either of them well yet.'

'Well, Emma can tell us. What does Ivor Lewis do for a living, for example?'

'He's an engineer of some sort, I'm not very clear about the details,' said Emma vaguely. 'It's funny about the Welsh, they're like the Scots ... a lot of them go into that line of work and most of them have to leave home to exercise their talents. That's what happened to Ivor, he's with Broadbent and Darcy, whose laboratory is on the outskirts of Rothershaw, the other side from here. And to complete the picture, in case you don't know, they're Dr Oaksley's next-door neighbours.'

'All right then, what about the Duttons?'

'They've lived in the village all their lives, I think, and they moved to one of the converted cottages in Parson's Row when Michael retired. They're tiny, of course – the cottages, I mean – but I think that's what they wanted and the ones that have been modernised are really rather attractive. They have a kitchen built out at the back, and a bathroom above. Anyway, I think Mary and Michael are very comfortable there, and it's much cheaper than trying to keep up a house and grounds, which is what they had before.'

'And until he retired, what did he do?'

'He was a civil servant in the Income Tax department, but tactful enough to keep well out of the picture if any query arose about his neighbours' affairs. Mary ... well they're an older couple, I don't think the question of her going to work ever arose. Peter is their only son, as I told you he's a friend of Roland Beaufort's. I think they have some tastes in common.'

'Such as a rather distorted sense of humour,' Maitland suggested.

'No, I didn't mean that. I meant they're both bookworms and fond of music. Before Peter got interested in Dilys he'd often go into Rothershaw with Roland to the concerts there.'

'And what does Peter do?'

'He works for a bookshop. He's only twenty-three, you know, I think he was born when his parents had practically given up hope of having children. Anyway he seems quite contented with his lot and there was nothing underhand about his courting Dilys and I can't – really I can't, Antony – see any reason why he should suddenly have changed so completely and attacked her.'

'You say you don't think she'd been leading him on.'

'No, I don't think that at all.'

'There's one thing I think you haven't considered,' said Maitland, looking from Emma to Stephen seriously. 'If she was as nice a girl as all that how did some stranger persuade her to go into the wood with him when she was supposed to be waiting for Peter? Unless, of course, she was killed where she stood and dragged among the trees for concealment afterwards.'

'That seems to be out of the question. Joe Kitchener told Hugh the ground had been gone over carefully, and there could be no doubt she'd been killed where she was found.'

'Well then!'

Stephen thought about that. 'I suppose you realise that's the best argument that could be put forward for Peter's guilt,' he said.

'I think it's devastating,' said Antony, and Stephen grinned at him.

'I'm not discounting that,' he said. 'It's a reasonable, logical, argument, though not, I must admit, exactly the conclusion I was hoping you'd reach. But you must remember I know all these people a little better than you do, and Emma knows them far better than either of us.'

'All right then, let's assume for the moment that Peter

27

Dutton isn't guilty. Why have the villagers got their collective knife into this man Wainwright? What's his full name, by the way?'

'Philip Wainwright. I don't think there's any reason really except that he's a stranger and keeps himself to himself and hasn't confided in anybody at all about his affairs.'

'Surely Caroline found out something about him when he bought Lane's End?'

'Not a thing, at least nothing that she's mentioned, though I did gather that it was a straightforward transaction, cash on the barrel head.'

'At least she must have known where he came from.'

'Birmingham, I believe, though I'm not sure about that. You don't have to give a *curriculum vitae* to buy a house, you know.'

'Of course not. Is that really all Caroline said about him?'

'No, but I wasn't particularly interested. He wanted a small property in a quiet village setting, so she told him about Lane's End. He could take over the furniture too if he liked; it was just as the Gillespies had left it. A bit of a mess, I suppose, but nothing much worse than dust and cobwebs. She said he seemed more interested in the surroundings than in the interior and agreed to buy the furniture with scarcely a look. It sounds as if all he was interested in was a roof over his head, though he got someone in to clean the place up before he moved in.'

'And that was all?'

'Absolutely all. According to Caroline he didn't dither about at all, just said Yes on the spot to everything. He moved in by the end of the month, if you remember, Emma, that is about two months ago. And of course,' he added with a slight smile, 'because I was already living at Burton Crook he seems like a newcomer to me.'

'I suppose you took some notice of him when you first saw him in the village.'

'Yes, I remember thinking what a strange-looking man he was, and now I'm not quite sure why he struck me that way. In fact, if you analyse his features he's almost good-looking. I

28

suppose it's because he strides along looking neither to right nor left and wears rather queer old-fashioned clothes that look as if they'd been made for somebody twice his size. Emma seems to be the only person to get anything approaching a smile out of him. But that's his affair after all, so I don't see why the village thinks so badly of him. He isn't the only newcomer, for instance.'

'If you mean the Hawthornes,' said Emma, 'it reminds me I've got an invitation to their house-warming. Drinks and a buffet supper this coming Saturday. I accepted for all of us,' she added, looking from Antony to Jenny. 'I hope you don't mind.'

'Of course not,' said Jenny. 'Where do they live?'

'Next to the shop.' No other description was necessary, it was the only one in the village. 'That is, next door but one to Dr Oaksley on the other side from the Lewises. They're all detached houses with quite large grounds, if you remember. He's . . . oh, in his late thirties I should think, but she's a very young thing and he told me he'd like her to make some friends in the neighbourhood.'

'Well, if being a stranger is the only criterion, I can't see why the village doesn't suspect him,' said Jenny.

'Now *you're* being logical, love,' said Antony reprovingly. 'Besides, the reason's obvious . . . a married man, everything above board.'

'He may turn out to be just as secretive as Mr Wainwright.'

'I doubt it if they're having a house-warming, but we shall know more about them on Saturday. And now, Stephen, what about your side of the story? I gather that you're acting for Peter Dutton and that the police suspect him of having killed his girlfriend.'

'They haven't made an arrest yet.'

'No, but what do they think?'

'What I'm sure you'll tell me any sensible person would think,' said Stephen. 'That Peter lost his head.'

'And strangled her with a cord with which he had thought-fully provided himself?'

'I put that badly. They think it was pre-meditated, that she wouldn't let him have his way with her and he was tired of her refusals. And if they're right about that, what on earth can be said in his favour? If it was a cold-blooded killing, not even a rape that went wrong or a sudden impulse ... I can't see the jury feeling much sympathy for him, can you?'

Maitland ignored the question. 'But you don't believe that's how it happened?'

'No, I don't. I'll go further than that, I don't believe he did it at all. But I'd better tell you—'

'Yes, I suppose that would be as well.'

'All right then. The police wanted to interview him so I arranged for them to come to my office, and that Peter would get there about a quarter of an hour before they did. He's ... how would you describe him Emma?'

'A thin, dark boy who looks as though he's outgrown his strength,' said Emma. 'And before you start, Stephen, why don't you get us all a drink of some kind?'

'Yes, of course.' He busied himself with that for a while and finally, when everyone was served, came back to his own chair and set down his glass beside him. 'I'll go into as much detail as I can about the interview, Mr Maitland,' he said, 'then you'll see what we're up against. Peter arrived a little before the time we'd arranged, and I must say just looking at him made me feel at least a hundred years his senior. He hesitated just inside the door as though unsure of his welcome ...'

Stephen was a good story-teller and as Antony listened he could visualise the scene well enough. It was, besides, quite obvious that its narrator had one qualification at least for his chosen profession, an excellent memory.

Peter came forward rather hesitantly and stood near the desk. 'It's very good of you to see me, Mr Anstey,' he said. 'I wasn't quite sure how you'd feel about taking me on as a client.'

Stephen ignored that. 'You'd better sit down, Peter,' he said. 'And I don't see why I should suddenly become Mr Anstey, just because for the moment I'm acting in a professional capacity.'

Peter obeyed as far as taking a chair was concerned, though still with that hesitant air. 'I'm very grateful,' he said.

'There's no need for that. Do you feel grateful to your doctor when you're ill?'

Peter thought about that. 'Yes, I think I do,' he said at last. 'But this . . . this is different. I'm telling the truth but I don't see why you should believe me,' he added in a rush.

'What shouldn't I believe you about?'

'That I didn't do it. As if I'd ever do anything to hurt Dilys. I loved her, I was going to marry her. It's queer, you know, that's the worst thing, much the worst. Not that the police seem to suspect me but that she's dead.'

'All the same you want my help.'

'Yes, I do. There's my mother and father to consider. I don't want them to be hurt as well. Besides . . .' He paused so long there that Stephen thought he had come to the end of what he was going to say but after he had waited patiently for a moment Peter went on in rather a shamefaced way. 'I've got to admit I'm frightened about what may happen.'

'So you're telling me that you're not guilty but in spite of that you feel that the police suspect you. Have they questioned you before?'

'Yes, of course. They woke us all up on Tuesday morning, and that was the first I'd heard about Dilys's murder. It was . . . I couldn't believe it!'

Guilty or not he was obviously upset by the recollection and Stephen gave him a few minutes to compose himself. Then he asked, 'I take it you're talking about the detectives from Rothershaw? 'What was their attitude?'

He thought about that. 'Sceptical,' he said at last, and his voice shook a little on the word.

'They didn't believe your story?'

'I don't think . . . you know I was too upset to tell them anything clearly. Except that I hadn't seen her that night. Do you suppose that's why they want to see me again? Or are they

31

going to arrest me?'

Stephen didn't answer that directly. 'I think you've got to be prepared for some really intensive questioning, Peter,' he told him. 'And a great deal will depend on how convincing your denials are.'

'They're true,' he insisted. 'Won't you at least believe me?'

'Until I've heard your story for myself that's hardly a fair question,' Stephen pointed out. 'But your instructions are quite clear, you're not guilty. So let's take it from there.'

That brought another silence. Finally Peter said, 'At first I thought – when I heard about Dilys, you know – that nothing mattered any more. Only then when I heard that Wentworth wanted to see me again I began to think about my parents and to become a bit scared about what might happen to me.'

He was repeating himself, but in the circumstances Stephen didn't blame him for that. 'If it makes you feel any better, opinion in the village is strongly in your favour,' he said.

'Is it?' Peter didn't seem to find the information very cheering. 'What do we do now?'

'That's up to you.' Stephen glanced at his watch. 'The police are due here at any moment, we can keep them waiting while we go over your story together or we can let them in and I'll hear it at the same time as they do. I think the latter course would make a slightly better impression and I'll put my oar in, of course, if necessary.'

'But it's hardly a story at all. And whether you believe it or not I've nothing to hide.'

At that moment the telephone rang and Stephen spoke to his client with his hand already on the receiver. 'That's probably to announce the detectives,' he said. 'Shall I ask them to wait?'

'No, let them come in.' When Stephen had passed on the message Peter gave him a rather shaky smile. 'Perhaps I'll convince you as well as them,' he said, 'that I'm telling the truth.'

When the detectives came in Stephen – whose first contact with the law in Rothershaw this was – looked at them pretty

32

closely. They were two big men, Inspector Wentworth a good deal older and a good deal heavier than his subordinate. Their greetings were polite enough but the inspector showed some surprise, whether genuine or not, at the sight of Stephen. 'Is Mr Marriott busy?' he inquired bluntly.

'He'll be retiring shortly, Inspector, and is in the course of handing over to me. This is one of the matters he has asked me to take care of.'

'A satisfactory arrangement from your point of view, Mr – Mr Anstey, isn't it? But I wonder if your client is quite as happy with it?' This was said with a geniality that rang distinctly false and Stephen answered him rather shortly.

'That's between the two of us, Inspector. As far as I know this interview is a mere formality to get Mr Dutton's statement. Are you telling me anything else is involved?'

'No.' He sounded doubtful. 'That seems a fair enough summing up of the position.'

'Very well then, you'd better sit down. You both know Mr Dutton already I understand, so I needn't introduce you.' The two detectives seated themselves obediently and Constable Tankard produced his note book. 'First of all I must ask you, are you going to warn us?'

'That would be going a little too fast I think, Mr Anstey,' said Wentworth slowly. 'Until we know what your client has to say—'

'I told you I didn't kill Dilys,' said Peter, 'and you didn't believe me.'

Wentworth turned and looked him very slowly up and down. 'You're willing now, I hope, to amplify that statement,' he said.

'Yes, of course, but there really isn't anything—'

'Let me decide about that. What I want from you, Mr Dutton, is an exact account of your movements on Monday evening, and some details of the arrangement you admit you had made with Miss Jones.'

That seemed reasonable enough so Stephen didn't try to interfere, though Peter cast a rather anguished look in his

33

direction as though pleading with him to do so. 'You must remember,' Stephen told him (but the statement was really made to impress the detectives), 'that I too am anxious to hear what you have to say.'

'All right then. But it can't do any good. Dilys is dead and nothing can change that.'

'Don't you want to help us find out who did it?' said Tankard, looking up unexpectedly from his notebook. Stephen thought he could hear the words, If you're telling the truth when you say you didn't see her that night, trembling on his lips, but wisely the constable didn't utter them.

'Of course I want to know, but it won't change anything really. She was so . . . she was so good,' said Peter earnestly. 'I know that sounds like sickly sentimentality, but she loved me, too.'

'Never mind how it sounds.' That was Wentworth again and he spoke more sharply than the constable had done. 'First of all tell us about yourself.'

'But you know—'

'Your name is Peter Dutton, and you are twenty-three years old. You live with your parents at Number Three, Parson's Row in Burton Cecil and work at Black's bookshop here in town. Don't you think that picture's capable of being amplified a little?'

Again Peter looked at Stephen, who gave him a nod that he hoped would prove encouraging. 'We've only lived in Parson's Row since my father retired,' he said, 'but always in Burton Cecil. I was born here. I went to the grammar school here and I got a scholarship to the university but I didn't take it up. It would have meant leaving home and there wasn't really enough money to supplement what the scholarship would have given me. Besides I like books and the chance came up of going to work at Black's. So I went there straight from school and I've been there ever since. Is that the kind of thing you want to know?'

'What would you say about your future prospects?'

'Reasonably good. I'm never going to make a fortune but I don't think that matters terribly.'

'Where did you meet Miss Dilys Jones?'

'I suppose I knew her by sight ever since she came to live with the Lewises. That's about two years, I think. But then I saw her one night at a concert ... that was here in Rothershaw too, I was with Roland Beaufort and he knew Dilys and introduced us during the interval. After that we went out once or twice, and then more often.'

'Regularly, in fact.'

'Yes, that's right, regularly.'

'Had you spoken of marriage to her?'

'I had, about two months ago I suppose. I don't think the Lewises were any too keen on the idea though. I went to see Ivor; he tried to persuade me we were still too young, but I knew my own mind and I knew Dilys did too.'

'The question is, what did she think of these prospects of yours?'

'I was quite open with her about what we could expect,' said Peter a little defiantly.

'I'm sure you were. What had she to say to the information?'

'She said it didn't matter. She wasn't a – a mercenary sort of girl, you know.'

'That's something I must take your word for,' said Wentworth with an edge of sarcasm in his voice. Stephen was to find that he was a man subject to quick changes of mood, sarcastic when the spirit moved him and not too fond of anything that savoured of contradiction. 'Well, if she didn't care about that had the wedding date been fixed?'

'No. She felt she shouldn't go too much against the Lewises' wishes as they'd been good to her. I did hope to persuade her that perhaps before next winter—'

'In fact you were more eager for the marriage to take place than she was. In the meantime' – Wentworth glanced at Stephen as though wondering how he would take the question – 'were you on intimate terms with her?'

'We were going to be married,' said Peter simply.

'I think we should get on more quickly if you were a little more explicit, Inspector,' Stephen said dryly. 'Mr Wentworth means, Peter, did you have sexual relations with her?'

'I . . . no, I didn't! Dilys wasn't that sort of girl.'

'A well-brought-up young lady in fact,' said Wentworth ironically. 'And how did you feel about that, Mr Dutton?'

'I respected her.'

'But the implication is, from what you've already said, that the matter had been raised between you.'

'No, it never was. Even if I'd wanted to . . . I suppose what I'm trying to say is that she had some very strict ideas. I'd never even taken her into the Mortal Man, though that's respectable enough. I think she'd probably have gone there with me after we were married, but she thought it wasn't suitable for a single girl.'

'A rather prim young lady. But we were talking about love-making, Mr Dutton. In matters of that sort was it you who called a halt or she?'

Peter closed his eyes for a moment as though some drama were being played before him that he just couldn't bear to see. 'Knowing how she felt I never tried to take things too far,' he said.

'In other words, you were pretty sure how your advances would have been received?'

'I suppose I was.'

'Did you like the idea of waiting for a wedding date that hadn't yet been fixed? Didn't that cause you some impatience?' Wentworth was pressing his questions now and Stephen felt it was time to call a halt.

'I think Peter has told you all he can on that point, Inspector,' he said. 'All you told me you wanted was an account of his movements on Monday evening last.'

'Very well, Mr Anstey.' The interruption obviously didn't please him, but Stephen didn't think it could prejudice him further against Peter Dutton.

36

'Tell us about that evening, Peter,' he prompted. 'You had an arrangement to meet Dilys, I believe.'

'Yes, at eight-thirty.'

'At Rowan Corner, I understand,' said Wentworth. 'Not very far from the wood where she was found . . . dead.'

Peter licked his lips as though they had suddenly become dry. 'I thought it was safe enough for her,' he insisted, 'in the summer when it's still light. We could walk down beside Farthing Gill and along the river path.'

'The one they call Lovers' Lane?'

'It's nice by the river at this time of year,' said Peter. 'When we first started to go out together it was still dark at eight-thirty, and we'd meet in the village outside the Mortal Man.'

'That doesn't quite square with your story that you never took the girl there.'

'It's quite true, I didn't. We met there because it was lighter than anywhere else in the village and I thought it was a safer place for her to be in case she ever had to wait.'

'Were you in the habit of keeping her waiting?'

'I tried not to. But Dilys never had much sense of time. She was inclined to leave the house as soon as she finished washing up after dinner. . . . I couldn't always be sure what time that would be.'

'And that particular evening?'

'I'm not exactly sure when I left home, except that I meant to be early. Probably it was about twenty past eight, but I know when I got to Rowan Corner I was in good time. Dilys wasn't there but I wasn't worried about it then; she was more likely to be early than late but she wasn't exact to a minute or two either way.'

'Why didn't you call for her at home? Surely that would have been the best thing to do since you were so particular about her safety?' Again Stephen didn't like the detective's tone, but this time he made no comment. Perhaps he was as curious as Wentworth was to know the answer to the question.

'She preferred it that way,' said Peter.

37

'I think you're going to have to explain that to us, Mr Dutton.'

'The Lewises didn't particularly like her coming out. I don't think it was me they objected to particularly,' said Peter, suddenly speaking rather quickly as though it were an explanation he was eager to make. 'I think she was useful to them and they didn't want to lose her. They knew she came out with me on Saturday nights; that's when we used to come over to Rothershaw and go either to a concert, if there was one, or a dance. But I think Dilys thought if she didn't stress the fact that it was me she was seeing the other evenings she came out they wouldn't mind it so much.'

'It seems very unlikely that in a place like Burton Cecil they didn't know who she was meeting.'

'Well, that's how Dilys wanted it anyway. She said it saved a lot of argument.'

'You say she was a little late that night. How late?'

'I told you I didn't see her.' Again there was that anguished look in his solicitor's direction, but he was doing pretty well and Stephen didn't want to interfere more than was necessary so he just gave another encouraging nod.

'That's what you say,' said Wentworth, sarcastic again, and Peter flushed. Stephen thought for a moment he was going to make some voluble protest but fortunately he kept his temper in check. 'What did you do those other evenings when it was too late to come into Rothershaw?' Wentworth went on.

'We'd go for a walk, I thought I explained that. There was always lots to talk about.'

'Since the Lewises objected to your meetings you didn't think of taking her to your parents' house?'

'I took her there sometimes but the cottages are very tiny. Just one small living-room. Quite often my parents would be wanting to watch something on the telly, something Dilys and I wouldn't be interested in. I didn't want to disturb them too much.'

'Very considerate of you, I'm sure. There would not, besides, be much opportunity for love-making in their presence, would there?'

'I told you—'

'You must forgive my short memory.' Though Stephen realised that the detective's suspicions were reasonable he was beginning to dislike Wentworth intensely. 'The young lady was high-minded,' the inspector went on, 'and didn't approve of that sort of thing.'

'Not – not if she thought it was going too far,' said Peter solemnly.

Stephen was pretty sure Wentworth had taken due note of this though he made no direct comment. 'You didn't like her refusals, did you?' he asked. 'So you planned—'

It was only too obvious where this was leading. 'Just a moment, Inspector.' Stephen's voice was as incisive as he knew how to make it. 'We agreed, didn't we, that there was no reason to warn my client as you hadn't heard his story yet?'

'And if I don't like his story?' Wentworth's tone was aggressive.

'That's your misfortune. I can't allow any bullying, particularly after the assurance that you gave.'

'Very well.' Stephen wondered briefly if Peter found the detective's tone as ominous as he did. 'So you were waiting for Dilys Jones,' Wentworth continued, 'and you say she never arrived. When did you start becoming uneasy?'

'I began to think she might not be coming ... I suppose at a quarter or ten to nine. I did look at my watch, but that wasn't until nearly nine o'clock.'

'You made a distinction there, Mr Dutton. I asked when you became anxious.'

'I was anxious in the sense that I thought she might not be coming and I badly wanted her to. But I thought, you see, that Mrs Lewis must have needed her for something and she couldn't get away. It never occurred to me that anything had happened to her.'

'You didn't think of going round to the Lewises' to inquire?'

'No, I didn't. I think what I've told you already explains that.'

'So what *did* you do?'

'We'd always arranged that if she couldn't get away I wouldn't wait longer than half an hour. After that she wouldn't be coming.'

'So you went home?'

'Not immediately. I was restless and I thought if I went for a brisk walk it would settle my mind before I went home.'

'Where did you go?'

'Back through the village and out on the Manningbridge Road. There was very little traffic about and I walked a bit further than I intended to. I suppose I got home again at about a quarter or ten to ten.'

'Your parents were in?'

'Yes, they were watching the telly. Mum seemed a bit surprised to see me but I don't think Dad noticed whether I was there or not. So I sat down and watched with them for a bit. No good asking me what was on, because I didn't notice. And then – it was really rather boring – there didn't seem much point in doing that so I went to bed with a book.'

'You weren't worried about the fact that Miss Jones didn't turn up, and yet you were too upset to notice what you were watching?'

'It wasn't quite like that. I told you I was upset at not seeing her. It never occurred to me that anything was wrong.'

'Let's go back a bit then. While you were waiting nearly half an hour, according to you, at Rowan Corner who did you see?'

Peter frowned over that. 'I know it sounds odd but I didn't see anybody at all. A few cars went past, but not ones I recognised.'

'Convenient.' Wentworth came to his feet, moving, although it was not yet lunch time, as though he was very tired. Constable Tankard followed suit slowly. 'That will be all for the present, Mr Dutton,' said the inspector. 'But I think you will realise, Mr Anstey, that I have by no means finished my questions to your client. Before I see him again I would advise

40

him, if I were you, to consider his position very carefully.'

Stephen got up himself and went to the door with them, trying not to seem too eager to see the back of them. When he returned to his room Peter was still sitting beside the desk; he didn't seem to have moved at all. 'What did he mean?' he asked almost before Stephen had had time to seat himself again. 'What have I got to consider?'

'I'm afraid he meant he wasn't really satisfied with your story. As for the rest, that's something I must talk to you about anyway.'

'I don't quite understand.'

'Think about it a little then. According to your story, Dilys must have been already dead by the time you arrived at Rowan Corner. I'm sorry if this distresses you, Peter,' he added, seeing Dutton's hands involuntarily clenching together, 'but it's something we can't avoid. If Dilys was really early for your appointment the murderer might have done what was done and got away before you arrived, or he might have been still hiding in the wood. Would you have noticed that?'

Peter thought about that for a little. This habit of his of thinking before he spoke was becoming familiar. 'I didn't notice anything,' he said slowly, 'but I might not have done, you know. Even in the country there are always small sounds, an animal moving in the underbrush for instance. I'm afraid that isn't very helpful.'

'Not helpful,' said Stephen, 'though quite natural I think. But we've got to face the fact that, even as it stands, the evidence against you is strong and unless the police find anything to confirm what you've told them I think you may take it that an arrest will follow in a day or two.'

'I . . . Dad said as much,' said Peter miserably.

'As I understand it you've told me you didn't do it and if what we fear happens I shall stipulate a Not Guilty plea when I brief counsel on your behalf. But I think what Inspector Wentworth meant was that if you changed your mind and considered pleading Guilty it might be possible to persuade the jury that the killing was done in a fit of passion when you were not completely responsible for your actions.'

'But I didn't kill her.'

'No, I know what you told me. Let me finish, Peter. I have to point out to you in that connection that to my mind such a plea could only be considered with manual strangulation or if you had used your tie or a scarf that you or Dilys was wearing. No jury would believe in anything but premeditation considering that the weapon used had been prepared beforehand.'

'And that was really all that's relevant,' said Stephen, coming to the end of his recital. 'Was there anything else I could have done? Did I let the police get away with too much?'

'From what you've told us, I'd say you handled the matter extremely well,' said Antony, 'and told your story very clearly too. But it does leave me with one question in mind. I know the village as a whole believes in Peter Dutton's innocence, I know that Emma is also a partisan of his, but what's your own opinion?'

Stephen hesitated. 'I know I'm going against the face of the evidence,' he said at last, 'but I believe what he says. You'll say that's guesswork, that there's nothing at all to support that opinion—'

'I've had those very words said to me far too often to be likely to attack you on those lines,' Maitland assured him. 'Are Hugh and Caroline also of your opinion?'

'Yes they are, and they know him far better than I do. I don't know what you think, Mr Maitland—'

'I've no opinion at all on that score yet, I can't have. But one thing stands out a mile, this Inspector Wentworth of yours is a formidable opponent.'

'Yes, there's no doubt about that. Emma said you wouldn't mind my asking your advice though. What should I do next?'

'Since you've told me you believe Peter Dutton's story you've two choices if he's arrested. Brief counsel and as – as you're about to remind me – you're not very experienced in these matters yet get him to attend the Magistrates' Court hearing and take it from there. There's no real need for that, though, because it's almost invariably the best thing to reserve your defence. Once the hearing is over you'll have some idea of the prosecution's case, and in any event they'll be bound to send you copies of all the statements by witnesses, and particularly proofs of any evidence they intend to produce at the trial.'

'You said I have another option.' Stephen spoke a little cautiously, as though he were both anxious and unwilling to hear the reply.

'Well, you can if you like make some preliminary inquiries about the matter, and if you decide on that course you should start on it straight away before the prohibition about approaching prosecution witnesses comes into force . . . that is before an arrest is made. It might be a good idea to talk to Peter Dutton's parents, and certainly to the Lewises, though I realise,' he added quickly, seeing Stephen's rather appalled expression, 'that it may be rather an unpleasant interview. What you want to know, of course, is what other friends Dilys had, and I think you'll find that one thing may lead to another.'

Stephen eyed him for a moment, and as clearly as if he had spoken the thought aloud he was weighing up the other man's possible reaction to what he was about to say. 'I suppose,' he said tentatively, 'you wouldn't be prepared to give me a hand, at least as far as those first interviews are concerned. After all, if one thing did lead to another as you put it, you'd be far more likely than I am to know what to do next.'

Maitland surveyed him in silence for a moment. 'I wonder how far this conspiracy extends,' he said, after a pause which Stephen obviously found uncomfortable. 'You and Chris and Emma. Are Hugh and Caroline in it too?' He managed with difficulty to keep both his expression and his voice completely serious as he spoke.

'They said they didn't think you'd mind,' said Stephen, with the air of one fighting in the last ditch.

Antony smiled, he couldn't help it. 'I know,' he said. 'They told you my ways are unorthodox, and therefore I wouldn't mind . . . it would be unusual, you know.'

'If you'd go one step further and agree to represent Peter—'

'Wait a bit! The poor chap hasn't even been arrested yet. Though I admit,' he added more slowly, 'from what you've told me it's the logical conclusion.'

'Nobody in the village would be in the slightest degree surprised at your helping me,' said Stephen encouragingly. 'They all know you cleared up that matter seven years ago when Jenny was staying with Emma.'

'Under false pretences,' said Jenny and exchanged a smile with her husband.

'I did nothing of the kind!' There was no amusement in Maitland's voice now. 'I may have reached the right conclusion, but if you know the full story, Stephen, you must realise that did nothing to help matters. And Jenny nearly got killed into the bargain.'

'But she wasn't,' said Stephen, 'and in any case this time it's quite different. I can quite see it's an imposition when you're supposed to be on holiday, but I did hope—'

'The trouble is, it seems so obvious that your friend is guilty,' Antony told him. 'But I've no right to make rash judgements, and you all know him while I don't. What do you think, Emma, what should I do?'

'I want you to help Stephen, of course.'

'And you, Jenny?'

Jenny smiled. 'I agree with Emma,' she said, 'but not perhaps for the same reason.'

'What then, love?'

'Because if you don't you'll be worrying about it for the rest of your life,' said Jenny. 'And you know that's true, even if you won't admit it.'

Antony laughed. *'Touché,'* he said. 'All right, Stephen, I'll give you a hand, but it's your show. How do you want to arrange matters?'

'I ought to go into the office tomorrow morning, but in any

event it might be best to do those interviews in the afternoon. Then if we see the Duttons first there's a chance that Ivor Lewis will be at home by the time we get to them.'

'That doesn't sound a very onerous programme, but when do I meet Peter Dutton? I told you I hardly know him.'

'He won't be home during the day. Tomorrow evening, perhaps?'

'You've forgotten, Stephen,' Emma put in. 'We're all coming to dinner at Burton Crook. Caroline and I arranged that ages ago. And I've also accepted an invitation for all of us to go to the Hawthornes' house-warming on Saturday, but that's in the evening too so it leaves the rest of the day to arrange a meeting with Peter.'

'All right, I'll remember,' Stephen promised. 'I can see you'd want to make up your mind about him for yourself.'

'A single meeting is hardly likely to do that,' said Antony, but seeing Stephen's cast-down look he relented a little. 'You're worried about your friend,' he said, 'but it's early days yet. All kinds of clues may have been discovered since you saw Inspector Wentworth and the constable with the attractive name. They may not be suspecting Peter any longer.'

'In any case, Stephen,' said Emma, who had obviously been considering ways and means, 'if you're going to conduct interviews in the village tomorrow afternoon you'd better come to lunch here first.'

'Yes, that would be the easiest thing,' said Stephen, his mind still engaged with more important matters. It was only belatedly that he remembered to thank her for the invitation.

FRIDAY, 27th August

I

The following morning Emma showed signs, which the Maitlands knew her well enough to interpret, of wanting to get at her typewriter. What her undutiful nephews called the Misadventures of Maltravers were obviously on her mind. So as soon as Jenny had tidied their bedroom, which took very little doing, and offered her services to Emma's new daily, Mrs Kitchener, and had them politely refused, she and Antony left the cottage together. That morning, by common consent, they avoided the village, following Farthing Gill as far as the river path and then turning downstream.

When they got back the typewriter was silent, Mrs Kitchener had departed to get lunch for her husband, Joe, who was also the village constable, and Emma was making some slight adjustments to the table which was already laid in the big kitchen. Stephen arrived about ten minutes later, having of necessity parked his car near the shop and walked from there. The subject of Dilys Jones's death was avoided while they ate, but Stephen was restless and anxious and as soon as they had had one cup of coffee suggested that he and Antony should leave for their talk with the Duttons.

Parson's Row was the obvious name for the six cottages that comprised it, as Number Six was practically joined to the churchyard wall. They were tiny but had all been beautifully modernised, and as Antony had visited Roland Beaufort in Number One, the cottage nearest to Farthing Lee, he was quite familiar with their very simple plan. Originally they had been

46

two up and two down; the living-room leading off a minute hall and a kitchen behind it, with two bedrooms upstairs. When they were brought back to life (as Emma put it, because she maintained they had been practically falling down before) a small scullery had been built out at the back with a bathroom over it, the back bedroom having been made still smaller by a narrow passage to reach this amenity.

Stephen seemed nervous, and when they had crossed the footbridge and were nearing Rowan Corner Antony said reassuringly, 'I'll keep my doubts to myself you know.'

Stephen turned to him eagerly. 'That wasn't worrying me,' he said, 'but I hoped . . . it would really be easiest if you conducted the interview.'

'If you like. Only—'

'I'll have to learn to stand on my own feet, I know that,' said Stephen, and allowed a little impatience to creep into his voice. 'Hugh says you hate people saying they've heard of you, but I have to in order to explain. I want very much to do my best for Peter, and obviously you know better than I do what questions need to be asked.'

'Yes, I see,' said Antony rather blankly. He was aware enough of his reputation, but it always gave him a jolt to be brought face to face with other people's opinion of his abilities. Still, so far as experience was concerned, it couldn't be denied that Stephen's suggestion was a practical one. 'Introduce me to the Duttons, and we'll take it from there,' he agreed.

It was the third cottage and looked, if anything, even neater than its companions. Antony wasn't surprised to find, when Mrs Dutton opened the door to them, that the room to which she led them, though tiny, was extremely attractive. Each cottage had, he knew, its own small garden at the back, which perhaps explained the profusion of flowers.

Mary Dutton was a small, round woman wearing a neat navy-blue dress into which Maitland was immediately certain she had changed after her morning chores were done. Her expression was grave but he thought a cheerful look would come more naturally to her. Her husband, Michael, was also very short but there was no comfortable stoutness about him. He gave the impression of having shrunk with the years, so that now the wool cardigan he wore even on that hot day was several sizes too large for him. Emma had said he was only two or three years past his retirement, but even bearing this in mind it was difficult to visualise him siring a son a mere twenty-three years before.

They received their visitors kindly and showed no surprise when Stephen introduced his companion, except that the introduction was followed by a short silence during which they regarded Antony, so that he felt rather as though he was an animal of some unknown species whose behaviour they couldn't predict. But then Mrs Dutton smiled. 'I've seen you in the village, of course, Mr Maitland,' she said, 'when you've been visiting Miss Anstey. It's good of you to help us ... to try to help us,' she added, which consoled Antony a little because he was already afraid that Peter Dutton's case was past praying for.

'And we're wondering,' said Michael Dutton, who turned out to have a surprisingly deep voice, 'what happened when the police interviewed Peter at your office, Mr Anstey.'

There was an anxiety behind the question and Stephen hastened to reassure him. 'Nothing definite emerged from it, they had no questions to ask that I didn't expect. But surely Peter—'

'He said it was quite obvious what Inspector Wentworth thought,' Mrs Dutton broke in. 'You're not telling us he was wrong about that?'

'I'm afraid not, only that I think the police would like a little more evidence before they go any further.'

'They can't find that, there can't be any. Peter would never do a thing like that.' She turned to Maitland as she spoke, obviously wanting his agreement, and unconsciously using the very phrase calculated to annoy him most.

He tried to smile back at her warmly, hoping that this would

48

be taken for agreement with her point of view. It was cowardly, he knew, but they were such a nice couple, and though he wouldn't in any case have said straight out that he thought Peter might well be guilty he didn't want them to have even an inkling of his opinion. 'Do you mind answering some questions for us?' he asked. 'Mr Anstey has suggested—'

She didn't wait for him to finish. 'No, not at all, if there's anything we can do to help.'

'Tell me about Monday evening then,' he invited. 'Did you know Peter was going to meet Dilys that night?'

'He didn't say ... young people are so secretive nowadays. Michael tells me I shouldn't blame him for that,' said Mrs Dutton. 'Peter is old enough to go his own way, and of course we never ask him.'

'I wonder if you realise, however,' Stephen put in, 'that his greatest concern is for how all this will affect you. Both of you.' There was a pause while they exchanged rather doubtful glances, and Maitland felt a sense of relief that Stephen hadn't after all been struck dumb by the difficulties of the situation. 'I'm telling you this because I know Peter never will. But it was quite obvious in every word he said to me.'

'Well, that's nice,' said Mary Dutton. 'But what is it that you're wanting to know, Mr Maitland?'

'About Monday evening,' he repeated. 'What time did Peter go out?'

'Now that I can't tell you exactly.' Mary Dutton seemed to have constituted herself as spokesman. 'We were watching the television, you see' - she indicated with one hand a rather large set that was mercifully mute in the corner – it's a great help in the winter when there's not much to be done outside, and even at this time of year we've reached the stage when we're glad enough to sit quietly in the evening. But I remember that we'd had supper, and everything was cleared away, and I asked Peter whether he was going to stay in. He said, No, but he wouldn't be late home, and he went up to his room to get ready. Our programme started at eight o'clock, and he went out some time while it was on.'

'More than half over,' said Michael Dutton suddenly. 'Eight-twenty probably.'

'And you didn't know where he was going or whom he was going to meet?'

'Not positively. We did know he was seeing Dilys, of course; he's brought her here once or twice, but he might just as easily have been going down to the pub with Roland that night.'

'What did you think of Dilys Jones?'

Again it was Mrs Dutton who answered. 'She seemed a very nice girl and I know they had a lot in common. But Peter was far too young to think of marrying.'

Maitland glanced at Michael Dutton and found him shaking his head. 'Mature enough,' he said, 'and I daresay the Jones girl would have done as well as another. As Mary says, their tastes seemed to run together. Not that they'd have had much to live on, not yet anyway, but I daresay his job at Black's is as safe as any other, seeing he didn't want to follow my advice and go into the civil service.'

'These tastes of Peter's that he and Dilys had in common?' Antony said, making the words a question.

'I don't know where he got them.' Michael smiled affectionately at his wife. 'We're a pair of lowbrows, Mary and I, and not ashamed to say so, but Peter grew up despising all the things we enjoy. This book business.... I'm all for a good read myself, but the reason he likes the shop is that he can talk to some of the customers about what he calls significant books. We enjoy a good show on the telly, but that wouldn't do for Peter. It had to be a concert in Rothershaw, classical stuff. He'd have liked his own collection of records, but you can see for yourself there's no room for that in this house, even if he could have afforded it.'

'If you want to know what I think,' said Mary Dutton, 'it was all because of his getting so friendly with that Roland.'

'Roland Beaufort?'

'Yes, he lives two doors away.' Antony knew that already but there was no point in saying so. 'He's a writer. The sort of books nobody understands, I can't believe he makes much from them but I think he has some private means as well.'

'He has all these high-falutin' notions about culture,' said Michael Dutton shaking his head, 'and somehow they've rubbed off on Peter.'

'And Dilys shared them?'

'I don't know about the books; I think that rather doubtful. A good girl, a kind girl, but not a great brain. But as for the music . . . well she was Welsh, wasn't she?'

'I suppose that would explain it. We seem to have got a long way from the subject, I'm afraid. You were telling me that Peter left the house at about twenty past eight and you didn't know where he was going.'

'That's right.'

'Peter says he wasn't worried when Dilys didn't turn up, even when it became quite obvious she wasn't going to. You'll understand that Mr Anstey has given me a careful account of their talk, and of the interview with the police. Apparently Peter just thought that Mrs Lewis had needed the girl for something and she couldn't get away. So he went for a walk instead, through the village and along the Manningbridge Road. Would you say that was typical behaviour?'

'Are you questioning his word, Mr Maitland?'

'That wasn't in my mind. He'd been waiting for her at Rowan Corner and he says he went for a walk because he felt restless. It's a pity he didn't go into the Mortal Man to join his friend there, because then someone would be able to substantiate that part of his story at least.'

He was relieved to find that they didn't question his attitude any further. 'He's a great one for walking is Peter,' said his father. 'Not that he doesn't like a drink now and then, but it's more the company he's after when he goes to the local.'

'So it was quite natural for him to go for a walk before he came home? Was he later than you expected him to be?'

'We didn't expect him, at least only because he'd said he

51

wouldn't be late home. If it had been Dilys he was meeting – yes, I know now that's what he meant to do, but we didn't know that at the time – he'd have taken her for a walk and got her back to the Lewises by about ten o'clock. After that he might have had a quick one if he found Roland in the pub and come home at closing time. I wouldn't have expected him to be later than that in any case.'

'But actually he was rather earlier.'

'Can you remember, Mary? I don't seem to call it to mind at all.'

'No,' said Mrs Dutton, 'I can't either.'

'Do you remember which programme you were watching? I think Peter said you were still watching television.' He glanced inquiringly at Stephen as he spoke.

'Yes, we were,' Mary Dutton responded readily. 'It was a film, an old film. I remember I was a little annoyed with him for interrupting, but whether it was in the middle or towards the end I just can't think.'

'I can't remember either,' her husband agreed. 'Naturally we broke off for a moment or two to ask him if he'd had a pleasant evening.'

'What had he to say to that?'

'I think he just said it was all right. Wasn't that it, Mary?'

'As if he'd found it rather boring,' said Mrs Dutton, nodding.

'So at least you can tell me how Peter seemed when he came in.'

'Not as if he had just been strangling that poor girl,' said Mary Dutton rather sharply. 'I think he'd been walking quickly, which was natural for him, because he was a little bit breathless. But apart from that he was just as usual. Don't you think I know him too well, Mr Maitland, for him to be able to hide a thing like that from me?'

'I'm sure you do, Mrs Dutton, but it may be important to be able to point out that there was nothing abnormal in his behaviour at a time that can't have been more than an hour and a half, or two hours at most, after someone strangled Dilys

Jones. There's also the question of the cord with which she was killed.'

'The police asked us about that. It was the kind that people use for drawing their curtains from the side. We've nothing of the sort here; you can see we don't need it with these tiny windows,' said Michael quickly.

'That's good. Did Peter stay up with you?'

'No, he didn't seem interested, just said he was going right to bed. And come to think of it, it must have been ten o'clock or earlier that he got in, because I did notice the time when Mr Lewis came round, eleven o'clock, and it certainly wasn't less than an hour before that.'

'What did Mr Lewis have to say?'

'He and his wife were a bit worried because the girl hadn't come home, and he thought she might have been here with Peter. Of course I had to say we hadn't seen her, and I called Peter down—'

'He'd been asleep, I can tell you that,' said Mrs Dutton.

'—and he'd said he'd been going to meet her but she hadn't turned up and he'd taken it for granted she'd never left home.'

'What did Mr Lewis have to say about that?'

'That she'd gone out after dinner.'

'Did she tell him who she was going to meet?'

'Not exactly. He said she was secretive about things like that but he knew well enough from talk in the village that Peter was the only one she ever went out with. So that's why he came here.'

'That must have worried you. I mean the fact that she seemed to be missing.'

'Yes, of course it did,' said Mary Dutton eagerly. 'The funny thing was that it didn't seem to affect Peter that way. He was puzzled, not worried.'

'Did Mr Lewis say he was going to the police?'

'Yes, that's what we understood.'

'I'd have thought the natural thing would be for Peter to go with him.'

53

'He explained that to us,' said Michael Dutton. 'He's never been one to talk much to us about his affairs, you know, but that night he was a little more open. He said he expected Dilys had got early to the meeting place – she never had any sense of time – and if somebody had come along while she was waiting, somebody with a car perhaps, she might have decided it would be more fun to go to the late show at the cinema in Rothershaw, than to wait for Peter. There was a film on that she wanted to see; in fact she'd asked him to take her on Saturday but he said it was sentimental trash and got tickets for a concert instead. So he thought perhaps she was angry with him, but she'd be home all right when the show was over.'

'He said nothing to me about that,' Stephen put in.

'No, he's a reticent one our Peter is.'

'Was Mr Lewis there when Peter told you what was in his mind?'

'Yes, and I don't think he found it reassuring. Anyway, off he went and Peter went back to bed again. As I've said it was only eleven o'clock when Mr Lewis came,' said Mr Dutton, obviously feeling that some further explanation was necessary. 'Peter had it all worked out. That was just about the time the picture would finish, and if they'd had a cup of coffee after the show it would probably be half past at least before they got back to Burton Cecil.'

'Yes, that all sounds very circumstantial, and it also sounds as though Peter had some idea who Dilys might have been with. That's something you'll have to ask him, Stephen.'

'Yes, of course.'

'I'll tell him you want to see him again,' Michael offered.

'That would be kind of you. But I'll have to get this quite clear: your minds were quite at rest after what he'd told you. Did you sit up much longer?'

'Only long enough to give him time to finish in the bathroom. And then at four o'clock there were the police hammering on the door to tell us what had happened.'

'That must have been a shock.'

'It certainly was. And Peter was stunned, you could see that; I think he was especially upset because he'd been thinking rather unkind things about Dilys for not showing up.'

'It was the detectives from Rothershaw who came, I believe.'

'That's right. They said they'd found her at two o'clock, that is the local men had, Sergeant Gilbey and Joe Kitchener. They hadn't called out a complete search until they'd looked in the obvious places, and Peter having told them where they were meaning to meet I suppose it was natural that they should look in the wood.'

'Poor child, poor child,' said Mary Dutton shaking her head sadly. 'And when Peter will get over it I can't think. But at least,' she added, 'people are being kind. They're going out of their way to be kind, I should say.'

'I'm sure they would be.' There was a small, cynical thought at the back of Maitland's mind that things might have been different if they hadn't already decided on another culprit. And then, oddly enough, for the first time a doubt of Peter Dutton's guilt crossed his mind. After all, the Ansteys knew him well, and Emma at least had watched him grow up. And if he was any judge Mary and Michael Dutton were a thoroughly decent couple. . . . Could they be capable of producing such a monster? In fact could Peter be a monster and impress everyone else with his innocence?

But he dismissed the idea almost before it was formulated. There was still the question he had propounded to Stephen: was Dilys Jones the kind of girl to go into the wood with a stranger? True, Peter, who presumably knew her very well, thought she might – in a fit of pique because he wouldn't take her to the pictures – have succumbed to the temptation to go to Rothershaw with someone else. But in that case a drive in a comfortable car might well have seemed more attractive than a rather dull walk by the river. And anyway that wasn't what had happened. Peter's freedom from concern in what should have seemed a quite worrying situation was just one more count against him in Antony's mind.

But none of this could be said to his parents. Though they talked a little longer nothing of interest emerged and Stephen looked dejected when they went out again into the village street and turned right towards the house where the Lewises lived.

II

Stephen's steps were lagging a little and Maitland thought he knew what was on his younger companion's mind. Talking to the Duttons whose son was under suspicion was bad enough; the Lewises had suffered a bereavement, and though it sounded from what he had heard of them that perhaps they hadn't been as concerned with Dilys's welfare as they might have been, still, sympathy seemed to be in order. Nothing much was said between them as they went along the village street, though there was a constant stream of greetings to be exchanged with almost everyone they passed. Beyond the shop there were four larger houses, each standing in its own grounds, and the one belonging to the Lewises was the last of them, a fairly modern, pleasant-looking place. 'I've been introduced to Mrs Lewis,' said Stephen as they turned in at the gate, 'but beyond that I can't say that I know them.'

It was evident, however, as soon as Myfanwy Lewis opened the door that she remembered him well enough. To Antony at least the recognition in her eyes was obvious, but for some reason she decided to suppress it and said merely, Yes? inquiringly, looking from one of them to the other as she spoke. She was one of those very fair Welsh women with a clear unblemished complexion and an oval face that had a faintly puffy look about it as though someone had intended to blow her up like a balloon and then thought better of the idea.

Stephen introduced himself and his companion and was prepared to explain their visit a little further until he saw there was no need. 'Mr Anstey! Of course we've met! And I've heard of Mr Maitland, and seen him in the village sometimes when he's been visiting your aunt.' She was almost gushing now. 'Do come in, so kind of you to call. Ivor nearly always comes home early on Friday so I was just going to make some tea.'

Perhaps because they had both found the previous interview difficult the prospect seemed inviting and the implied invitation was accepted with pleasure. In a way, thought Maitland, it was perhaps a good thing that Ivor Lewis had not yet arrived home; there would be no harm in having a gossip first with Myfanwy.

She was still prattling away when she led them into the drawing-room. Antony generally mistrusted modern furniture, but this for a change looked quite comfortable and lived up to its looks when he accepted the chair she indicated. 'We sent the children to Ivor's sister,' she was saying. 'All this going on, it wasn't a proper environment for them though of course they can't understand how really horrible it is.'

'That was the first thing I wanted to say to you, Mrs Lewis,' said Stephen, finding his tongue and following the unmistakable lead her greeting had given him. 'I should like to offer you my sincere sympathy in your loss, and that of my aunt and brother and sister-in-law too. They all asked me to tell you that if there was anything they could do—'

'Oh yes, of course. So kind.' She received the carefully prepared speech in rather an offhand way, so that Maitland, beyond murmuring something almost inaudible, felt that nothing further was called for from the stranger in their midst. 'Dilys was a dear girl and so good with the children,' Myfanwy went on. 'I can't believe she's gone, and in that ghastly way.'

Obviously she thought that to offer condolences was the sole purpose of their visit, and it seemed advisable to lead up gradually to the real reason. At any moment now she'd be saying that it was a relief to know that nothing had happened before the murder. To Antony's relief it seemed that Stephen agreed with this conclusion. 'How old are the children, Mrs Lewis?' he asked, which had at least the effect of heading off that possibility.

'David is nine and Llewellyn is seven,' she told them. 'But we're neighbours now that you've come to live at Burton Crook and I can't go on calling you Mr Anstey; it's quite ridiculous when I say Hugh and Caroline to your brother and sister-in-law. So I shall call you Stephen, and my name is Myfanwy, which I'm quite sure you don't know how to spell.'

Stephen obviously decided to ignore that; perhaps he felt it was time he stopped sailing under false colours. 'I'm here professionally, as a matter of fact,' he said, 'besides wishing to offer our condolences. And Mr Maitland agreed to accompany me, in view of his greater experience in these matters. I'm representing Peter Dutton.'

'Peter? Why?'

'So far it's only been a question of sitting in on an interview he had with the police.'

'You mean they suspect him of having killed Dilys?' This seemed to be quite a new idea to her. 'Ivor says—'

'What does Ivor say?' Maitland asked when she hesitated, and Stephen also seemed to be at a loss for words.

She smiled at him. What he had heard of her before had definitely prejudiced him against her, but he was beginning to like her now. 'Well, one thing he says is that I quote him too much,' she admitted. 'But I was going to tell you he thinks that strange man Wainwright must have done it. He says nothing like this ever happened before he came to live in Burton Cecil.'

'Are you forgetting what happened seven years ago?' Antony asked, returning her smile, though it was the last subject he wanted to dwell on.

'No – how could I? – but this is different. A young girl. . . . Ivor says there doesn't have to be a motive, not in the way that is generally understood. It must be someone who is not quite all there, and Ivor thinks there may be more deaths.'

This idea had already occurred to Maitland though he still found Peter Dutton a more believable suspect. This other possibility, besides, was even more unpleasant. 'Tell me about Dilys,' he invited. 'It might be important to know what sort of girl she was.'

Myfanwy showed no unwillingness. 'She lived with us for about two years,' she told them. 'Before that I managed with some help in the village. We still have that, of course. Dilys looked after the boys mainly. As for the household chores, I do the cooking and she does – did – the clearing away. That seemed to be a fair arrangement.'

'What I really want to know is what she was like,' Maitland explained.

'A bit dreamy. That could be annoying, as a matter of fact, but I suppose I shouldn't say that now. As for this idea of her marrying Peter Dutton, she was far too young.'

'I don't think I even knew her by sight, did you, Stephen? How old was she?' he went on, without waiting for a reply.

'Twenty. You're going to tell me that's old enough for a girl to be thinking of marriage,' she added shrewdly, 'and perhaps it would have been better to say that Peter was too young. He may know his own mind at twenty-three, I don't know. He certainly couldn't have supported her in any great comfort.'

'Then you didn't like her going out with Peter?'

'I didn't quite say that ... after all she had to have some friends nearer her own age. And the Duttons are a respectable family, I wasn't afraid for her virtue or anything like that.' (Really she did use the most incredible phrases.) 'Maisie Jerrold – the vicar's wife – accused me once of being afraid to lose her, and I can't deny she was very very useful to us.' Again there was that smile, this time as though she had some secret source of amusement. 'So I examined my conscience thoroughly, but I don't think it was true.'

'They used to go into Rothershaw on Saturday evening?'

'Yes. Other days Dilys wasn't free until after dinner and by that time it was too late for them to take the bus. The Duttons don't have a car—'

'It never occurred to me before,' Antony interrupted, turning to Stephen. 'How does Peter get to work?'

'By bicycle. A boy his age thinks nothing of ten miles a day,' said Stephen, as though his client were somebody of quite another generation than his own.

'No, I suppose not.' He turned back to Mrs Lewis again. 'Forgive me for interrupting you, I gather you knew about the Saturday meetings but Peter thought you didn't know that Dilys was meeting him the other evenings she came out.'

'Then Peter was wrong. She didn't always say where she was going, and I didn't ask her, but if you think you can hide a thing like that in a place like Burton Cecil you don't know us very well in spite of your regular visits. In any case I'd no reason to make a fuss. From what I was told they'd just go for walks together, and she was generally home by ten o'clock or ten-thirty at the latest.'

'How often was she seeing him then?'

'Besides the Saturday evenings when they'd go to Rother-shaw, about twice a week.'

Antony had the feeling she was about to add something but at that moment there came the sound of a car drawing into the drive. 'That'll be Ivor!' she exclaimed. 'And I still haven't made the tea I promised you.' She rushed from the room as if the devil himself was after her and they heard her heels clicking down the hall away from the front door.

So there were just the two of them in the room when Ivor Lewis came in, and they had to sustain a momentary look of incredulity. But when Stephen introduced himself and his companion it was obvious that they were both known to the newcomer by sight. 'We haven't met but I'm Ivor Lewis, as I'm sure you've guessed. It was very kind of you to come.'

'Not kind at all, really,' Stephen told him. 'We've both expressed our regrets to Mrs Lewis for what happened, it was a terrible thing and must have been a great shock to you, as well as a grief. But I'm really here professionally, and Mr Maitland very kindly offered to lend me a little moral support.'

'Ah yes, very understandable.' There was a note of mockery in his voice. 'Where's Myfanwy?' he inquired rather abruptly, looking round as though he might find her hiding behind the sofa or in one of the corners of the room.

'I think she went to make the tea. Don't you want me to explain—?'

'Is it really necessary?' Now he sounded more bored than anything else. 'The police are about to arrest the wrong person and Mr Maitland – and you too I suppose – are all set to put them right.'

Antony thought it was time to take a hand. In view of his doubts the statement was inaccurate, but he found the knowledge it conveyed of his own affairs too near the bone to be comfortable. 'I think from what Mr Anstey tells me that their inquiries are in a preliminary stage,' he said, 'but Peter Dutton is his client and, as he told you, I agreed to lend him what assistance I could on a purely friendly basis.'

'You mean that's the way Wentworth's mind is turning? You do surprise me.'

'Do I, Mr Lewis?'

'You certainly do. I don't like the boy . . . well, I don't exactly dislike him either. But I should have thought it would have been obvious to anyone – even the police – that he isn't the guilty party.'

'Then you won't mind answering a few questions for us,' Maitland said hopefully.

'No, not at all.' This time his smile was more friendly. 'You must realise you're a bit of a – a conversation piece, Mr Maitland, ever since what happened the first time you came to Burton Cecil. It will be interesting to see at first hand how you set about things.'

At that moment Myfanwy returned with a tray, which was just as well because – as Stephen said afterwards – Maitland was almost visibly breathing fire. There was an interval while she poured the tea and Ivor passed round sandwiches, which gave Antony more time to study his host and hostess a little more closely. Her blue dress was obviously expensive and he was equally well turned out . . . dressed with perfect propriety for the country, but much more elegantly than was usual in that

61

part of the world. In addition, the tea service was of the most delicate china, so that if Jenny had been present she would undoubtedly have been longing to turn over the saucer to see from which famous maker it came. There was no lack of money, he decided, which was interesting in its way but not much help.

'It's so nice to have Ivor home as early as this,' said Myfanwy. Maitland had been listening for a Welsh lilt in her voice without being able to detect it, though it was only too apparent in Ivor's. 'It makes such a nice start to the weekend. By the way, darling, do you know the house on the other side of Doctor Oaksley's has been sold?'

'Of course I do, I saw them moving in about a month ago.'

'Yes, of course. I was only leading up to the fact that we've been asked to a house-warming party tomorrow. I suppose it's the modern way,' added Myfanwy rather regretfully. 'People don't wait to be called on any more.'

'I haven't any patience with those old-fashioned ideas,' said Ivor. He had finished his errand of mercy now and seated himself again. 'You'd better tell me, Mr Maitland, what is it exactly you want me to do for you?'

Antony glanced at his hostess. 'It seems a poor return for your kindness – this tea is delicious – but Mrs Lewis has promised to answer some questions for me. Do you mind?'

'Myfanwy never minds talking,' said Ivor, a fact which either of the visitors might have deduced for themselves from their conversation so far. 'What are these questions of yours?'

'Very simple really. I'd just like an account of Monday evening from your point of view.'

'I don't see how that's going to help Peter, which I suppose is the idea. However, here goes. Dilys left here just before eight o'clock.'

'Wait a bit! I understood it was eight-thirty when she was to meet Peter.'

'That may be so, but it was certainly no more than five to eight when she left here. That was earlier than usual and I know she was rather vague about time so I glanced at my watch – it was three minutes to eight, but it might be a couple of minutes fast – and told her to wait a while. It was Peter's place to wait for her rather than the other way around.'

'But she went anyway?'

'She did. I think, to tell you the truth,' said Ivor a little ruefully, 'that she thought I was just making an excuse to delay her because she knew we weren't too keen on these walks she used to take with young Peter. She'd never told us who she was going to meet, but you can't keep anything to yourself in Burton Cecil.'

'Then she must have reached Rowan Corner by a quarter past eight at the latest.'

'I'd put it earlier than that if anything. When she was alone she walked rather quickly. Ten past eight would be more like it.'

'Peter says he aimed to be there before half past, because he rather expected her to be early. What do you think could have happened in the meantime?'

'Somebody came along and invited her to walk into the shade of the wood with him. And I don't think you've very far to look for that somebody.'

'If you mean this Mr Wainwright I keep hearing about, would she have gone with him? I mean, she could hardly have known him, could she?'

'Only by sight. But you didn't know Dilys, Mr Maitland; she was a very credulous girl. Anybody could spin her a yarn, and however outrageous it was she'd believe it.'

'I still think you're making too much of the fact that he's a stranger.'

'Tell him what you think, Ivor,' Myfanwy urged apparently forgetting that she'd already done so.

'It's quite simple. I think it was a sex murder, despite the fact that she hadn't been molested. That doesn't always happen, as I'm sure you know. And whatever Peter Dutton's shortcomings might have been as a prospective husband, I've never had any doubts about the fact that Dilys was quite safe with him. So I'm afraid, I'm very much afraid, that what happened may not be the end of it.'

'I sincerely hope you're wrong,' said Antony, forgetting for the moment Peter Dutton's interests. But even Stephen, that strong partisan, would hardly wish his client to be proved innocent by some other girl being killed. Maitland looked round at his companions. 'You all know Burton Cecil so much better than I do. I pass the wood where she was found every day when I'm staying with Emma, but I've never actually been in it. Is walking there pleasant, or is there a lot of undergrowth?'

It was Stephen who took it upon himself to answer. 'It's quite pleasant walking, but from what the police told me – which I should have passed on to you along with the rest – though Dilys's body was out of sight of where Peter would have been standing waiting for her, it was really only a few feet into the wood.'

'That's just what I wanted to know. I was thinking of the time element, of course. It's quite obvious that she could have been dead quite a while before Peter arrived at Rowan Corner.'

'I think you're quite right,' said Ivor. 'In any case, I've always understood that strangulation is quite quick.'

'I hate it when you talk like that,' said Myfanwy. 'It brings it all home to me.'

'I know it does, my dear, but it's no use blinking at facts. And, come to think of it, I've another reason for remembering what time Dilys left. I went out a few moments later to the wood pile, the Jerrolds were coming in for an after-dinner drink and if there's one thing Maisie likes more than another it's an open fire. It's only really today that it's got warm enough to do without one in the evening.'

'I didn't see Dilys go,' Myfanwy put in. 'I was upstairs putting the boys to bed and when I came down I couldn't think where you'd got to. And then the next thing I knew you were bumping on the door with your arms full of firewood. Maisie's a darling, but really rather a nuisance in that way. The fire makes so much mess.'

That was incontrovertible, though Antony at least was inclined to think it was worth it. 'Have you met the Jerrolds?' Ivor asked.

'Yes, on a number of occasions. Emma says they've been here for ever.'

'I often think that Tom ought to apply for a parish nearer to town,' said Myfanwy. 'The vicarage is far too big for them now that the children are all grown up and gone. But then again I think Maisie would miss Burton Cecil and her friends here. And one can't live other people's lives for them.'

'That is only too true, my dear,' said Ivor, with a shade of meaning in his voice that perhaps wasn't quite kind. 'But Mr Maitland is wanting to hear an account of our evening.' He didn't add, of our alibis, though from his tone it was quite obvious that he realised this. 'The Jerrolds arrived a little later than we expected, about nine o'clock I should say but one doesn't notice things like that exactly. We had a drink and some conversation ... you know how it is when you know people very well, there's always a lot to talk about. I don't think Myfanwy had realised how late it was getting but I was beginning to listen for Dilys. And when it got to eleven o'clock I was quite sure that something must be wrong.'

'Yet you had thought she was out with Peter Dutton?'

'Yes, I had. I had no qualms about her if she was, as I think I've told you, but she hadn't said in so many words that it was Peter she was meeting.'

'So what did you do?'

'Excused myself to Tom and Maisie and went round to the Duttons' cottage. Mary and Michael were watching one of their inevitable television shows, I thought at first nobody was going to answer the door, they didn't hear me knocking. When I explained what had happened they were quite shocked and said they hadn't seen Dilys that evening and Michael went to the bottom of the stairs to call Peter down. It was a few minutes before he came, he looked as if he'd been asleep, and he didn't seem to take in straight away what I was getting at.'

'Did he tell you his side of the story?'

'Yes, and I believed him. I mean insofar as the fact that he hadn't seen Dilys that evening. What I couldn't credit was the explanation he gave for her disappearance.'

'You thought Peter's idea was unreasonable?'

'I couldn't understand his entertaining it for a moment. It made me wonder whether he was quite as fond of Dilys as I had previously thought.'

That didn't sound too good. If the case ever came to court Peter's lack of worry over Dilys's disappearance was going to be a material point. 'If Dilys was vague about the time she might have thought Peter was standing her up,' Stephen hazarded, trying the idea out for size as it were. 'That might have been what was in Peter's mind.'

'It might have been,' said Ivor grudgingly. 'Anyway, as it wasn't what happened, it doesn't really matter, does it?'

'It might matter to Peter,' Maitland pointed out. 'I gather that you were alone when you left the Duttons' cottage.'

'Yes, I was. I went straight to the police station. Joe Kitchener and his wife live there, you know.'

'Yes I know, I used to visit Hugh there, seven years ago, and Emma tells me that Mrs Kitchener works for her now.'

'Of course, I'd forgotten. Anyway, I aroused Joe with some difficulty and we phoned Sergeant Gilbey. I wanted to get up a search party but they persuaded me it would be best for them to have a look around first and that I should go back to my guests. I must say I was a bit reluctant to do so, but when I thought it over I understood they were trying to be kind. To have seen her like that.... It was bad enough later when I had to identify her.'

'I'm sorry to make you go back over all this,' said Antony.

'I may as well finish now that I've started. Joe Kitchener came to tell us, perhaps an hour later. I'm a bit vague about that. He said the sergeant was getting in touch with the Criminal Investigation Department at Rothershaw, and if we weren't too tired they'd be glad if we stayed up to talk to them.

Of course we agreed. It was a bit of a shock to know Dilys couldn't be brought home, but of course when we thought about it we realised it was the best thing because of the boys. I don't think there's really anything more to tell you.'

'You've been very helpful.'

'Helpful?' he said doubtfully. 'I don't see how all this can help you.'

'If the police arrest Peter Dutton—'

'That's ridiculous! You're something of a detective yourself, I understand,' said Ivor, more or less as he had done before. 'Present them with the true culprit and Peter will be home and dry.'

'You're still meaning Philip Wainwright,' Maitland said. 'There's not a thing against him except that he's a stranger here. I can understand the villagers thinking that's suspicious,' he added bluntly, 'but not a man of your intelligence.'

Ivor had a rather wry smile for that. 'I can only say, Mr Maitland, when you know us all better you'll realise I'm not being quite as stupid as you think.'

'I didn't say—'

'No, but you thought it. Don't worry, I'm not offended, I can quite see how it looks from your point of view. But you'll find that I'm right, and that the wiseacres at the Mortal Man are right too. You see if you don't.'

After that they finished their tea and took their leave of the Lewises about half an hour later. Nothing else had come to light; come to think of it nothing had come to light either in the question and answer part of the conversation. But Antony was relieved at least that they'd taken his curiosity so well, and was inclined to like both of them better than he had expected. But Stephen gave the impression of being far from happy. Perhaps, thought Maitland, with some amusement, he was beginning to question for the first time his wisdom in asking for help.

III

As they left the short drive that led up to the Lewises' garage and stepped into the village street again Stephen paused and glanced at his watch. 'We ought to talk,' he said, 'but it's too early for the pub to be open.' And then, looking up, 'There's Peter now, you said you wanted to meet him.'

Maitland glanced in the same direction. The cyclist who was approaching them must, he supposed, be Stephen's client. He was coming up rather quickly, and almost fell off his bike when he saw them, which seemed to indicate surprise rather than consternation because his voice was reasonably casual as he spoke. 'I was just on my way to see you, Stephen.'

'Well, here I am,' said Stephen, apparently unconscious that he was stating the obvious. 'And this is Mr Maitland, who has kindly agreed to give me a hand with the preliminary inquiries I wanted to make.'

Peter turned to look at Antony, who recognised him now as someone whom he had seen about the village from time to time. It was perfectly obvious that the younger man knew exactly who he was, but whether from tact or awe he made no comment on the fact, saying only, 'That's very good of you.'

'You're early today, aren't you?' said Stephen.

For a moment Peter scowled. 'That's what I wanted to see you about,' he said rather solemnly. 'The police have been asking more questions.'

'Then you shouldn't have answered them. Inspector Wentworth understands the position perfectly well.'

'I didn't mean asking me,' said Peter. 'They came round to the shop asking Mr Black what kind of a person I am. So of course, when they'd gone, he wanted to know what it was all about and when I told him he said I'd better take a few days off. And that's what I wanted to know, Stephen, have they any right going round blackening people's characters?'

'I'm afraid in the circumstances they've every right to ask

68

some questions about you, Peter, and from what you say they made no defamatory remarks to Mr Black about you. I'm sorry about it, but I'm afraid for the moment you'll have to put up with that kind of thing.'

Maitland had been occupying himself by wondering idly where Peter Dutton had got his height, but now the young man surprised him by abandoning the resentment he obviously felt for an outburst of sentiment that equally obviously came straight from the heart. 'The trouble is, it gives me all that more time to think about Dilys. You wouldn't believe how I miss her. Mum says, You're young and you'll get over it, but things don't hurt you any the less because of that.'

As he spoke he had been looking from one to the other of his companions, so that the remark was addressed equally to both of them. It was Maitland who replied, for the moment forgetting his suspicions. 'I sometimes think,' he said quietly, 'that they hurt you more. But there's something in what your mother says all the same.'

'Have you been to see them?'

'Yes, we have. Stephen was kind enough to let me go with him. Didn't you understand that was what he meant to do?'

'They couldn't tell you anything I haven't told him already.'

'They told us one thing, Mr Dutton. About why you weren't worried about Dilys, even after Mr Lewis's visit at eleven o'clock.'

'Oh that! I hadn't a lot to offer her, Stephen will have told you that. I know she said it didn't matter, but suppose that while she was waiting someone came along with a car, don't you think she might have been tempted to go with him? Particularly if she resented my refusing to take her to that silly film.'

'Yes, I can see your train of thought. But in that case you must have some idea whom she would be likely to go with?'

'One of the lads,' said Peter vaguely.

'That doesn't help me very much. If you mean someone from Burton Cecil—'

'If he was driving towards Rothershaw it could have been

69

someone from anywhere along the Manningbridge Road. But that isn't what happened, Mr Maitland, so what are you asking me all this for?'

'Because if Dilys had some other friends besides yourself—'

Again he was interrupted. 'Of course she did, but they were people she'd met when she was out with me. I did think that might have happened, but I didn't think it meant anything serious. And I haven't the faintest idea who might have wanted to kill her, unless Roland's right about what they're saying in the pub and it was that chap Wainwright. He looks queer enough for anything.'

'If it was this Mr Wainwright the police will know about it soon enough,' Maitland said non-committally. He was beginning to feel tired of countering this particular argument. 'In the meantime, try not to feel too resentful of your employer. Look at it from his point of view.'

'I can understand that all right now I've cooled off a bit. I can't say it cheers me much though,' said Peter. 'Is that all you wanted to ask me, because if it is I'd better be getting along home? If either Mother or Dad saw me from the window as I passed they'll be wondering what's happened.'

Stephen glanced inquiringly at Maitland, who returned his look with a slight shake of the head. Interpreting this correctly, the solicitor turned back to Peter. 'That seems to be all, except that I might add one bit of advice,' he said. 'Your parents are of a different generation, but they feel things just as deeply as you do.'

'And they didn't care two pins about Dilys,' Peter retorted.

'That may be so, except in the sense that any decent person must feel sorry at the tragic death of anyone as young as she was. What I meant is they're worried about you, just as you told me you were concerned about them. If they want to talk, let them. It might have a therapeutic value for you too.'

Peter grinned suddenly, surprisingly. 'I'll bear it in mind,' he promised and swung a leg across his bicycle. 'I hope you're not regretting taking me on,' he said then, 'because I'm beginning to be very glad you did.' He sketched a brief gesture of farewell that included the pair of them and began to cycle back towards his parents' home.

'I wonder how much of that last remark was due to the fact that you're helping me,' said Stephen. 'The trouble with that lad is he makes me feel older by the moment, and as far as I know we're practically the same age.'

'I shouldn't worry about that,' said Maitland. He was thinking that not many men of Stephen's age would have spoken so understandingly about the Duttons or even felt any sympathy for their point of view. 'As for talking, you heard Emma tell us that Caroline had invited us for dinner tonight. Will you be at home?'

'Yes, I shall.'

'Then we shall have a chance to discuss the very meagre information at our disposal,' Antony told him. 'And it will give me a chance to sort things out first.'

'What did you make of Peter?'

Antony smiled at him. 'That's one of the things I want to think about,' he said.

They had been walking towards the shop where Stephen's car was parked while they were speaking, but now as they reached the open space Stephen halted and said earnestly, 'He's a good chap.'

'One of the things our profession will teach you,' said Maitland, feeling in his turn about a hundred years old, 'is that you can't take anybody at face value. Or practically anybody,' he added conscientiously.

'They say murder's the one crime anybody might commit,' said Stephen. 'Do you think that's true?'

Antony took his time to think that out. 'In a sense I'm inclined to think it is,' he said at last. 'But there's a difference between a murder committed in the heat of the moment, and one that's carefully planned.' He began to turn away and then stopped and added seriously, 'That's why I'm beginning to think you may be right about your friend Peter.'

71

IV

When Antony and Stephen had left them after lunch Jenny expected that Emma would be drawn back immediately to her typewriter as though by a magnet. She had provided herself with plenty of reading matter, and as the weather had turned so warm had proposed to spend the afternoon sitting by Farthing Gill, probably dabbling her feet in the water at the same time, and reading a book that had been chosen for the amusement it was likely to provide, rather than for any instructional value. Emma however had other ideas.

'Maltravers is perfectly comfortable for the moment,' she said, so that Jenny remembered with amusement the first time she had heard that remark: the poor man, as far as she could recall, had been given some drug of Emma's own invention and was suffering from a rather unpleasant series of hallucinations. 'I forgot to get coffee beans when I did my shopping yesterday, so I'd better do it now before I forget again. Will you come with me?'

'I know my own way perfectly well,' said Jenny. 'I'll go for you, Emma, and then you can get on with your work.'

'The walk will do me good,' said Emma firmly, 'and the whole thing won't take us more than half an hour at most.' This Jenny doubted, knowing that they would probably have to stop and speak to everyone they met, and that, in any case Mrs Ryder at the shop would have some questions to ask about her own and her family's well being. However, Emma seemed determined so she went along without further argument.

As it turned out the street was surprisingly quiet and they reached their destination with no more than three interruptions. Nor were they delayed in the way Jenny had expected at the shop. By the time Emma's forgotten coffee beans had been weighed out and ground to specification four other people were waiting to be served and they got away without any further conversation.

They had only just begun to retrace their steps towards

Rowan Corner when a man turned out of the lane that led up to the church and vicarage, and beyond that, as Jenny remembered, to a cottage called Lane's End. 'Philip Wainwright,' said Emma under her breath. 'The one everybody's talking about.' Jenny, not unnaturally, eyed him with more interest than she would usually have given to a casually met acquaintance of her hostess.

He was a very tall man and extremely thin, and – like Mr Dutton – he wore clothes that hung on him as though they had been made for a larger man. Oddly, on that hot day, he was wearing a raincoat that flapped around him as he stalked rapidly towards them, so that Jenny was immediately reminded of a huge bat. He wore a felt hat with the brim turned down all round, and this he raised politely as he came up to them so that she could see that his hair was lank and a little too long, though it showed no signs yet of retreating at the temples. She thought that perhaps it wasn't altogether surprising that the village had cast him for a sinister role; perhaps if she hadn't had a good deal of opportunity since her marriage of acquiring some knowledge of the laws of evidence she might, in the circumstances, have done so herself.

'Good evening, Mr Wainwright,' said Emma and was about to pass on when, to her obvious surprise, he not only returned her salutation but stopped and spoke.

'Dreadful doings in the village, Miss Anstey,' he said. It occurred to Jenny that perhaps he didn't use his voice very often, it had something in common with the croaking of a raven.

'Yes indeed, Mr Wainwright,' said Emma, coming to a halt. 'This is a new neighbour, Jenny,' she added. 'Mr Wainwright, Mrs Maitland, who is staying with me for a short holiday.'

'I'm glad to meet you, Mrs Maitland. Your husband is here too, and in the thick of our mystery I hear.'

It occurred to Jenny to wonder how he had heard anything at all, even the fact there had been a murder, if what they had been told was right and he rarely spoke to anyone. Still, it

73

sometimes seemed to her that the country grapevine was a wordless affair, thoughts and ideas being communicated by some advanced form of ESP. 'It's a very nasty business, Mr Wainwright,' she agreed seriously. 'But there's no case yet for Antony to be in the middle of, as far as I know.'

'And according to Burton Cecil there never will be,' he said, which made her wonder again about his source of information. 'Fool of a girl, whatever possessed her. . .? But I mustn't keep you standing, Miss Anstey, so I'll say good day to you both.'

Neither of them spoke for a little while after that, and then Emma said, 'You see?' And Jenny replied, 'Yes,' in a rather doubtful tone. She was thinking of their encounter with Philip Wainwright as they went along, and oddly enough her first impression of him seemed to be undergoing a change.

When they got back to Farthing Lee Emma handed her packages to Jenny. 'I'm going to get straight back to work, my dear,' she said, 'because if I know you you've got a book waiting for you anyway. But will you put these away for me first?'

'Yes, of course, Emma.' She took the bag and made for the kitchen, where she found that Emma's daily (Monday to Friday really) had arrived back, her husband presumably fed, and was starting preparations for dinner. She was willing enough to break off to tell Jenny where the various items should be stored, and obviously ready for a good gossip while they were being put away. 'They tell me, Mrs M,' she said, 'that your husband's mixing himself up in police matters again.'

She had no doubt heard that from her husband, Joe, but how *he* had learned it was another mystery. 'Do you disapprove of that?' Jenny asked, putting the butter away in the small refrigerator that, like the telephone, had been added to the amenities of Farthing Lee since first she stayed there seven years before.

'Nay, why should I? Everyone's a right to his own opinion. Though I ought to warn you, this time he's picked a loser.'

'Everyone has a right to representation,' Jenny said, and was amused to hear herself putting the other side of an argument she'd had often enough with Antony. But the aptly named Mrs Kitchener seemed ready to talk, and because she was really curious she went on, 'Do your husband and Sergeant Gilbey really agree that Peter Dutton is guilty? If so, they must be just about the only people in the village that do.'

'Inside information,' said Mrs Kitchener importantly. 'You've got to go by t' evidence, Joe always says.'

This statement was one Jenny thought she couldn't quarrel with, but an idea came into her head uninvited and she asked as casually as she could, 'What do you think of the theory that there might be a sex maniac at large in Burton Cecil?'

'Nothing to support it,' Mrs Kitchener pointed out. 'And if you're thinking about Mr Wainwright I shouldn't be surprised if he wasn't a bit weak in t' head, but not in that way.'

'You've heard the gossip then?'

'Of course I have. I hear everything, don't I?' This was said without the glimmer of a smile. 'Still, there's one good thing about it, there won't be any awkwardness, or owt of that, about Mr M taking a hand. T' village will be on young Mr Dutton's side.'

'They believe in his innocence, don't they? Will that make a difference do you think?'

'Bound to.'

'But you don't believe in him? You and your husband and Sergeant Gilbey, and of course the detectives from Rother-shaw?'

'That's right, dear.'

'You've been here a long time, Mrs Kitchener.'

'Nigh on six years now, ever since Mr Hugh retired and took up farming.'

'You must know Peter Dutton as well as the others do. Is this the can Emma keeps the coffee in?'

'That's right. You might say I know him pretty well.'

'It's his character that all the people who know him are basing their opinion on.'

'If there's one thing I've learned,' said Mrs Kitchener emphatically, 'it's not to trust appearances. If you'll pardon my saying so, Mrs M, you haven't gotten t' experience of human nature that I've got. And you can take it from me, anybody may do anything at any time.'

'Oh dear, I hope not,' said Jenny and heard an echo of Emma in her voice as she spoke. But she couldn't help smiling at the sweeping statement.

'You mark my words, when sex comes into it—'

'But you said—'

'You was talking about a maniac. I don't think there's anything of that about young Peter. Frustrated, that's what he was, frustrated.' She sounded pleased with the word.

'If he's arrested he'll plead Not Guilty,' Jenny said. 'But I daresay you know that already, it's what he told Inspector Wentworth.'

Her answer to that was a snort, not of disbelief – she didn't doubt Jenny's word – but perhaps of disgust at the coming waste of the taxpayer's time and money. 'Well, dear, we've all got to live,' she said, which Jenny took to be some sort of absolution for Antony's part in the affair. 'Give me that bag and I'll get rid of it,' she added, seeing that Jenny had finished what she came into the kitchen to do, 'and then I'd better get on with what I'm doing.'

Jenny suddenly realised that a gigantic steak and kidney pie was under construction. 'Mrs Kitchener,' she said, 'didn't Miss Anstey tell you we'd be out to dinner tonight, and tomorrow as well?'

'Oh yes, Miss Emma told me all right. This is for Sunday, because she didn't want to be tied up with cooking with you and Mr M here. I'll just pop it into t' freezer and it'll come out a treat and no trouble to anyone.'

The rest of the afternoon was as peaceful as Jenny had expected. Her book was amusing *and* instructive, which was more than she had expected, and she didn't notice Antony's return until he had crossed the footbridge and was walking downstream towards her. She looked up and smiled at him. 'How did you get along this afternoon?' she asked.

'If you want to know the truth, love, I haven't the faintest idea,' he said, and sat down on the grass beside her. 'I went with Stephen to see the Duttons and then the Lewises, whom I like by the way.'

'Didn't you like the Duttons?'

'Yes, very much indeed as a matter of fact. To tell you the truth, love, I rather fell for both of them. But I had a prejudice against the Lewises for some reason until I met them, which I have a feeling you shared, though of course being the charitable soul you are you'd never say so.'

'I did think,' said Jenny slowly, 'that perhaps they hadn't been quite kind to Dilys ... or kind only because it was convenient for them.'

'Yes, that's what I thought but I changed my mind when I talked to them. And then we met Peter Dutton and had a word with him to clear up a point that had arisen when we talked to his parents. He's got the sack ... no, I should say he's been suspended from his job until things are cleared up.'

'What did you think of him, Antony? I know he's well liked in the village and Emma and all her family share the same opinion, but you've always told me—'

'Not to jump to conclusions,' said Antony smiling at her. 'That's quite right, love, and I have to tell you I'm in a complete muddle myself now. There's no doubt at all that, judging by appearances, he's a nice lad, and reacting to the police's suspicions in a completely normal way. But there's the evidence, and that's going to be something that's very difficult to get round.'

'What do *you* think?' Jenny insisted.

'I liked him, but ... you know how difficult it is for me to make my mind up about anything like that, Jenny. Apart from anything else I'd like to help Stephen Anstey, not just because we like Emma and Hugh and Caroline but because he's a nice chap himself and the more I see of him the more I like him. I'd better tell you just what happened . . .'

When he had finished Jenny thought for a moment and then said rather tentatively, 'I've a little bit to add to that myself, Antony. Emma and I walked down to the shop after lunch and met Philip Wainwright.'

'Did you indeed? That's interesting.'

'Not particularly. We only really exchanged the time of day. Only he wasn't quite what I'd expected. I'm sure he likes Emma, and she says he's always polite to her. And though he was a little abrupt I think he liked me too.' She paused and smiled. 'Perhaps that's why I have to say I rather took to him myself.'

'Did you indeed, love? And that I *do* find interesting,' said Antony with complete sincerity, though he knew well enough her tendency to think well of everyone.

Jenny frowned a little over that, seeming to find it incomprehensible. 'When we came home I talked to Mrs Kitchener,' she said.

'That's Joe Kitchener's wife, isn't it, who's now working for Emma?' said Antony. 'It's rather funny that we've never met her before, but of course we've passed the time of day with him often enough.'

'She was making a pie for Sunday evening's supper,' said Jenny inconsequently.

'What sort of pie?' asked Antony suspiciously.

'A steak and kidney pie. If our meal last night was anything to go on I should think it will be very good,' said Jenny encouragingly. 'And you've only to look at Joe Kitchener to see that he thrives on her cooking. Have you ever thought, Antony, that Kitchener is rather an odd name for a daily? I mean she spends so much time in the kitchen.'

'It hadn't occurred to me, and I don't think it's very interesting now that it has,' said Antony bluntly. Jenny knew what the trouble was, of course, he wanted to know whether the good lady had had anything interesting to tell her. So she repeated the conversation as well as she could remember it, adding, 'It's no more than we knew, really.'

'Not really helpful,' he agreed when she had finished. 'About what I told you, Jenny, is there anything that strikes you particularly?'

'Ivor Lewis's suggestion that Burton Cecil may be in for a series of similar murders,' Jenny said. 'It may have been telepathy, but the idea came to me some time this afternoon that that might be the case. He's quite right, I suppose, the absence of sexual interference doesn't rule it out.'

'No, it certainly doesn't, and it's an interesting idea,' said Antony. 'Does that mean you're coming round to the village's way of thinking, love, about Peter Dutton's innocence?'

'I suppose I'm a little bit influenced by the . . . the unanimity of opinion in his favour,' said Jenny. 'And if they're right – everyone except the police, I mean – a sex maniac does seem to be the only possible alternative.'

'I imagine it hadn't occurred to you before, love, but what did you think the people down at the pub had in mind when they were talking last night about Philip Wainwright?'

'That, I suppose.' Jenny shivered suddenly in spite of the warmth of the afternoon. 'He's a strange man, Antony, though as I told you I did rather like him. But I wish we knew more about him.'

'Now you're going from one extreme to the other,' Antony told her. 'If we continue with this investigation' - Jenny had a private smile for that 'we' - 'as I suppose we must considering my commitment to Stephen, we may or may not find that Peter Dutton is the guilty party. But I don't necessarily believe in Wainwright as a possible alternative.'

'Who then?'

'Hasn't it occurred to you that it needn't be anybody from the village? The Lewises told us that Dilys was a credulous girl; she might have been enticed into the woods by some sort of specious tale.'

'Considering the kind of girl everyone says she was, it doesn't seem very likely to me,' said Jenny.

'Who lives may learn,' said Antony lightly. He listened a moment. 'Emma seems to have stopped working,' he added then. 'Do you think she'd mind calling in at the Mortal Man for a quick one before we went to Burton Crook this evening? I know there's no need in view of Caroline's idea of hospitality, but it seems we might learn a thing or two if we did.'

V

Maitland wasn't surprised to find that anything in the nature of a scandal brought the *habitués* of the Mortal Man out in full force. He had noticed before that such occasions were far more frequent in a country district than might have been supposed and they were invariably followed by a drawing together of the local population, but coming originally from the country himself that caused him no surprise. A murder, of course ... well, there they all were, and the arrival of Emma and her party was greeted with what could only be described as a sort of appreciative murmur. Jenny said afterwards that she thought she distinguished the words 'We're with you,' but she couldn't be sure who had uttered them. Emma caught sight of Cyril Lansing and made a bee-line for his table, and once they were settled their presence didn't inhibit the talk at all. It was far too juicy a topic of conversation to be lightly dropped.

Apart from the aforementioned greeting, Cyril Lansing was the only one who referred directly to Antony's connection with the case. 'At it again?' he asked with a quizzical look in Maitland's direction.

Antony knew him well enough by now to realise that he didn't expect any indiscretion, so he only said mildly, 'A little friendly help to Stephen Anstey, that's all,' and gave him his blandest smile.

'On a purely friendly basis,' Cyril agreed. 'But if I know you, you've come here tonight with some purpose in mind.'

'Nothing very sinister. I wanted a word with Roland, but

we're due at Burton Crook so if he doesn't arrive soon I'll be out of luck.'

'He's late already. But I can tell you one thing, as long as you and Stephen are on Peter's side everybody in the village will be falling over themselves to help you.'

Antony looked at him for a long moment. 'I think you mean something more than that, Cyril,' he said. 'Out with it!'

'Only that this business has stirred up feelings. More feelings even than that affair you were mixed up in before. Talk about Philip Wainwright mainly. But if you're going to dinner with Caroline and Hugh she'll be able to tell you something about him. After all, she sold him Lane's End.'

'I don't imagine that gave her an intimate knowledge of the chap.'

'I can only say there are some nasty feelings about, very nasty. And you can't wonder, a young girl like Dilys.'

'No, you can't wonder,' Maitland agreed.

For a while after that they sipped their drinks in silence. Cyril was an old friend by now, even to the Maitlands, and there was no need to make conversation. But gradually Antony became aware that he was being studied. 'What is it?' he asked.

'A question I think I may properly ask you since it concerns Stephen's client's affairs only indirectly. Are you going to set about Peter's defence in the way you usually do?'

'I'm not quite sure I know what you mean.' In spite of himself a little stiffness had crept into Maitland's voice.

'It's very simple.' Emma came to his rescue. 'He means, are you going to try and find out who the real culprit is?'

'I'm only giving Stephen a little friendly advice, you know, but in any case that isn't part of his instructions. It may never come to an arrest.'

'And if it does?' Cryil insisted.

'If it does, whoever Stephen briefs as counsel will explain to the jury that they must be convinced beyond reasonable doubt, and the judge will repeat that to them in his summing up. That's all that's necessary for an acquittal.'

'I seem to remember your saying once,' said Emma, 'that the Scottish Not Proven verdict left the defendant almost as badly off as before. Wouldn't that be the equivalent?'

'I hope not,' said Maitland uneasily. Cyril's eyes were much too sharp, he'd be guessing next how he really felt about this business and though Antony thought he could trust the other man's discretion he didn't feel it would be fair to Peter Dutton. But at that moment, to his relief, the door was pushed open and Roland Beaufort came in.

He paused at the bar to order a straight whisky, which was his usual drink. When he reached the table he greeted them all in turn punctiliously. 'Let me guess,' he said, 'you were discussing foreign policy.' He slipped into a chair between Emma and Jenny.

'Not exactly.' Cyril glanced around the room. 'You're not telling us that you think that's the main topic of conversation in here this evening.'

'I'll answer in your own words . . . not exactly,' said Roland, grinning. 'It's nice to see you, Emma, but I have a nasty feeling. . . . Is there any ulterior motive in your being here this evening?'

'I was hoping for a word with you,' said Maitland before Emma could reply.

'Let me get you a refill.'

'No thanks. We're on our way to Burton Crook.'

'I'd really be more comfortable if you'd let me. It would make this interrogation seem less official.'

Antony smiled. 'Official is just what it isn't,' he said. 'I offered a little friendly help to Stephen Anstey,' he repeated, 'and as everyone seems to be on the side of his client there seems to be no harm in asking a few questions.'

'Oh, very well! I suppose you want to talk to me about that unfortunate child, Dilys Jones.'

'As far as I can tell you were the last person to see her alive . . . except her murderer of course.'

'Thank you for that small addition,' Roland said dryly. 'But I

82

suppose you're going to ask me about the time and that's almost as bad as accusing me of murdering her. You know I never have the faintest idea of what o'clock it is.'

'Come off it, Roland,' said Cyril. 'You're conscious enough of the time to catch the bus to Rothershaw when you want to, and I've never seen you trying to get in here outside opening hours.'

'That's true. I can only put it down to instinct.' He paused a moment to consider. 'All the same, I can't be sure to a minute or two. I left home at eight o'clock or soon after, that's the best I can do. And she had just gone past in the direction of Rowan Corner.'

'How long would it take to reach there from the time you saw her?'

'You're in a very exacting mood this evening. A minute or two, not more, and if you're going to ask me if I'm sure it was Dilys you needn't bother, my eyesight isn't that bad.'

'But she didn't stop to have a word with you?'

'No, why should she? I told you I don't even know if she heard me call out a greeting. Anyway, I'd nothing against the girl, but we'd nothing in common.'

'No, I suppose you wouldn't have. So you came straight in here and didn't leave again until closing time?'

'You're right about that, but if you're looking for an alibi,' said Roland bluntly, 'it won't work. Unless Lily or Adam recorded my time of arrival exactly I could have turned back with Dilys, escorted her to Rowan Corner and then into the wood, and been back here with the horrid deed done before Peter arrived on the scene.'

'I wasn't thinking that as a matter of fact,' said Antony, smiling, 'and even now you've pointed it out the idea doesn't appeal to me much. I do think though, Roland, that this affectation of yours about not knowing the time is just that . . . an affectation. You're clear enough about the events of that evening.'

'Well, I've been talking to Peter. Besides – I think I've

told you this before – what Adam doesn't tell me about what's going on in the village Lily does.'

'Tell me about Peter then,' Maitland invited. 'I understand he's by way of being a friend of yours, and to tell you the truth I shouldn't have thought you'd have any more in common with him than you had with Dilys.'

'Peter has a mind,' said Roland consideringly, 'and our interests run along the same lines. It's bad enough to be an only child, I imagine, and when your parents are rather elderly too—'

'Yes, I see what you mean.' Antony smiled again, but not without a little gentle malice. 'You've been playing a paternal role? Or taking the place of an elder brother perhaps?'

'Nothing of the kind!' Roland sounded genuinely revolted. 'But I think I got it across to him that there's more to life than a job with the civil service, and if books are what he likes he might as well work among them. It would be better, of course, if he'd no need to earn a living but one can't have everything.'

'I'm glad to know you retain so much grasp on reality,' said Cryil, as though, where Roland was concerned, he was sometimes doubtful about this. 'How's your latest book coming along?' he added.

'Slowly,' said Roland. He gave his companions a look in which amusement and defiance were nicely blended. 'You can't hurry genius, you know.'

There seemed to be no answer to this and Antony didn't try to find one. 'Let's get back to Peter,' he said. 'What do you think about this complete conviction the village has of his innocence?'

'I agree with them,' said Roland, perhaps a little too promptly.

'Then I can only hope the police will come round to your point of view.'

'Don't tell me you're doubting your own client.'

'Stephen's client,' Antony murmured. He was thinking that

he should have remembered that Roland was an exceptionally intelligent man, and quite capable of picking up any nuance there might be in his voice. 'It isn't a matter of doubt,' he added, 'but it will be hard to defend him if they do proceed to an arrest.'

'Well – it's funny, isn't it, how one always talks about the village as if it were a single entity? – we've all known Peter a long time. And I'll tell you something that I doubt he'll be able to convey to you, Antony: he was genuinely very much in love with Dilys.'

'To tell that to the court might not be the best way of defending him,' said Maitland thoughtfully.

'Forget about all these legal angles and concentrate on the facts for a bit,' Roland advised rather impatiently.

'All right then, why are you so sure he was genuinely in love?'

'Because I – we need another round,' said Roland in his inconsequential way. 'Come and help me carry the glasses, Antony.'

In view of Maitland's disability he was the last person who should have been chosen for this particular job, but he was in no doubt of the other man's intention in separating him from the others. 'I expect Adam will give us a tray,' he said as he followed Roland towards the bar.

'I expect he will.' He gave the order and then turned to face Antony squarely. 'What I was going to say was that our visits to Rothershaw – Peter's and mine – haven't always been to attend concerts or go to the library. You accused me a moment ago of being parental towards him and though I don't agree with you in the slightest I have to admit that what sexual education he's had has been from me. Michael Dutton was no use to him there.'

'You're trying to tell me you introduced him to his first popsy,' said Antony, becoming impatient with all this circumlocution.

'That's rather an old-fashioned way of putting it, but I should have remembered your fondness for calling a spade a spade,' said Roland. 'Yes, I do mean exactly that.'

'What has it got to do with his feelings for Dilys?'

'Merely that ever since he became interested in her there have been no more adventures in Rothershaw,' said Roland. 'I should think myself that was pretty good evidence that he was really serious about her.'

'Yes, I see. You realise you're likely to be called as a witness for the prosecution if it comes to a trial?'

'Because of seeing Dilys?'

'Yes, that's right. You were the last person to see her,' said Antony again.

'I wish you wouldn't keep stressing that. Well, I won't tell them all this if you don't think I should, though I can't see anybody thinking to ask me. And I can't see, either, what difference it makes.'

'I think the motive cited would be Peter's frustration over Dilys's attitude.'

Roland thought about that for a moment. 'I see now what you mean,' he said at last. 'I don't think I can be much use to Stephen, or to him, in that case. I'm hardly the type to make a good character witness.'

'You underestimate yourself. It's just that that particular angle. . . .' Maitland broke off there. He was beginning to doubt whether his first impression, that Roland doubted Peter's innocence in spite of his protestations, was the correct one. 'May I take it,' he asked, 'that Peter has confided to you in some detail what he told the police?'

'So far as I know, yes.'

'Then I may as well tell you there's one thing that bothers me about his story of that evening.'

'What's that?'

'When Ivor Lewis went round to the Duttons and said Dilys was missing Peter doesn't seem to have been worried at all. That doesn't seem natural to me particularly in view of what you told me about the genuineness of his feelings for the girl. He gave us an explanation—'

'I know all about that too. Perhaps it would help you to believe him if I tell you that from time to time I've given him the benefit of my worldly wisdom in other things besides purely sexual matters.'

'I didn't know you had any.' Adam Shaw came up then with the tray, but he left it on the counter beside them and went away again out of earshot. 'In any case,' Antony added, 'I don't quite know what you mean.'

'Very simply that I told him that the quiet sort – meaning Dilys in this case – were always deep ones. I didn't quite like to see him putting all his eggs in one basket.'

'Had you anything against the girl?'

'Not a thing. I introduced them at a concert, so perhaps I felt a little responsible for the way their relationship developed. She had a genuine love for music, but I don't suppose she'd ever opened a book in her life. Seeing her three times a week or so was one thing, Peter would have been bored stiff in a month if he'd had to live with her.'

'You've been very helpful, Roland.'

'I like Peter,' said Roland simply, which made Antony doubt all over again what his real opinion was. He nearly said, But who else could have done it? but stopped himself in time. Roland, however, seemed to divine his thought.

'There are other possibilities,' he pointed out. 'For instance, Ivor is just at the age where some people might say he was ready for an affair with a younger woman.'

'Some people might charge you with slander,' Maitland reminded him, allowing the amusement he felt to creep into his voice.

'Yes, there's that of course. However, anything you want to know about the village—' He waved his hand expansively. 'They say the onlooker sees most of the game.'

'Tell me then, what do you think about this feeling against Philip Wainwright?'

'If you mean do I subscribe to it, no I don't. But country people will get some funny ideas, comes of having too much time to think, I daresay. Wainwright is a stranger in our midst and has made no attempt at all to get to know his neighbours or to mix in village life. They might just as easily have fixed on me just because I'm different – and I don't mean that in a boasting way, as I'm sure you realise – if they weren't so used to seeing me around for the last I don't know how many years.'

'It isn't reasonable,' Maitland said. Something in Roland's tone had worried him.

'No, it isn't. Not at this stage anyway. And I'll tell you another thing,' said Roland, serious again, which he hardly ever was. 'It could lead to trouble.'

'If Peter were arrested, you mean?'

'That wasn't exactly what I had in mind. I was thinking more that if anything else happens—' He broke off there, eyeing his companion shrewdly. 'I see that idea has occurred to you too.'

'It has occurred to me, and you're not the first person to mention it either,' said Maitland. 'You don't like the situation at all, do you?'

'I think,' said Roland slowly, 'that if I were the village I'd follow the old advice, lock up your daughters. And that's almost as much for Mr Wainwright's sake as for the girls concerned.' He turned and picked up the tray. 'The ice in Emma's gin and tonic will be melting,' he said. 'We'd better go back and join our friends.'

VI

The party from Farthing Lee didn't stay long after that, but said Good Night to their companions, and a general Good Night to the assembled company, and proceeded on foot towards Burton Crook. Jenny offered to pick up the car, which was still parked in front of the shop, but Emma was inclined to be indignant at the idea that the walk to her nephew's house might be beyond her. She pointed out various landmarks that might be unfamiliar to them as they went: the house next to the shop that had stood empty for almost a year now; the one next to that had been bought by the Hawthornes and where they would be dining the following evening; Dr Oaksley's house beyond that. 'And you'd better be careful, my dears, he's the sort of man who thinks that when he gets into his car he has the right to do exactly as he likes.' (They negotiated the driveway in safety, however.) Beyond that again was the Lewises' house where Antony had been with Stephen Anstey that afternoon.

The next thing they came to was a farm gate opening onto the rugged track which led to Willie Barnes's farm. 'Hugh is on quite good terms with Willie again now that he's farming himself,' Emma confided. 'I'm afraid he used to be rather jealous of him, and annoyed because he didn't take advantage of his opportunities. You have to admit his land is a disgrace.' But she hadn't time to expand on the subject because they came next upon a group of cottages very like Parson's Row, though rather larger, and in the garden of the first Jenny recognised an old acquaintance in the witchlike figure of Miss Murgatroyd.

Her cottage, in contrast to the others which were extraordinarily neat, had an overgrown garden and one of those larch trees that have been so twisted by the wind that they look as though they are deliberately trying to scare anyone who comes near them. The cat was there too, just as it had been first time she walked that way, sitting on the gatepost and eyeing the approaching party balefully. They all greeted the old woman politely and received in return the rather obscure remark, 'An evil and adulterous generation seeks after a sign.'

'Does she mean us?' asked Antony in a low voice when they got a little way past, and Emma said reassuringly,

'She always talks like that.'

'The first time I saw her she told me to "keep innocency", or something like that,' said Jenny. 'I think on the whole she must take a dim view of strangers but I didn't realise you hadn't come across her before, Antony.'

'I've seen her,' her husband assured her, 'but she hasn't

89

honoured me with any advice. However,' he added, still amused, 'you reassure me. It must be you and Emma she was talking about.'

Burton Crook lay at the west end of the village, though there were farms beyond whose address was also probably Burton Cecil. There was an ash tree opposite the end of the drive, which wound up towards the house between an avenue of horse-chestnuts, and as they came out from under the trees there was a sweep of lawn between them and the house, the grass as smooth as a bowling-green. It was a handsome place and they had all got used by this time to the changes indoors. It had seemed to come alive in the years since Caroline Anstey inherited it from her uncle, in the same way as the surrounding fields were now in excellent heart since the lease Willie Barnes had held on them had run out.

Burton Crook was said to be so named after a bend in the river, but it was hard to see why this particular curve should have been singled out as the Eller is erratic throughout its comparatively short course. However, as Caroline had once said in a burst of frankness, it was better to stick firmly to this explanation in case the name should become associated with the house's former owner, her uncle, whom it would have fitted like a glove.

Elsie, who had been in Emma's employ until recently, let them in, and greeted each one of them in turn with an enthusiastic hug, which was hardly orthodox but surprised none of them. 'I'll take you and Mrs Maitland upstairs Missemma,' she offered. 'And when you've done your hair,' (in Emma's case this was very necessary, the Spanish comb being quite incapable of withstanding the walk from Farthing Lee) 'I'll let you have a peep at the twins. They're asleep by now, but I know Mrs Anstey won't mind being as it's you. She went back to t' kitchen to make sure everything was all right.'

This was obviously a treat not, in Elsie's estimation, to be missed, and Jenny and Emma followed her willingly enough, leaving Antony to make his way to the big drawing-room,

90

where he found Hugh and Stephen arguing amicably over the merits of two rival brands of Scotch. Hugh came forward immediately, greeting Antony like the old friend he was. They were much of a height these two though Hugh, even without an ounce of fat on him was a much bigger man. He had dark hair and brown eyes and a far more relaxed attitude to life than his brother, who was really, when Antony came to think about it, more like their cousin Chris Conway in temperament. 'I didn't hear you come,' said Hugh. 'Is Caroline looking after Jenny and Emma?'

'Elsie has taken them to view your offspring,' Antony told him. 'She said Caroline was in the kitchen.'

'I hope that doesn't mean a crisis,' said Hugh. 'Come and sit down, Antony, I've got some of your favourite sherry. And I have to thank you, I understand, for giving a helping hand to my little brother here.'

'The spirit is willing,' said Maitland seating himself, 'but I'm afraid the results weren't particularly happy.'

'What exactly does that mean?' Hugh had his back to them now, pouring the promised sherry. 'Stephen says you think Peter Dutton's guilty. Is that right?'

'I don't know,' said Antony weakly.

'Come now!' Hugh came across the room with a glass in his hand. 'That isn't like you, Antony.'

'On the contrary, it's an only too frequent state of mind with me.'

Hugh ignored that. 'You haven't had much chance of weighing Stephen up yet,' he said, 'but you know me well enough. Would you say I was a particularly credulous person?'

'No, I don't think so,' said Maitland consideringly.

'The thing is we know Peter Dutton, you don't.'

'We met him this afternoon,' said Stephen. 'I told you that.'

'I liked what I saw of him,' Maitland agreed, 'but ... you must realise, both of you, that it isn't enough to say, He wouldn't do a thing like that. Now think of it, Hugh. Would you ever have dreamed Mrs Gillespie would write poison pen letters, or that her husband would kill her when he found out because he didn't want anyone to know?'

'It took you to work that one out,' Hugh admitted, 'but this is hardly the same thing.'

'No, very different, and potentially even more unpleasant. I've just been talking to Roland,' he said. 'We stopped at the Mortal Man on the way here because I wanted to have a word with him, not because I doubted your hospitality,' he added, smiling.

'Roland knows Peter Dutton better than either of us,' said Stephen.

'Yes, and he's just as sure he didn't kill Dilys, but he seems to be basing his opinion on the fact that Peter was genuinely in love with her and you must both see – Stephen will anyway – that if it came to a trial that wouldn't help at all. Even without the evidence Roland could give they'd cite frustration as the motive.'

'Yes, I realise that.' Stephen sounded dejected. 'But at least you can tell me, Antony, is there anything else I can do?'

'Unless you can get a line on someone else who'd fallen for Dilys and was jealous because she preferred Peter, I can't think of anything that would help. If he's arrested—'

'You think he will be, don't you?'

'I'm sure of it,' said Maitland with rather brutal frankness. 'By his own story he must have been standing only a few yards from where her body was found for at least half an hour. It's quite possible that she was killed before he arrived at Rowan Corner, but there's nothing in the world to prove it.'

'Well—' Stephen hesitated, and then said in a rush, 'if it does come to a trial will you defend him?'

'If it can be fitted in with any other commitments Mallory has made for me during the vacation, certainly I will.' He thought for a moment. 'I don't know that that's altogether a wise decision on your part though. In the absence of any further evidence – which I admit might make all the difference – it will be mainly a matter of advocacy, and if we could persuade my uncle he'd do a much better job of it than I would.'

'Sir Nicholas Harding?'

'You needn't sound so nervous, Stephen. He doesn't know you yet, so there's no chance of his treating you as one of the family ... which I admit might be a little daunting. Mallory wouldn't accept the brief without his consent because he hates going out of town, but I think with Vera's help – you've heard us speak of her, Hugh, she's been my aunt for the last five years – I think I might be able to persuade him.'

'I'm in your hands,' said Stephen rather helplessly. 'If you really think that would be best—'

'I really do. But we needn't worry about that yet, the rumours in the village about this chap Wainwright may have the effect of discouraging the police from any further action. I haven't met him myself but Jenny and Emma encountered him briefly this afternoon and Jenny seems to have taken a liking to him.'

'I reckon nowt to that,' said Hugh, relaxing into the local idiom. 'Jenny likes everybody.'

'Nearly everybody,' Maitland admitted. 'In the meantime the only thing I can advise – and this can be carried out best by Hugh and Caroline – is that you try to find out what other friends of the male sex Dilys Jones had. To go back, though, what do you really think of this chap, Wainwright?'

'Nobody knows him really. The villagers had been talking about a mystery man long before this happened. And I admit his being a stranger is no reason to accuse him of murder, but to my mind anyone would be a better choice than Peter.'

At that moment Caroline Anstey came in, a little flushed but not unbecomingly so. She was as slim as ever and even prettier than she had been when the Maitlands first knew her seven years ago – or so Antony thought – with dark hair and eyes. She was also rather tall for a woman, so that when Jenny and Emma followed her almost immediately into the room the two younger women seemed to tower over Miss Anstey. There was a chorus of greetings, and it was several minutes before they were all seated and supplied with drinks. Then Hugh asked laughingly, 'What dreadful things has Mrs Dally been perpetrating in the kitchen?'

'Nothing really. She just got a little fussed because the ice cream she'd made hadn't set properly. I told her we'd enjoy it just as much as cream poured over the fruit, after all the raspberries are fresh from the garden.'

'We've just been looking at the twins,' said Jenny. 'Emma thinks they're sweet,' she added with a teasing glance in Miss Anstey's direction, 'but I think they're enormous. When they're awake they must be a pretty handful.'

'Yes they are, and that's why I'm so grateful to Emma for letting me have Elsie. You wouldn't believe how good she is with them. I haven't asked how you two are,' she added, looking from one of the Maitlands to the other, 'but you both look marvellous. And Antony's being kind to Stephen in allowing himself to be imposed on. I only hope it won't spoil your holiday too much.'

'Oh, I say!' said Stephen. 'That's hardly fair!'

'It's perfectly fair,' said Caroline. It was obvious that she was on excellent terms already with this brother-in-law of hers, who after all hadn't shared their home for very long. 'But I may as well make it clear from the beginning that discussion of poor Dilys's murder is absolutely off the agenda for this evening.'

'Very well then,' said Hugh immediately, 'you suggest something else to talk about.'

This remark, deliberately calculated to put a stop to all conversation for the moment, left Caroline speechless, but not for long. 'Tell us about Mr Maltravers, Emma,' she suggested. It was always a safe bet that Miss Anstey would have something to say on that subject. 'How is he getting on?'

'Not too badly,' said Emma, but she sounded a little doubtful.

'He was all right after lunch,' Jenny volunteered. 'Has something happened since then?'

'I hope you've incorporated our suggestions,' said Antony.

'They should have put you on the right track.'

Emma looked at him in silence for a moment. 'In view of the body in the library,' she said severely, 'frivolity would be out of place.' But then she relented. 'I have to admit though, the telephone wires *had* been cut.'

'Well, I'm still worried about the police,' said Jenny. 'Even if they didn't fall into – what was it? – the third bog on the left, there'd still be the dogs to cope with.'

'Dogs?' said Emma, obviously puzzled.

'You don't mean to tell us you haven't provided Sir Jasper with any dogs,' said Antony, obviously shocked by the idea. 'I thought no Yorkshire landowner would feel himself properly equipped without a savage pack of dogs to protect him against the menace of the odd hiker, or the man selling the *Encyclopedia Britannica*. A kind of insurance,' he explained. 'If the bogs don't get them the dogs will.'

'Sir Jasper has a dog,' said Emma. 'A cocker spaniel,' she added.

'That won't do at all. Why, even Hugh—'

'I don't think Cedric has ever bitten a policeman,' said Hugh. 'Perhaps he senses that I was once a member of the force myself. And even Dick Rawsthorne' (Dick Rawsthorne was the local postman) 'seems to be safe from his attentions, though I think if anyone deserves biting he does.'

'What's he been up to now?'

'Nothing particular, I'm just speaking on general principles. However,' he added, entering into the spirit of the conversation, 'if ever we do have a body in the library—'

'We haven't got a library,' Caroline objected.

'—I couldn't answer for the behaviour of the two ghouls, should the police happen to pass the family vault. The last time I walked in that direction they were looking very sullen.'

'If you go on like this,' Emma complained, 'you'll have me thoroughly muddled.'

'I'm sorry,' said Antony untruthfully. 'We were only trying to help. You did sound a bit doubtful, you know, when you assured us that all was well with Maltravers.'

'Maltravers hasn't actually arrived yet, but there's a party of guests, of course.'

'Of course,' echoed Caroline encouragingly. 'Who are they?'

'Well, one's a big game hunter, I visualised him as a strong silent man, and the trouble is that makes it difficult to get a conversation going.'

'I know,' said Antony. 'Sometimes he seems about to speak, but none of his friends can ever remember his having actually done so.'

'It isn't *quite* as bad as that,' said Emma seriously. 'I'll just have to make the other people very talkative.'

'Well to begin with,' said Jenny, 'there has to be a girl to shatter the brooding quiet of the hall by a series of piercing screams.'

'There is a girl, and she did scream,' Emma admitted.

'There was bound to be.' It was Hugh's turn to embroider on the subject. 'An enchanting blonde with eyes wide with terror ran distractedly down the staircase and flung herself upon the butler's chest. He fielded her neatly and passed her to Sir Jasper's not unwilling embrace. "The grey monk!" she panted.'

'Yes, that's pretty good. I hope you're making notes, Emma.'

Emma smiled. 'I have an excellent memory,' she assured him. 'Do go on one of you, I can't wait to hear what happens next.'

Hugh was the first one to accept the invitation. ' "You'll feel better for your dinner," the baronet told the girl, his tone giving no inkling of the passions which seethed within him. (Drat that ghost, he was thinking. No sense of timing.)'

'And then,' said Antony impressively, ' "Did you get up a bottle of the '47 Château Margaux?" Sir Jasper asked. "I regret sir," said the butler at his stiffest, "I was unable to do so. I feel it only right to inform you that the faceless horror is in the wine cellar again.' "

'I like that,' said Hugh approvingly, but it was Jenny who took up the story.

'For one terror-filled moment his employer looked at him and then he pulled himself together. "Oh well," he said, "make the best of it, what?" And now,' she added, 'I think we've teased Emma long enough.'

They all looked at the great authoress, who appeared to be lost in thought. 'I don't mean the faceless horror in the wine cellar,' she said, 'but a ghost might be a good idea. What do you think?'

The ensuing discussion effectively dismissed more serious matters from their conversation for that evening at least.

SATURDAY, 28th August

At Farthing Lee they were none of them up very early the next morning. Emma made one of her gigantic breakfasts, but whatever she might do when she was alone, when visitors came she kept strictly to a Monday to Friday working week, so they were able to sit over the meal as long as they liked discussing the pleasant evening they had spent at Burton Crook. All the more pleasant, as they had discovered that Hugh and Caroline were also bidden to the Hawthornes' party that evening. Which was only natural, as Emma assured them, as Caroline had sold the house and therefore was the first person the newcomers had known in Burton Cecil. After that they spent a lazy day. It was hotter than ever, and though Antony and Jenny took a short walk by the river they soon came back to the coolness of the old stone cottage.

The Hawthornes were expecting them at eight o'clock. There were to be drinks and a buffet supper. Mrs Kitchener had confided to Emma that she was responsible for the latter, young Mrs Hawthorne being quite inexperienced and Mr Hawthorne (presumably) having made it worth her while. It was a little cooler by the time they set off. The Hawthornes lived next door but one to the Lewises, between Dr Oaksley and another large house that stood empty.

As they passed Roland Beaufort's cottage he came out and walked with them as far as the Mortal Man. They talked of nothing in particular, but Antony was distracted by the thought that for a man who professed to have no sense of time Roland was remarkably regular in his habits. But then they were saying Good Night, and a few moments later turned into the driveway. It was another big house though quite unlike the Lewises', and Jenny found herself wondering whether its new tenants intended to start a family.

Samuel Hawthorne let them in and his wife was hovering in the hall not far behind him, and even at a glance the disparity in their ages was very pronounced. Samuel looked to be in his late thirties, a tall man, very thin, so that even his handshake, though firm enough, rather gave the impression that a skeleton was greeting them. He had straight, dark hair and his features were almost regular enough to deserve the word 'handsome' if he'd put on a little weight. But when he smiled at Jenny she thought she knew what his young wife must have seen in him to attract her; it was a charming smile and genuinely welcoming.

Emma introduced the two Maitlands and Samuel introduced Mabel to them. Whatever Antony was thinking, Jenny's mind immediately turned to her age. She could easily have passed for sixteen, but this seemed unlikely, and after observing her for a while, Jenny came to the conclusion that it was partly her manner that accounted for this. Mabel had fair, curly hair, genuinely blonde unless she was very much mistaken, and round blue eyes with a guileless expression that seemed altogether too good to be true. In fact, in any description of her the word round would have to recur not that she was the slightest bit plump, just gently rounded, and with a round, smiling childlike face. She, too, obviously desired to be friendly and her pride in her new home and her new husband was touching.

When they took the visitors into the drawing-room Hugh and Caroline were already there. Even though they had met so recently there was the usual babble of greetings, the usual uncertainty about where they should all sit, the usual inquiries as to what everyone would like to drink. 'Two other couples are coming whom I'm sure you know,' said Samuel, returning with their glasses. 'The vicar and his wife, and Ivor and Myfanwy Lewis.'

'I know them, of course,' said Emma, 'and so do the others I think except that Jenny may not have met the Lewises.' Perhaps Samuel Hawthorne misinterpreted the doubtful note in her voice because he smiled at her.

'You're wondering about the Lewises coming out so soon after that dreadful thing happened to their cousin. It was Tom Jerrold who suggested that we should include them in the invitation as a matter of fact. They're our close neighbours, as you know, the children are away, and Mrs Lewis has been so upset he felt the change might be of benefit to her.'

Antony had his own thoughts about that, but of course he joined in the general murmur of agreement. For that matter he liked both the Lewises and would be glad to meet them again under less of a strain. But one of those small silences had followed Samuel's remarks and to break it Jenny turned to Mabel.

'How long have you been married?' she asked.

'Six months. Well, a little more. We were married at the end of February.' She turned an adoring look on her husband. 'But sometimes I think we've been married for ever,' she said.

'Now, how do I take that?' His tone was indulgent, teasing.

'I think,' said Caroline, 'you may take it as a compliment.'

'I think so too,' said Hugh. 'And now, as a resident of a whole month's duration, what do you think of Burton Cecil?'

'Oh, we love it.' Mabel thought for a moment before she elaborated on that. 'Everything is so different.'

'How do you mean different?' Caroline's tone was amused but not unkindly. Jenny found that Mabel had rather that effect on her too, a desire to protect her; and that was the one thing she seemed least in need of. It only took a glance around the big room to see the lavish way it had been furnished, and that money was obviously the last thing the Hawthornes had to worry about. As for their difference in age, Mabel's appealing quality made that seem more natural.

At the moment their hostess was frowning over the question. 'Well, you know we lived in Manchester,' she said. 'A big town, even if it doesn't seem so to Mr and Mrs Maitland, living in London as I believe they do.'

'We haven't always lived there,' said Jenny. 'We were both born in the same small town, in Sussex. And I don't remember that I've ever been to Manchester. Is it nice?' She thought she knew the answer to that, but of course it might seem very different to people who had lived there.

'Not bad,' said Mabel. 'Sam lived with his mother until we were married. Mrs Hawthorne was the dearest person, and so kind to me. It seemed the obvious thing for us to take a flat quite near her house so that she wouldn't miss his company too much. My parents are younger and they have each other, and my brothers and sisters for company besides.'

Perhaps both Caroline and Jenny thought that last remark rather tactless, for they both rushed into speech together. Each of them naturally immediately offered to give way to the other, and it was Caroline who went on with what she had to say. 'How many brothers and sisters, Mabel? You must miss them.'

'In a way, but they're only children, all of them. It's not like having grown-up companionship,' said Mabel, still looking as though she ought to have been in the schoolroom.

'But still,' said Hugh, who had the habit of asking pertinent questions and in any case was interested in his new neighbours, 'you decided after all that you'd prefer to live in the country?'

To the horror of all the visitors Mabel's eyes filled with tears. 'That was so sad,' she said.

Her husband took up the story. 'It certainly was a tragedy, and quite unexpected. We hadn't been married a month when my mother died. I'd always wanted to move to the country and now that I have no ties it seemed the obvious thing to do. Besides there were memories. . . . Mother was a great old girl and I was glad to get away.'

'It must have taken you a little while to decide where you wanted to settle,' said Caroline, 'but at least you had good weather for your move.'

'We saw your advertisement, and when I came up here to look at the house you told me everything was in good order,' said Samuel. 'And I must say we found it so; the house couldn't be more comfortable. We didn't bother to look any further, we'd given up the flat and moved into Mother's house until it was sold and that happened more quickly than I expected. Still, I'm quite sure now we made the right decision.' He glanced at Mabel and smiled. 'In spite of what happened in the village a few days ago,' he said. 'Thank goodness Mabel has her head screwed on the right way and it didn't give her a distaste for the place.'

They all of them looked rather curiously at young Mrs Hawthorne at that moment. 'I think it's romantic to live in a village where a murder has been committed,' she said. Thinking of Dilys, Jenny decided that perhaps after all Mabel added a lack of imagination to her other qualities. 'And the house next door, the one that's still standing empty, isn't nearly as nice as this one.'

'Besides being a good deal more expensive,' said Samuel, smiling. 'As you pointed out to me, Mrs Anstey, this is the better value for money. I must say it's refreshing to do business with an honest woman.'

It was obvious that both Caroline and Hugh found this remark embarrassing, but fortunately at that moment the bell rang and Samuel went out to answer it. 'I wonder which of our other guests that is,' said Mabel. 'You know Mrs Jerrold has been so kind to me since we came here. She noticed me the first time I went to church and spoke to me afterwards. But I'd better go out and greet them.'

As it happened, both couples had arrived together. Mr and Mrs Jerrold came into the room first. The vicar, though short and inclined to be stout, was by far and away the most handsome man in the parish, particularly when seen in profile. Maisie Jerrold was a little taller than her husband, and was a woman whose appearance Jenny had always particularly admired. She had an air of chic that was not too common in the

102

country – or anywhere else for that matter – a figure that was well nigh perfect and an excellent taste in dress. Seven years ago . . . but that was another story. She had bloomed since then into a mature loveliness that could only be explained by extreme contentment.

They seemed pleased to see the Maitlands and the various members of the Anstey family, all of whom, of course, they knew much better. There was some reference from Tom to an auspicious occasion, presumably the welcoming of newcomers to the district. The Lewises, just behind them, joined in all this, but Ivor, at least, had a rather hang-dog air, as though he felt his presence at such a festivity might be misconstrued. The thought had obviously never occurred to Myfanwy, who looked as placid as ever.

They had their drinks and they had Mrs Kitchener's excellent buffet, and then they sat down to discuss such impersonal matters as the current state of Britain's economy. To Antony, it didn't seem the easiest party he'd ever attended, though he imagined that in normal circumstances they would have formed a reasonably congenial group. The trouble was, it was only too obvious that almost everybody present was itching to discuss Dilys's murder and was inhibited from doing so by the presence of her cousin. He thought himself that Ivor felt the girl's death more than his wife did, but even so the proprieties must be observed and the subject was no more than skirted gingerly until Myfanwy herself brought it up.

'Maisie persuaded us to come, and Tom thought we should. We did want to get to know you both better,' she added, smiling from one of the Hawthornes to the other. 'But I do hope you don't think it's dreadful of us so soon after—'

She let the sentence trail there, and her husband took it up in a rallying tone. 'Nonsense, my dear, it's no use sitting at home brooding. If it would help matters . . . but it won't.'

'I must say,' said Tom in his deep voice, 'I do wish the police didn't think all the clues they've got pointed so inevitably to Peter Dutton. He's a nice boy and I was looking forward to a marriage that—' He broke off there, glancing with obvious embarrassment towards his hostess, but Maitland was pretty sure he could have completed the sentence for him . . . where the parties didn't *have* to get married. But that thought he kept to himself.

'You know I wasn't too pleased with Peter's association with Dilys,' said Ivor, sinking back in his chair as though prepared for a lengthy discussion. 'But I do agree with you and it will take more than the fact that they were friendly to make me suspect him.'

Hugh glanced at Antony, but this was one conversation he intended to keep well out of. It was Caroline who interposed. 'Should we be discussing this at all? Myfanwy—'

'I'd really rather you did than keep on so obviously avoiding the subject,' said Myfanwy in her placid way. 'It's on my mind every minute, of course, how could it be otherwise? So I don't blame anyone for being curious.'

'It would be interesting to know,' said Maisie Jerrold, 'what Mr Maitland thinks about the case against Peter.' She obviously knew nothing of the fact that Stephen Anstey had asked for Antony's help, but the vicar, who was obviously better versed in village affairs and had a good grasp of their significance, interrupted her quickly.

'My dear, we mustn't ask him that. Hugh's brother is professionally engaged in the matter and Ivor told me that Mr Maitland had consented to advise him. It isn't right to ask for his opinion.'

Antony smiled at him gratefully but said nothing. 'All the same,' said Hugh, 'there's no harm in our picking your brains. What do *you* think, Vicar, of this lunacy that's going round the village?'

'Which lunacy?' asked Tom cautiously.

'But nowt like this happened until that Wainwright came here,' said Hugh, in a very fair imitation of the local accent. 'I'm hearing that, or something very like it, on every side.'

'I don't know Mr Wainwright and I certainly know nothing

against him,' said Mr Jerrold. 'A man who likes his solitude, which is certainly his privilege. But I don't think you can blame the villagers too much; strangers are never accepted immediately, and when nothing is known about them it just makes matters worse.'

'Who is Mr Wainwright?' asked Mabel.

'That tall man you may have seen striding through the village and taking no notice of anybody. Except for Emma,' added the vicar with a smile, reminding Antony all over again that very little goes on in the country that isn't observed by someone.

'But we're strangers too, we've only been here a month.'

'That's a little different,' said Myfanwy. Jenny was amused to see that she too seemed to have caught some of the prevailing protective attitude towards the young Mrs Hawthorne. 'You're trying to become part of the village life, not cutting yourselves off from everyone completely.'

'I have a theory that might vindicate the villagers' opinion in this matter,' said Ivor. 'Mr Maitland knows it already but I hope he won't mind listening to it all over again. If Peter is innocent – and I told you I think he is – this could be the start of something very nasty.'

'You're trying to suggest that this man Wainwright is a mass murderer,' said Tom Jerrold aghast. 'Come now, Ivor, I really think that's going too far. Just because he likes his solitude—'

'Time will tell,' said Ivor stubbornly, and shrugged.

'Well, I think it was a passing tramp,' said Maisie firmly.

'Are there any tramps nowadays?'

'There are always some strange people about and it's really the only explanation,' Maisie elaborated. 'No one we know would do a thing like that.'

Antony exchanged a glance with his wife indicative of despair. 'Well, saving your presence, Vicar,' said Hugh coming to his rescue, 'I think this is one subject we've had enough of. Isn't it about time we drank the health of our host and hostess, and wished them a long life and happiness in their new home?'

To Antony's relief that rather heavy-handed hint was taken

and there was no further discussion of Dilys Jones's death that night. Later, as they were making their farewells, Maisie reminded Mabel that the evening service was at six-thirty the next evening and she was expecting her for tea first, and Tom asked Samuel half laughingly whether on this occasion he wouldn't accompany his wife.

'I'm afraid I'm not much of a church-goer,' Samuel told him lightly. 'Sorry, Padre.' A moment later the door closed behind them; Hugh and Caroline turned right with the Lewises, who only had a step or two to go to their own gate, and the others turned left through the village.

'An admirable young couple,' said Tom appreciatively, 'and I don't despair of bringing him to another way of thinking, I don't despair at all.' And indeed the last sight they had of the Hawthornes in the lighted doorway had been a pleasant one, Samuel was standing with his arm around his wife's shoulders, rather as though he couldn't wait to be alone with her again. Antony didn't somehow think the vicar's arguments would have too much effect on him, but Mabel's persuasion might be a different matter.

It wasn't long before the Jerrolds turned up towards the vicarage, and the other three walked along in a contented silence until they reached Farthing Lee. 'I won't bother opening the window,' said Emma. 'Just leave the door open, Antony. Would you like a night-cap?'

'Cocoa?' asked Antony cautiously.

'You know perfectly well I've never offered *you* cocoa in my life,' said Emma indignantly.

'No but sometimes when you indulge yourself I feel a kind of moral pressure ... but I think after such a long walk we all stand in need of fortifying.' Emma grinned at him and went to the cupboard where she kept the drinks.

'What do you think of our new friends?' Antony asked.

Jenny had subsided onto the sofa. 'I thought Mabel was rather a dear. But so young,' she added, sighing.

'If you like that type,' said Maitland rather dryly, coming to

106

sit beside her. 'Hawthorne's an interesting chap. He struck me as a man . . . well' – he paused, choosing his words carefully – 'a man under a great strain.'

'I think perhaps he doesn't like to meet strangers, but realised he must for Mabel's sake,' said Emma, returning with her trophies which she put down on the desk, turning them tacitly over to Antony's ministrations.

'Yes, that was my impression so far as it goes. He smiled a lot,' said Jenny, 'but I didn't really think he has much sense of humour. But it might have been just nervousness.'

'True my love, but typical.'

'If you mean because I don't hate everybody I meet on sight—' She sounded indignant, but had obviously forgotten all about it before the sentence was completed. 'Did I ask you this before, Emma, because if I did I've forgotten the answer. What does Samuel Hawthorne do for his living? He's too young to be retired, and though it isn't all that far from Manchester it was quite a big step moving here, and much too far to travel to business every day.'

'I gather he has independent means,' said Emma. 'Caroline told me he didn't take a mortgage out on the house, anyway.'

'How nice for them. There's one thing though, Mabel isn't mercenary. I think she absolutely dotes on him and she'd have married him if he hadn't a penny.'

'Yes, that's what I thought too,' said Emma. Maitland, for the moment, was strangely silent. 'I was rather surprised to see the Lewises there though. Maisie had told me they'd been asked, but I thought they'd back out at the last moment.'

'I think Ivor Lewis would rather have been anywhere else,' said Antony, 'but his wife doesn't strike me as having exactly a sensitive nature. Which is not, my love, a criticism,' he added, forestalling any protest Jenny might have been about to make. 'Did I tell you about my talk with Roland when he so obviously lured me from your side at the Mortal Man last night?'

'Not a word,' said Emma. 'And if it was anything interesting I think you should have *some* regard for our feelings.'

'Yes, I know you're both curious,' said Maitland annoyingly. 'As for Roland, the trouble is I don't know how serious he was being. He suggested that Ivor had just about got to the age when a man might prefer a rather younger woman to his wife. Or at least like a change.'

'Roland had better be careful,' said Emma seriously.

'There was no one within earshot, and he took care to wait until Adam was at the other end of the bar. I think he trusts me by now, and certainly he'd like to help Peter. And then he said – I think I've got this right – that if the villagers really believed what they were saying about Philip Wainwright they'd lock up their daughters.'

'That isn't the first time the possibility of a series of murders has been mentioned,' Jenny pointed out rather uneasily. 'You told us yourself that Ivor Lewis had said.... I wonder if Inspector Wentworth has thought of it.'

'I'm sure he has, and dismissed it in favour of Peter's guilt. Leaving that aside for the moment, it isn't a nice idea.'

'Not at all nice,' said Emma soberly. 'But you needn't let it worry you, you still believe in Peter's guilt, don't you?'

'I still think it's the most obvious thing,' said Antony. 'He's a nice boy, I'll go so far as that with you. But . . . oh, I wouldn't have any doubts at all of his guilt if it weren't for your belief in him.'

'I'm not the only one,' Emma reminded him.

'No but . . . let's leave it at that, shall we? All we can do now – and I've tried to explain this to Stephen – is to wait and see what happens. And if we talk horrors until we go to bed, we shall none of us sleep a wink,' he added.

Emma took this rather heavy-handed hint, and turned the conversation to the subject of the twins at Burton Crook. But Antony was interested in Hugh and Caroline's offspring, so if this was intended as a penance it missed its mark.

SUNDAY, 29th August

I

On Sunday morning Emma decided to attend the early service at St Anselm's, while Antony and Jenny collected the car and drove over to Manningbridge. When they got back Emma had coffee waiting, but she suggested that instead of making breakfast they should go to the Fighting Cock at Burford Bridge for an early lunch. Burford Bridge was only three miles downstream from Farthing Lee and the Maitlands had often been there on foot by the river path; by car, however, it was a good ten miles, starting up Burton Bank and leaving the moor road to Rothershaw to take a rather bumpy track down to the village that had grown up to take advantage of one of the few crossing places of the Eller.

This seemed a good idea, and neither of them had any hesitation about agreeing to it, and the outing proved as enjoyable as they had expected. When they got back and Jenny had parked the car Antony went round to the side door of the shop (Mrs Ryder opened in the morning, rather to Mr Jerrold's dissatisfaction, but that redoubtable lady insisted it was easier that way and if people arrived after she had closed she was never one to be disobliging). He was able to obtain a fair selection of the Sunday papers, and when they had walked back to Farthing Lee these occupied them with reading and discussion almost until dinnertime. Mrs Kitchener's steak and kidney pie was excellent, and when everything had been cleared away ready for that good lady's attention in the morning Antony and Jenny would have been perfectly satisfied to spend a quiet evening with their hostess. But they knew Emma's ways pretty well by now, and when Antony caught her eyes straying towards her working table for the third time he asked her, 'Have you left Maltravers in difficulties again?'

'Not really,' said Emma. 'It's just ... well to be honest, my dears, it's that ghost.'

'What ghost?' asked Antony, surprised. He had forgotten all about the conversation at Burton Crook.

'Oh, not the grey monk,' Emma assured him. 'But I did think, you know, it might add a little atmosphere to the scene. And I shan't do any real writing but I should like, if you don't mind, to get one or two ideas down on paper.'

'Of course we don't mind,' said Jenny quickly. 'Why don't we go down to the Mortal Man, Antony, there's always someone to talk to there?'

'Good idea,' Maitland agreed. 'We'll leave you to wrestle with your ghost, Emma, but we shan't be late. Is there anything you'd like us to bring back for you?'

'Not on Sunday,' said Emma, shocked. 'Adam has an off-licence, but I don't think it would allow him to sell anything to you today.'

'Perhaps not, but I bet he'd be only too ready to all the same. Is it breaking the law or breaking the Sabbath that worries you, Emma?' he added curiously.

Emma gave him a brilliant smile. 'Neither really,' she confided. 'Anything you feel like for a nightcap, and I really think you should take a cardigan with you, Jenny, it may get cold later on.'

This was a perennial argument, or would have been if Jenny hadn't given in gracefully years ago and consented to take the unnecessary garment with her. Emma was at her desk already when they left the cottage. 'Come to think of it,' said Jenny when they had crossed the narrow footbridge and were walking past the wood, 'she needn't really look very far for her ghost. Poor Dilys! But I think on the whole it's a good thing country people are so matter-of-fact about death.'

110

'In one way they are,' her husband agreed. He posssessed himself of her hand and tucked it under his left arm. 'But I wouldn't call the kind of talk that's going on in the village at the moment exactly matter-of-fact.'

'No, of course not,' said Jenny. But she broke off there, perhaps because they had reached Rowan Corner and were entering the village street. It was very quiet, which in spite of their infrequent visits they had learned to expect on a Sunday evening. The people who attended the evening service at the church would have dispersed at about a quarter past seven and by now were either safely in the pub, if they had had high tea earlier, or at home having their dinner. As they passed the cottages they noticed two men walking ahead of them, probably bound for the same destination. As they were talking neither of them was paying much attention, but then Jenny suddenly felt Antony's hand on her arm pulling her to a standstill. Then she heard one of the men ahead exclaim sharply, there was a muffled oath, and Peter Dutton's voice saying in a rather high-pitched tone, 'Who is it, Roland, what's happened?'

'Stay there, Jenny,' Antony commanded, though he must have known there wasn't much chance she would obey him. She did let him go ahead of her, however, but halted when she saw two figures crouched over another, stiller one which lay almost at the spot where the lane from the church entered the village street.

Antony went forward to join the group. It was a woman who lay crumpled up in the roadway and when Roland turned her over gently it was only her curly blonde hair that made it possible to recognise her at all. Her face was so distorted as to seem to have lost all touch with humanity. Maitland was no stranger to violent death, and it would have been obvious that she was a victim of strangulation even if the cord around her neck hadn't told its own story. 'It's Mabel Hawthorne,' he said, and bent over her for a moment, confirming a fact of which he was already perfectly sure. Then he took two quick steps back to Jenny's side and pulled her into the shelter of his arm so that

111

she could hide her face against his shoulder. 'From the look of her—' he said, and then broke off. 'We'd better get Dr Oaksley.' He was suddenly at his most decisive. 'Will you go, Peter? And perhaps you'll fetch Constable Kitchener, Roland. I don't want to leave Jenny alone.'

They both set out on their errands immediately, and Peter and the doctor were back in an unbelievably short space of time. It needed no more than a brief examination to confirm what Antony had known already must be true. Dr Oaksley stood up again and looked around him. 'We can't leave her here,' he said.

'Nothing should be touched,' Antony objected.

'Who's that? Oh, Mr Maitland. I'm going to override you I'm afraid, anyone may come along and I understand from Peter that she's been moved already. Go to the side door of the Mortal Man, Peter, there's a good lad, and see if we can take her into one of the rooms in the back. I'll take full responsibility,' he added, unnecessarily. Maitland's protest had been automatic and he didn't really think that leaving the body where it was would do the investigation the slightest good. As for Jenny, all she could think of was Mabel as she had been the night before, as happy in her short-lived marriage as she herself was in her much longer-lasting one.

'Who'll break it to her husband?' she asked.

'I'll have my hands full for a while,' said the doctor. 'Why don't you go to the vicarage? Tom's the obvious person, he knew the Hawthornes, didn't he?'

'Yes, of course. We could do that now couldn't we, Antony?' said Jenny eagerly. 'I mean Roland and Mr Dutton can tell the police whatever they need to know about finding her.'

Dr Oaksley agreed to that, probably his main concern was to get out of having to perform an unpleasant task himself. A moment later light was streaming out of the side door of the Mortal Man. Adam and Peter returned, and together they took up their sad burden. 'A good idea of yours, love,' said Antony as they turned to walk up to the vicarage.

'Yes I . . . I suppose that must have been Peter Dutton,' said Jenny. 'With Roland, I mean.'

'Yes, it was. I think I told you Roland's an old friend of his.'

'Well, I admit I'm glad to get away for the moment; it would be horrible to have to hang around until the detectives arrive, though I suppose they'll want to see us later. But, Antony, do you think this means it's happening?'

'If by that characteristically vague question, my love, you mean, Is Burton Cecil in for a succession of sex murders? the answer is, I just don't know, but it looks as if it might be happening.'

'Doesn't this change your mind about Peter Dutton?'

'That's something else I can't give you an answer to,' said Maitland slowly. 'I'll have to know something about the timing to be able to say whether this lets him out.'

'It's quite obvious – at least that's what I thought and I imagine you did too – that Roland had called for him to go down to the pub. Doesn't that put it out of the question that he could have killed poor Mabel?'

'Not necessarily, it would depend . . . let's just wait and see. We shall hear all about it soon enough.'

And when it came to the point of breaking the news to Maisie Jerrold it turned out to be almost as bad as breaking it to a near relation. It was obvious to Jenny that Mabel Hawthorne's knack of arousing a desire to protect her from life's difficulties had made a deep impression, particularly perhaps on the women who were present the evening before, and of them all Mrs Jerrold had known her by far the best. They had asked first for her husband, of course, but he was still in the church, so there was nothing for it but to tell her the purpose of their visit. 'That poor child!' she kept exclaiming.

Antony offered to fetch Mr Jerrold. He had a naturally helpful nature, but in this case Jenny couldn't altogether acquit him of a longing to get away. As for her, it was as much from a desire to distract Maisie from her distress as it was out of curiosity that she asked as soon as he had gone, 'I can't understand how it could have happened. There are usually quite a few people at the evening service, aren't there, and they all leave more or less at the same time?'

'That makes me feel as if it was all my fault,' mourned Maisie Jerrold.

'Why on earth should you think that?'

'Because she'd forgotten her gloves and came back to the vicarage to fetch them. You know she was having tea with me this afternoon, I'm sure you heard us make the arrangement last night. And I kept her talking, so that I daresay there would be nobody about when she actually left.'

'Have you any idea what time that would be?'

'I don't know exactly, except that we usually get out of church about seven-fifteen. I shouldn't think it was more than a quarter of an hour that she was with me, but time enough for the rest of the congregation to disperse, I expect.'

Jenny thought, Someone could have waited for her, but wisely did not say it aloud. It occurred to her, however, as a veteran of goodness-knows-how-many legal discussions between Antony and his uncle when they were at home, that it was a question the police would be asking the vicar later . . . who had attended church that evening? 'It's a terrible tragedy,' she said aloud, 'and I know you were particularly friendly with her. But you mustn't add to your grief by blaming yourself, that's quite unnecessary.'

'I suppose I'm being silly,' Maisie said, still tragically.

'At least she couldn't have suffered,' said Jenny, with all the confidence she could muster. She wasn't at all sure that she was telling the truth, though she had an idea she'd read something of the sort, but it seemed the best thing to say in the circumstances, and to her relief Mrs Jerrold seemed to accept the assurance.

'Yes, we must be thankful for that. Can you tell me, my dear, where was she?'

'She must have come down the lane from the vicarage and just reached the main street. Roland Beaufort and Peter

Dutton were walking ahead of us, they'd just found her when Antony and I came along.'

'Well, I may as well say this while we're alone,' said Maisie confidentially. 'Tom doesn't like me to say this, which is why I talked about a tramp last night, but this just confirms what everyone's saying about that man Wainwright. I only hope the police will do something about him before he does any more harm.'

Somehow Jenny didn't feel it was quite as simple as that. As Antony had pointed out, Peter might not yet be in the clear himself. But there was no point in arguing and to her relief the two men came back then. Tom Jerrold couldn't have been far to seek, in fact Antony told her later when they were exchanging notes that the vicar had been leaving the church and actually in the act of locking the door behind him when he got there. Of course there were more lamentations. Jenny wished Maisie Jerrold would stop because she felt pretty miserable about the whole affair herself. But she had to admire the way that Mr Jerrold took charge of everything, including the unpleasant task they had wished on him at Dr Oaksley's suggestion.

'I'll go along and see Samuel straight away,' he said, 'and perhaps,' he added doubtfully, 'I shall be able to find some words to comfort him. In any case, he must be informed before the police want to see him.'

So they all left the house together, the vicar admonishing his wife to lock the door carefully behind them, a precaution that seemed reasonable enough in the circumstances. They encountered Sergeant Gilbey and Constable Kitchener at the bottom of the lane, the vicar told them his errand, which seemed to be a great relief to them, and Antony paused to ask them if they wanted his and Jenny's story now or whether it would wait till the detectives arrived from Rothershaw. 'Better wait,' said the sergeant. 'The only question is, where will you be?'

'Well, we were on our way to the Mortal Man, but I don't think either of us feels much like that now. We'll be at Farthing Lee if it's all right with you.'

That too, for some reason seemed to relieve the sergeant. 'T' body shouldn't have been moved, of course,' he confided. 'But there, Dr Oaksley he's always had a mind of his own. There'll be going and coming around here, no good trying to keep things quiet then. So this way t' inspector can take your statement nice and peaceful like.'

'For heaven's sake,' Jenny said rather crossly as they went back along the road, 'does the poor girl have to become "the body" so quickly? Only last night—'

'Take it easy, love. You can't blame Gilbey, it's just a job to him. Just be thankful Tom Jerrold has taken it on himself to break the news to Hawthorne, that's something I wouldn't like to be doing myself.'

'Neither would I. I wonder if they have dinner or high tea,' Jenny added inconsequently.

'Who?'

'The Jerrolds. There was a smell of cooking, so I think it must have been dinner,' Jenny said, trying to distract herself with this minor puzzle. 'So I wondered why he stayed so long at the church.'

Antony began to laugh. 'My dearest love,' he said, 'if you're going to begin looking for clues and making deductions I doubt if I shall be able to stand the strain.'

'I was only wondering—' said Jenny.

'In any case, there's no secret about it. He's prayer and she's good works, if you know what I mean. There's glory for you!'

Jenny didn't need that explaining, but she wasn't yet quite in the mood to be distracted from the unpleasantness they had witnessed. 'When I use a word it means what I want it to mean,' she said vaguely. 'Do you realise, Antony, we've still to tell Emma? And as we never got to the Mortal Man you'll probably be condemned to drinking cocoa after all.'

116

II

Telling Emma was just as unpleasant as they had expected, but fortunately there was a little cognac left, some *crème de menthe*, and almost half a bottle of Grand Marnier, so they weren't condemned to the cocoa with which Jenny had threatened her husband. Emma had obviously been in the throes of composition. The Spanish comb had given up its job entirely and was lying beside the typewriter. She reminded Jenny sometimes of Vera; they both had hair that wouldn't stay arranged for two minutes together, though in every other way she was the complete antithesis of Lady Harding. But where Jenny was accustomed to playing Alice to the White Queen where her aunt was concerned, Emma never seemed to notice her own state of disarray. She left an untidy pile of papers on her desk and thought of them no more that evening, but it cannot be said that the discussion that followed added very much to anyone's knowledge.

It wasn't until nearly eleven o'clock that Inspector Wentworth and his shadow Constable Tankard reached the cottage and by that time the cognac bottle had been consigned to outer darkness (that is to say the dustbin) and they had all turned their attention to the Grand Marnier. 'Well Mr Maitland,' said Wentworth, surging in front of his subordinate into the living-room, 'this will make a change for you, won't it? To be answering questions yourself instead of trying to trip up the poor unfortunate in the witness box.'

For a moment Maitland was distracted by a vision of what might have been. He had a particular dislike for answering questions, though he had been fated to have to do so on countless occasions during his career. But he pulled himself together to respond to the inspector's greeting before turning to speak to the silent constable, who was producing his inevitable notebook. 'There's very little we can tell you, I'm afraid, but such as it is, of course, we're at your disposal.'

'And Miss Anstey wasn't with you on this occasion?'

'No, she stayed at home to work.'

'I'll go into the kitchen if you like, Inspector,' Emma offered, 'but I think you'll find that I know as much by now of what happened as Mr and Mrs Maitland do themselves.'

'My dear Miss Anstey, we wouldn't dream of turning you from your own hearth,' said Wentworth, which on an evening that was still very warm was an odd way of putting it. And that was all very fine, but Antony sensed a certain reservation in the detective's manner towards him which – as it was seven years since their last encounter – could only be due to his having heard more than Maitland cared about his recent activities.

'I think Peter Dutton and Roland Beaufort will have already told you more than we can, and Dr Oaksley more than any of us,' he said.

'That may be true enough, but it doesn't dispense with the formality of a statement,' said Wentworth a little heavily. 'As you can imagine we're very concerned with the actual time you found Mrs Hawthorne.'

'You haven't got that quite right,' Maitland corrected him. 'It was the other two who made the discovery, we were a few yards behind them. As for the time, we left the cottage at about a quarter to eight. I can't be sure that's absolutely exact, but it was certainly no later than that.'

'And you'd been together all evening until then? And Miss Anstey too?'

'Certainly we had. All day for that matter.'

'And you can't be more sure about the time you left the house?'

'I'm sorry about that. That's one of the joys of being on holiday, not having to watch the clock. But assuming I'm right, I should imagine the discovery must have been made at about seven fifty-five.'

'Thank you, Mr Maitland, that's all very clear. Do you agree with your husband, Mrs Maitland?'

'Yes I do, even to the extent of being a little vague about the time.'

118

'Have you found anybody who saw anything, Inspector,' Antony asked, 'during the period after she left the vicarage on her way home and the time she was found?' He knew he was risking a snub, but it seemed worthwhile to take the chance.

'I'm sure your inquiring mind has led you to the answer to that question already,' said Wentworth. 'The church-goers had long since departed, and unless someone was going to the pub, as you and Mrs Maitland were, and as Dutton and Beaufort also claim to have been doing, it wasn't likely there would be anybody about.'

'Someone was,' said Jenny and shivered. 'Someone killed her.'

'I'm not forgetting that. Which brings me to another point I want to ask you about. I understand you were all at the Hawthornes last night. Who knew that Mrs Hawthorne would be attending the evening service?'

'All of us, I suppose.' Antony looked questioningly at Emma, who nodded her agreement. 'It was mentioned as we were leaving, but it wouldn't have been a very good time to plan to kill her, if that's what somebody did, because unless she'd gone back for her gloves, which Mrs Jerrold says she'd left at the vicarage, she'd have been leaving the church in company with several other people.'

'You don't go to St Anselm's do you, Mr Maitland?'

'No, as a matter of fact we don't, and Miss Anstey, I've observed, prefers the morning service.'

'If you did you'd probably be aware there weren't too many people to disperse. Besides Mrs Hawthorne, and Mrs Jerrold of course, six people in all attended this evening.'

'I see.' For some reason the information surprised Antony and it showed in his voice. 'But I gather Mrs Hawthorne had made a habit of going since they moved here,' he said after a moment's hesitation, 'so anyone in the village might have known that she'd be there. I don't see that the fact that it was mentioned at the Hawthornes' house-warming is relevant at all.'

''Appen you're right.' For some reason of his own Wentworth

119

made the agreement sound almost indulgent. 'Perhaps you could describe again exactly what you heard and saw when Mrs Hawthorne's body was discovered.'

'I can, of course, but I don't think in this case Jenny can confirm what I say,' Maitland replied. 'She didn't notice anything was wrong as quickly as I did and then I tried my best to keep her at a little distance. It wasn't a pretty sight you know.'

'I know that very well,' said Wentworth coldly, 'but I should be glad to have your help, Mr Maitland.'

So Antony went over the matter again, as concisely as he could. 'There's just one thing, Inspector,' he added, as Wentworth got up and Constable Tankard, tucking away his notebook, followed suit. 'Don't you feel that this makes a difference to the way Dilys Jones's murder must be regarded? Unless you're going to postulate two murders by different people in Burton Cecil within a week it must be obvious that Peter Dutton isn't implicated.'

'You're going a little too fast, Mr Maitland,' said Wentworth, not stopping on his way to the door. 'Our inquiries have barely started.'

'I realise that, but surely as Peter Dutton was with Roland Beaufort—'

'Don't take anything for granted, then you won't be disappointed,' Wentworth advised as he opened the front door. And added, by way of a rather unsettling valediction, 'Things aren't always what they seem.'

Constable Tankard followed and as soon as the door had closed behind him Jenny said uneasily, 'What do you think he meant by that?'

'Exactly what he said, I should think,' said Maitland, adding for good measure, 'condescending bastard. Sorry, Emma, but really—'

'You needn't apologise, Antony, I quite agree with you,' said Emma sedately. 'I suppose he meant that we don't know how long Peter and Roland had been together.'

120

'But—' Jenny started.

'This is a beastly business, love,' Antony told her. 'It's got to be stopped, you must see that.'

'That's the affair of the two gentlemen who just left us,' said Emma rather tartly. 'Like the rest of the people who know him well I've maintained Peter's innocence all along, though I'm quite aware that you gave your help to Stephen rather reluctantly.'

'I agreed to take over the defence if it came to a trial,' Maitland protested, 'though I did suggest Uncle Nick might manage it better. But whatever Wentworth says this changes matters. I can't see Peter Dutton as a mass murderer. All the same if there's the slightest chance . . . I'll have to get hold of Stephen, because as his lawyer he's got a certain responsibility before things get altogether out of hand. Do you mind if I use the telephone, Emma?'

'Of course not. Jenny dear,' said Emma, confirming Antony's worst fears, 'I really think some cocoa would be a good idea tonight after all we've been through. Shall we go and make it?'

So Maitland was alone when he crossed to the desk and pulled the telephone towards him. He got through quickly to Burton Crook and wasn't surprised to find that the news of Mabel Hawthorne's death had already reached there by way of Elsie's brother, Eric, who had been in the pub and couldn't wait to pour out his story on his return. When Stephen was fetched he grasped Maitland's point readily enough. 'You're quite right, I must see him as soon as I can tomorrow and find out what his story is about this evening. From Wentworth's attitude as you describe it I imagine it wasn't altogether satisfactory.'

'That's what I thought too. I have to admit, though, that what's happened has changed my own feelings about him a little.'

'I can understand that, but I also agree with you that the matter's far too serious for us to take any chances. If he *has* done this as well as the other he must be mad. Will you come with me, Antony? Perhaps you and I together could persuade him to plead insanity, that way no one else will get hurt.'

'I'll accompany you with pleasure.'

'All the same, we don't want to bully him into a confession,' said Stephen, worried again.

'Give me credit for a little sense,' said Antony, not trying to hide his amusement. 'I only meant to convey that all the possibilities should be put clearly before him. And his story about tonight may prove his innocence for all we know.'

'Yes, of course it may,' said Stephen more cheerfully. 'How shall we arrange it?'

'I think it will be better to see him at your office, there's no point in worrying his parents unduly. What time do you usually go in, because I'd like a lift.'

'I'll pick you up at Rowan Corner at eight-thirty,' Stephen promised. 'But how will you get back again? It isn't market day, so there won't be a bus.'

'I'll get Jenny to come over and meet me for lunch. Perhaps you'll join us?'

'That sounds a good idea. Tell Jenny to go to the Boar's Head, and we'll meet her there about twelve o'clock.'

Antony put down the receiver, and went into the kitchen in time to prevent a third cup of cocoa from being poured for his use. 'I know we never finished our errand at the Mortal Man,' he said, 'but as you seem to be content with that stuff I shall take the liberty of going back to the Grand Marnier. I want to take the taste of Inspector Wentworth out of my mouth.'

MONDAY, 30th August
I

The programme as outlined went without a hitch the following morning. Stephen had stopped at the Duttons' cottage before picking Maitland up at Rowan Corner, and arranged for Peter to come into Rothershaw on his bike as soon as he had finished his breakfast. 'The request worried him, I could tell,' he told Antony as they drove up Burton Bank, 'but he was doing his best to hide it. As for Mr and Mrs Dutton, they're not ones to show their feelings but they must be worried to death.'

Maitland agreed, but he'd already got the impression that Stephen preferred to be silent as he drove so nothing further was said until they reached their destination. There he was introduced to the venerable gentleman from whom Stephen was taking over, and then repaired to Stephen's office where they spent the time until Peter's arrival in going over the story of the interview with Inspector Wentworth the evening before. Not that anything helpful emerged from their conversation, but as Antony pointed out nothing could until they had seen their client.

Peter came in hesitantly and said Good Morning politely to both of them before he seated himself. Then he burst out, as though he couldn't contain himself any longer, 'I don't quite understand why you want to see me again, Mr Anstey.'

'About last night, Peter,' Stephen told him.

'But I thought . . . it was horrible,' said Peter, and it was hard to believe that he wasn't sincere. 'I've never seen anything like that before, she looked like one of the gargoyles on the church.

123

Is that what Dilys looked like when they found her? I can't bear the thought of it.'

'I'm sorry, you're upset, which is very understandable, but I do want you to tell us all you can about yesterday evening,' Stephen said. 'Mr Maitland agrees with me; as your legal advisors it's essential we should know every detail.'

'But . . . I still don't understand! It was horrible,' he said again, 'and I don't think I shall ever forget it, but I did think as far as the police were concerned it would put me in the clear.' His nervousness made it obvious, however, that this last statement wasn't altogether true.

'That's what we want to find out,' said Maitland smoothly. 'So if you do as Mr Anstey says and tell us about the evening from your point of view we can come to a decision as to what is best to be done. Or, indeed, if you need our help any longer.'

'All right.' Peter still sounded doubtful. 'Roland said I was brooding and I ought to snap out of it; it would help if I came down to the pub with him. I haven't been there much since I started going out with Dilys, but there's nothing else to do in Burton Cecil on a Sunday night.'

'And?' said Stephen, when Peter paused. For a moment it seemed that he might have to formulate another question, but his client went on without further prompting.

'Roland was going to call for me on the way, you know he lives just two doors away from us. He said he'd come about ten to eight, and that's what he did, so I suppose we reached the place where we – where we found her only a few moments later. You know what happened then, Mr Maitland, you were there.'

'Yes I know that quite well, and I've explained it to Mr Anstey. I've also made a statement to the police, as I'm sure you have. But what they didn't tell me, and we'd both like to know, concerns the time before Roland called for you. Where were you then?'

'At home.'

'With your parents?' Maitland had taken over the questioning, but Stephen – though less used to his ways than most of the

124

solicitors he worked with – seemed content enough that this should be so.

'No, they had the telly on so I stayed up in my room reading. I was listening for Roland's knock though and went down as soon as I heard it.'

'Unless Mrs Hawthorne stood talking to her assailant before he killed her, the time of her death must have coincided approximately with the time she arrived at the bottom of the lane from St Anselm's. That is, not earlier than seven-thirty-five and not later than seven-forty if Mrs Jerrold's right about the time. If you had left the house and returned during the ten or fifteen minutes before Roland called for you, do you think your parents would have heard you?'

'You can't think—!'

'I'm not thinking anything,' said Maitland inaccurately. 'I want to know whether there's any possibility of the police alleging that that is what you did.'

There was a long pause there. Then Peter said abruptly, 'I'd better tell you the truth, hadn't I?'

'Neither Mr Anstey nor I can help you unless you do,' Antony pointed out.

'Well then, when they get watching one of their programmes there's nothing they notice. In fact, when I went home last night they were surprised to know I'd been out at all. But this – this is like a nightmare.' He broke off, looking from one of them to the other. 'There's no reason why I should have killed Dilys, though the police won't believe that. And I didn't even know Mrs Hawthorne.'

'That isn't quite the point,' Maitland told him. 'I think with two murders within a week in Burton Cecil, both of the victims young women, we've gone beyond the realm of what might be called a reasonable motive into the realm of insanity.'

'But Dilys wasn't. . . . Was Mrs Hawthorne raped?'

'We've no information about that so far. I should say not, considering the time element and the place where she was found. But there are many different motives for multiple murders, for instance a man might get sexual satisfaction out of the mere fact of a killing.'

'I see why you talked about insanity,' said Peter in a shaking tone, 'but if you're thinking I . . . I'm not mad, Mr Maitland!'

'Will you listen to me for a moment? Neither Mr Anstey nor I is making an accusation, but you're our client and we're bound to do our best for you. So we have to point out that in certain circumstances it might be most advantageous for you to plead Not Guilty by reason of insanity.'

'You mean, if I killed them? That would be as good as admitting it.' Peter's voice had gone up almost an octave and he turned to Stephen with a kind of desperation. 'Do you agree with him? Is he telling me I ought to go to the police and confess?'

'Not unless you're guilty, Peter.'

'I'm not!'

Stephen took up the explanation. 'You must understand that besides our duty to you we have a duty to the public as well, and if by any unhappy chance that plea would be the correct one we want to prevent anybody else from getting hurt. I think from what I know of you that you would wish that yourself.'

'Yes, I would. But I couldn't have done it without knowing, could I? Could I?' he repeated, and this time his glance from one to the other of them held a frantic inquiry.

'I'm not a psychiatrist, Peter, but I don't think so.'

'Let me add something,' said Maitland, doing his best to sound reassuring. 'I think it's possible to suffer from amnesia after a very traumatic incident—'

'Such as murdering someone, for instance,' said Peter bitterly.

'—but I don't think you could forget all about the motive. If you had no feelings of resentment towards Dilys, or towards women in general—'

'I didn't, I didn't!'

'Then I think, Stephen, we may take his word for it. Do you agree with me?'

'You know I do, but I'm thankful to hear you say it,' said Stephen. 'You'll have to forgive us, Peter, but I think you'll understand that in a case like this we have to be sure.'

'Yes, I understand.' Oddly enough Peter's tone was now almost without resentment. 'You have a duty to the general public as well as to me as your client. But there's a chance the police won't see it that way, I suppose.'

'I'm sure they talked to you last night.' Maitland took up the questioning again.

'Yes, they did. They wanted a statement.'

'And asked you the same things I've asked you today?'

'Exactly the same.'

'Then I'm afraid you'll still be on their list of suspects. But I'm also sure – and I think Mr Anstey will agree with me – that that list will be a good deal expanded by this latest happening. Meanwhile, if they approach you again, you should refuse to answer any questions until you can do so in Mr Anstey's presence.'

'I'd have made sure he was with me last night, only I thought Mrs Hawthorne's being killed made a difference.'

'Yes, I can understand that. Try not to worry, he'll be there if you need him, and for the next few days at least so shall I.' But he turned to Stephen Anstey as soon as Peter had gone. 'What's happening to us, Stephen? What's happening to the peaceful life in Burton Cecil which Jenny and I have always valued so much in spite of what happened seven years ago?'

'I don't know,' said Stephen helplessly.

'Before that there hadn't been a murder since seventeen hundred and something,' Maitland went on. 'Adam says that lightning doesn't strike in the same place twice.'

'It seems he was wrong,' said Stephen dryly.

'All the same, I wonder—' He broke off there, staring into space.

'If you're wondering whether a ghost murdered these two girls I thought better of you, Antony,' said Stephen amused in his turn.

127

'No, that wasn't what was in my mind,' Maitland answered with perfect seriousness.

'What then?'

'Just that if somebody was in a jam,' said Antony slowly, 'knowing what had happened here before might have made him think of this way out.'

He wasn't surprised when Stephen trampled over that idea briskly. 'You're letting your imagination run away with you,' he said. 'These are as near to being motiveless murders as you can get. I mean, the victims might have been anybody young and of the right sex.'

'You're beginning to sound exactly like Uncle Nick,' Antony complained. 'But of course you're right. I hope the police let up on Peter Dutton though, it could be awkward.'

'He's safe for a while anyway. This second death will cause a full scale hue and cry, you can rely on that, and they won't be making an arrest until they're sure. And as I have every confidence in Peter's innocence, as I gather you now have too, there shouldn't be any more incriminating facts turning up about him.'

'No, that's true.' (But already Maitland's confidence was waning. Jenny would have told him to trust his instincts in the matter of Peter's innocence, but for himself he had a profound distrust of anything in the nature of intuition.) 'The police asked us who knew that Mabel would be going to the evening service,' he went on. 'Of course it was mentioned at the party, but the question did make me wonder who was at church that evening? Inspector Wentworth said only six people besides Mrs Jerrold and Mabel.'

'I'll put Caroline on to find out from Mrs Jerrold who they were,' Stephen promised. 'Not that I think it'll be the slightest use. And now I suppose there's nothing whatever we can do except wait and see what happens.'

II

It was no surprise to Jenny that Emma made her way to the typewriter as soon as they had finished breakfast. They knew one another well enough by now to make an apology unnecessary. The beds were already made so she started clearing the dishes in a rather desultory way until she was interrupted by Mrs Kitchener's arrival. That good lady was as ready as ever to talk, and having refused Jenny's offer of help urged her to sit down and make herself comfortable while 'she got on with pots'. Jenny had realised by now that she preferred to do everything herself, and obeyed quite meekly.

'Well, this is a fine kettle of fish,' said Mrs Kitchener, holding one hand under the hot tap while she waited for the water to become warm. 'And you finding the poor girl. I was reet sorry to hear about that, Mrs M.'

'I didn't exactly find her,' said Jenny. 'I mean, I was there but I left everything to the men. And I was sorrier still about poor Mrs Hawthorne,' she added ruefully. 'I suppose your house has been turned into a sort of murder headquarters again.'

'Well, that's fair enough, it's a police station, isn't it? Not that Joe doesn't get tired with all the extra there is to do, and that inspector thinking him and t' sergeant ought to know everything.'

'Don't they?' Jenny asked, hoping that Mrs Kitchener would take the question as it was interded.

She may have done, though she answered as seriously as though the small attempt at humour had gone unnoticed. 'Not about a business like this,' she said. 'That's a thing no normal person can tell you about. And I'll tell you something, dear, nobody touched Mrs Hawthorne.'

'But—'

'Not that way I mean,' she said euphemistically. 'Just like that poor little Dilys Jones, even to the cord that was used. But someone's mad and there's going to be trouble, you mark my words about that.'

'What on earth do you mean?' Jenny didn't remind her of her previous confident assertion of Peter Dutton's guilt.

'You've heard t' talk about that Mr Wainwright. Stalking through t' village at all hours and never speaking to a soul.'

'He spoke to me the other day when I was with Miss Anstey. I think he usually greets her too.'

'Well, and so he may have done but he didn't say much I'll be bound.' Jenny had to admit to herself that that was correct. 'And nothing like this happened before he came here. There's a lot of bad feeling, and I don't wonder at that.'

'There's also no proof,' Jenny pointed out.

'That's lawyer talk you learned from your husband,' said Mrs Kitchener wisely. 'Commonsense, that's what I go by. Well, they've sent some chaps over from Rothershaw and one of them will be on duty every night with Joe, patrolling t' village. Until all this is cleared up, you know.'

'What if it never is?' Jenny couldn't resist asking.

'Bound to be, I'd say. Look, dear, it's just a week ago tonight since Dilys Jones was killed. This chap can't help himself, it'll not be long before he tries again and when he does they'll catch him.'

'Well, that's a relief anyway. Unless of course, Mrs Kitchener, Joe and the other man happen to be at the other end of the village. Still, surely everyone will be taking care now.' (She thought again of Roland and his 'lock up your daughters'.)

'I daresay. But that Mr Wainwright, he's about t' village at all hours. Even though he's been here so short a time he must know our ways,' said Mrs Kitchener apparently quite unconscious that this more or less contradicted her previous statement.

'Then perhaps the most sensible thing would be for Joe and his colleague to keep an eye on him.' That last comment of hers made more sense to Jenny than she cared to admit, though she couldn't forget that she had liked Philip Wainwright and there was still the undeniable fact that there was no real evidence.

'General surveillance,' said Mrs Kitchener grandly. 'That's what they're calling for and that's what they'll get. What they're doing,' she added, 'is casting their net wide.' (Jenny couldn't help wondering where she had come by this unlikely expression.)

'How do you mean?'

'They're asking all the men in the village for alibis. Every one!'

'Not the women?' Jenny asked, it must be admitted with mischievous intent, because Emma had told her that Mrs Kitchener, for all her domestic qualities, was a strong advocate of women's lib.

'Not a woman's crime, is it dear?' she asked, rather as though the fact saddened her.

'No, of course not. But what you've told me looks as though Inspector Wentworth isn't by any means sure of Mr Wainwright's guilt,' Jenny said.

'Well, he's like your husband, he likes to see some proof.' She paused there, rubbing at one of last night's plates to which some morsel of food seemed to have got stuck, and Jenny took the opportunity to probe the matter a little further.

'Among the evidence the inspector wanted,' she said, 'was information about who knew that Mrs Hawthorne would be at the evening service.' She knew perfectly well that she shouldn't be pumping Mrs Kitchener, and Mrs Kitchener knew perfectly well that she shouldn't be talking out of turn, but for the moment both of them chose to ignore that.

'Yes, and they wanted to know who had been at church. I couldn't help them there but I think they got a list from Mr Jerrold. Only a few people, it seems a pity, doesn't it?' Jenny couldn't be sure whether she was referring to Mabel's death or to the poor church attendance.

'Do you know who they were?' she asked, as casually as she could.

'Of course I do.' It was already quite obvious that when Mrs Kitchener wanted to know something she was quite capable of finding it out. 'There was Mr and Mrs Lewis t' children are still away; Miss Murgatroyd – you must know Miss Murgatroyd – and Lily Foster from telephone exchange; and besides them John Bull and that daughter of his, Ethel. Nancy was indisposed as usual.' There was some scorn in her voice over that last description, which was the usual excuse given for Mrs Bull's absence from any village activities. John Bull, unlikely as it may seem, was the local butcher. His shop was in Rothershaw, but he brought his van to the village every Thursday to supply his neighbours with their weekend joint.

Jenny thought about that for a moment. 'I don't suppose Inspector Wentworth found that very helpful,' she said at last, and was at a loss to explain to herself the trace of satisfaction in her tone. Mrs Kitchener looked at her sharply.

'That's right,' she agreed. 'Mr and Mrs Lewis would be home long before Mrs Hawthorne left the vicarage. As for Miss Murgatroyd and Lily Foster, it's hardly worth mentioning them. And unless John Bull sent Ethel on home, which is a thing which would be easy to find out, he couldn't have waited for Mrs Hawthorne either.'

'Oh well, so far everything is pure speculation,' Jenny said.

'Not all of it, Mrs M,' Mrs. Kitchener reminded her. 'You can't have forgotten what I said before, that this Mr Wainwright came to live in Burton Cecil and *then* this sort of thing began to happen.'

'He's been here for several months,' Jenny protested.

'Learning the lay of the land,' said Mrs Kitchener in a sinister tone. 'And don't you be going anywhere in the dark alone Mrs M, don't you do it!'

For some reason their talk left Jenny depressed and she wasn't sorry when it was time to leave for Rothershaw, a little early so as to give herself time to locate the Boar's Head. This took a little longer than she had expected, and Antony and Stephen were already installed in the dining-room by the time she joined them.

They had already discussed their talk with Peter Dutton *ad nauseam*, but Antony obliged by giving her a brief account of what had been said. 'I'm glad you believe him now,' she said when he had finished, her eyes daring him to express any further doubts aloud. 'And you won't have to worry Caroline about who was in church, Stephen, because I found out from Mrs Kitchener.'

'We're both agreed it won't help, but we ought to know as much as the police,' Antony told her.

Jenny repeated the information, and added Mrs Kitchener's comments. 'What else did she have to say?' asked Stephen when she had finished; and then he smiled at her. 'I seem to be getting two sleuths for the price of one,' he added.

'There's a full scale manhunt going on in the village, so you were right in saying, Stephen, that at least it will delay matters a little as far as Peter Dutton is concerned. And Joe Kitchener and a constable from Rothershaw will be patrolling the village at night until things are cleared up. And I don't know how the police will look at it – Inspector Wentworth didn't seem at all convinced of Peter Dutton's innocence, did he? – but Mrs Kitchener has now made up her mind like the rest of the village of poor Mr Wainwright's guilt. And I suppose,' she added with a sigh, 'it isn't impossible that he's a homicidal maniac.'

'Forget about it for the moment, love,' Antony advised her.

'I can't,' said Jenny. 'And don't you realise, we must pay a visit of condolence on poor Samuel Hawthorne.'

'I'm afraid we must. Let's do it this afternoon and get it over. Or I can go alone if you like?'

'And say I'm indisposed like poor Mrs Bull. No, of course I'll come with you, Antony. Emma's working so we'll go this afternoon as you suggest,' she added with more determination. 'And if we get some flowers – I think I saw a florist just down the road – we can say she sent them, and give him all the proper messages from her, and that should take care of it for a time, shouldn't it?'

'An excellent plan, my love,' Antony approved. 'And ... Stephen, do you think it would be considered in very bad taste if the three of us went to the Mortal Man this evening? It seems to me, from what Jenny tells us of Mrs Kitchener's information, that alibis may be bandied about pretty freely at the pub this evening, so it might be interesting to hear what's being said.'

'If you tell me what time I'll join you,' Stephen offered, 'and Jenny needn't come unless she wants to.'

'I could stay with Emma,' said Jenny doubtfully. 'Unless Maltravers has been particularly tiresome she won't be going back to work after dinner. But perhaps—'

'Come with us, love,' Antony told her. 'Unless you really feel you can't bear it. It may make our presence there a little less – a little less pointed.'

When they got back to Burton Cecil and had parked the car there preparatory to walking along to the Hawthornes' house, there seemed to be more children than usual in the street. Whatever game they were playing it seemed to involve a great deal of jumping about and shouting, and when they passed 'Wicked' Ramsay's cowman he called out to them, 'That's right, Mr Maitland, you take care of her.' (There were two farmers called Ramsay in the vicinity, uncle and nephew, and the older of the two was invariably known as 'Wicked' because of his habit of allowing his cows to stray, a thing he carefully never discovered until they had had a good feed at his neighbours' expense; this – as both the Maitlands were well aware – being regarded as a cardinal sin in a country district.)

'I will,' Antony promised. He already had hold of Jenny's arm and she felt his grip tighten a little. 'They're getting nervous,' he said.

'Can you wonder?'

'No, it doesn't surprise me at all. I just don't know where it will lead, that's the trouble.'

'Do you think the children—?'

'I think the children are playing a new game. Not cops and robbers, something more like vigilantes. They're acting out what they've heard their parents say they'd like to do to the man who committed these murders.'

'Won't one of them get hurt that way?'

'I don't think so, love. Have you noticed the lad who's playing the part of the suspect, he's half a head taller than any of the others. I expect he chose the part himself, *he* won't get hurt.'

'Unfortunately "suspect" doesn't seem to be the right word. They seem to have made their minds up already.'

'*I'll be judge, I'll be jury*,' said Antony, who often found that quotation coming into his mind in the course of his professional duties. '*I'll try the whole cause and condemn you to death.*'

'Don't Antony! You're making my flesh creep.'

'Sorry, love.' But by that time they had reached the Hawthornes' house and were glad enough to turn in at the gate.

Samuel let them in and took them into the drawing-room. He seemed glad to see them, as glad as he could be of anything just then. Jenny gave him the flowers and found herself making a speech to him which she realised went on far too long but she couldn't think of any way of finishing it. Eventually to her relief her voice – over which she seemed no longer to have any control – trailed into silence.

'Everyone has been so kind,' said Samuel. 'I'm afraid just yet I cannot take it in.' But it seemed obvious that this last statement wasn't quite the truth; he looked as if he had lost weight overnight and aged by at least ten years since he and Mabel had entertained them. If he felt shocked it wasn't surprising, but he certainly realised what had happened clearly enough to feel a very deep sorrow.

'You'd better sit down,' he said now, recalling himself with difficulty to his duties as a host. But when they had done so he fixed his eyes on Jenny sadly. 'I feel so guilty, you see,' he confessed. 'If I'd known it was that sort of a murder—'

It didn't look as if that sentence was ever going to be finished so she ventured to prompt him. 'I don't quite understand what you mean,' she said, though she thought she had a very good idea.

'Someone preying on women. I could have gone with her to

135

church. As it was I meant to go and meet her, but I got reading and didn't realise the time. So don't you think I'm right to blame myself?'

'Not at all right, is he, Antony? There was no possible way you could have known that such a thing would happen.'

'No way at all,' Antony echoed.

'You found her, didn't you?' All at once Hawthorne sounded eager. 'Mr Jerrold told me—'

'Yes, we did,' Maitland admitted, though he sounded reluctant.

'Did you see anybody around? Anyone at all?'

'Only Peter Dutton and Roland Beaufort. We all arrived on the scene at almost the same moment. And if it's any consolation to you,' said Antony, improvising as Jenny had done when talking to Myfanwy Lewis, 'it must have been terribly quick, it's unlikely she knew anything about it at all.' (But he was remembering as he spoke that Hawthorne must have had the ordeal of identifying his wife, and had seen for himself the dreadful distortion of her childlike good looks.)

'That's a relief, of course. And the other thing is a relief,' said Samuel, obviously alluding to what Antony remembered somebody referring to as the fact that she hadn't been interfered with. 'But there's my point of view too. A selfish one, but I can't help that. We'd been married for six months and now I'm alone. And I loved her.'

'I don't think it's good for you, staying in this house all by yourself,' Jenny said. 'Isn't there anybody who could come to be with you?'

'Nobody I'd want,' said Samuel emphatically. 'But I shan't stay here, I couldn't bear that. As soon as the funeral is over – and I suppose that can't be until after the inquest – I shall go away.'

'To friends, I hope.'

'Yes, perhaps.'

'You mean to leave Burton Cecil altogether?' Jenny persisted. Anything seemed better than silence, even at the risk of seeming inquisitive, and besides she was genuinely concerned.

'Oh yes, certainly. You can see, I'm sure, I couldn't stay here now. So you see your friend, Mrs Anstey, will probably have the house on her hands again in record time,' he added with a rather twisted smile . . . a smile, as Jenny said afterwards, that seemed to have changed its mind half way.

'I think you're wise,' said Antony, 'though I suppose you realise that with the house next door empty too it may be difficult to sell.' Obviously he was as conscious as Jenny was of the need to keep some sort of conversation going.

'That, fortunately, is a matter of no importance. It can stand here and rot for all I care.' Hawthorne suddenly sounded almost vicious. Not that either of his visitors blamed him, if ever a man had a right to feel aggrieved it was he.

'Will you go back to Manchester?' Jenny asked.

'I don't know. I haven't thought about it yet.' Suddenly he was speaking quickly, as though he realised that the question was an important one but hadn't given it any thought yet.

'Your friends are there, surely.'

'Mother and I led a fairly isolated existence, until I met Mabel. And I've been wondering' – now he was speaking more slowly – 'all the publicity. People would want to talk about it, it might be more difficult to forget.'

'Yes, that's true.' Jenny spoke slowly as though considering the matter, but in fact she was still talking for the sake of talking, and for once Antony seemed almost as much at a loss as she was for something to say. 'It might be nice to go south for a while,' she suggested. 'Somewhere where the sun is shining even when winter comes.'

To her surprise the idea seemed to appeal to Samuel. 'That's a good idea,' he said slowly. 'Somewhere where I didn't know anyone, where there would be no memories at all and I could make new friends.' He sat quietly for a moment, apparently contemplating this rather desolate future, and then he stirred himself to offer them a drink. Neither of them wanted one, just then, though tea would have been welcome. But, as Jenny

137

confided afterwards, she didn't like to suggest it in case he didn't know exactly how to go about making it, which she thought was only too likely. However, it put her in mind of another question.

'Is there someone to look after you for the rest of the time you're here?'

'A girl called Gloria, who I believe is Mrs Kitchener's niece,' he said. 'She was doing our cleaning, but now she says she'll look after my meals as well, so I've got to be grateful to her. I hope it won't be for long.'

They made a little more desultory conversation, but were interrupted eventually, to their relief, by Gloria's arrival to fix Mr Hawthorne's supper. It was obvious that for the time being he was going to have to resign himself to village habits, rather than to the later dinner hour he probably favoured. 'There's one thing I shall never forget,' said Samuel, following them to the door. 'Among all the unpleasant memories of Burton Cecil there'll be some happy ones too. The kindness everyone showed to me and particularly to Mabel when we came here as strangers. I don't think one should forget things like that, however painful the memories are that they're mixed up with.'

There didn't seem to be much to say to that. Both Antony and Jenny were silent on the way back to Farthing Lee. When they got there they found that Emma had put the cover on her typewriter, so they were able to tell her something of the day's activities, of the messages they had conveyed to Samuel Hawthorne on her behalf, and of the arrangements they had made to meet Stephen at the Mortal Man that evening. 'Would you like to come with us?' Antony asked.

'If you're hoping that you'll hear the local people talking fairly freely among themselves I think the fewer in the party the better,' said Emma. 'I'll phone Caroline to see if they'll be in this evening, and I'll come with you as far as the pub and then go on to Burton Crook.'

The Maitlands exchanged glances. 'I'll collect the car at the shop and drive you there,' said Jenny, with more firmness than she usually displayed. 'It will save Stephen a walk too, because I can bring him back with us, and take him home again when I collect you.'

'There's really no need—' Emma started, then she seemed to realise the significance of their silent consultation. 'I'm not a young girl,' she said, 'nobody's going to murder me. In any case, Jenny walked into the village by herself.'

'In mid-morning, with everyone shopping for things they'd run out of during the weekend,' said Antony. 'That's quite different. But this place is pretty dead in the evening, you might not see a soul the whole way.'

'I suppose you're right,' said Emma reluctantly, 'but I do hate being coddled. Anyway, the first thing is to find out whether Caroline and Hugh will be at home.'

III

There were no difficulties in the way, the arrangement was made as suggested, with the addition of a promise from Antony and Jenny to go in for a while when they brought Stephen home. When they pushed open the door to the bar parlour of the Mortal Man that evening they were greeted by a roar of talk, and it didn't take any great intelligence to realise that the subject under discussion wasn't the recent developments in world affairs but something much nearer home. Jenny found herself edging a little closer to Antony, as though in some way the new mood in the village, of which the company in this room was a good cross-section, formed some sort of a threat.

Cyril Lansing and Roland Beaufort were already there, seated at a table for two, but at Stephen's suggestion they moved to one nearer the window that would accommodate five people. Jenny and Antony seated themselves and Stephen went up to the bar. 'Well, Antony?' asked Cyril quizzically.

'What does that mean?' Maitland asked him, smiling. He

didn't much care for what seemed to be happening, but they were there in the hope of gaining some information after all.

'I was wondering how you feel about things now,' said Cyril Lansing. He saw Antony's surprised look and went on, smiling himself. 'For all your tact I'm quite aware you didn't believe a word of Peter's denials until last night's unfortunate happening. Has that changed your mind?'

'Without prejudice,' said Antony, 'I think it has. But that doesn't absolve either Stephen or me from continued responsibility.'

'Aren't you curious to know who the village have hit on in his place?'

'I think we all know that already. There was enough talk the other night when we were here, even before poor Mabel Hawthorne was killed.'

'Do you find that surprising?'

'I don't wonder they're shocked,' said Antony rather evasively.

'It isn't shock,' Roland put in suddenly, 'as much as sheer, furious anger.'

'And that doesn't make it any better,' said a loud voice over Jenny's left shoulder, 'though the police don't seem to agree with us.' They all turned to look up at the man who was standing there, tankard in hand, and the Maitlands at least were surprised to see that it was Mr Bull, the butcher, one of the people who had attended the service at St Anselm's the night before. He was the last person they'd expected to see that evening, a piece of luck they hadn't expected, and it also occurred to Antony that it was surprising he had been at church the evening before. He'd heard him express some very puritanical views from time to time while cutting up Emma's weekend order, and had supposed he'd be more likely to be a fellow parishioner of Sarah Benson at the chapel in Manningbridge.

'How do you know that Mr Bull?' he asked. Stephen came back at that moment and slipped into his seat without speaking, putting the glasses he had carried on a small tray in front of the people they belonged to.

'They're asking every man jack of us in the village for an alibi,' said John Bull aggressively. 'They must have been to see you, Mr Maitland, and I'll bet you know all about that.'

'You're forgetting,' said Maitland quietly, 'we were two of the people who found Mrs Hawthorne. Naturally we had to make a statement about that.'

'Didn't they ask you about your alibi?' Bull repeated.

'We told them we'd been together all the evening, in Miss Anstey's company, and I suppose that covered it.'

'Anyway,' said Cyril, 'you've got nothing to worry about, John. You went straight home with young Ethel, I suppose.'

'Well, I didn't then. I went back to Benson's farm to get some more milk for Nancy. Didn't seem there was anything else she could keep down and that's nourishing, or so they say.'

'I'm sure that would be good enough for the police,' Jenny put in gently, with some vague idea of placating him since he seemed in such a belligerent mood.

'Maybe it was and maybe it wasn't. Most people were at home, of course. Them as weren't here.'

'Did you all leave together after the service?' Antony asked, at his most casual.

'Nothing to hang about for, was there? Vicar did, of course, but that's usual for him, and that little Mrs Hawthorne, poor lass, turned into the vicarage with Mrs Jerrold. Mr and Mrs Lewis were both with us down to the main street, then she went along home with Ethel and Miss Murgatroyd, they all live close enough together, and Mr Lewis came the other way with Lizzie Foster and me, said he was going to see her home. A bit more sense than some I could name.'

'Yes, that was a good idea as it turned out,' said Maitland, and didn't add his private thought that it would be a brave man indeed who tackled Mrs Foster.

'And there's you, Mr Beaufort.' Mr Bull was swaying a little on his feet, so that Jenny began to feel uncomfortably sure she wouldn't get away without having some of his beer splashed down her dress. 'I suppose all they wanted from you was an account of how you found her.'

'Nothing of the sort.' Roland's tone was as negligent as usual, but his glass of scotch had hardly been touched. Of course it might not have been his first one. 'It's quite possible, you know, that I walked along to the corner of the lane up to the church before I called for Peter, and then went back and knocked on the Duttons' door. It would have to have been after you and Ivor Lewis and Lizzie Foster passed, of course.'

Mr Bull gave a bark of laughter, 'Having done the dreadful deed,' he said, and for once in her life Jenny took him up rather sharply.

'It *was* dreadful, Mr Bull. She was so young, they were both so young.'

'Only nineteen,' put in Cyril, who had a way of knowing everything. 'You may as well tell us, Roland, were the Duttons at home when you called?'

'I didn't see anything of Michael or Mary, though the television was going full blast. Peter ran downstairs and came straight out to join me. But as I daresay you realise already' – he was looking straight at Maitland now – 'with the row that infernal machine was making he could have been in and out of the house quite easily without his parents' knowledge.'

'Is that what you think?' Antony asked him, still in the rather vague tone he seemed to have adopted that evening and that came so easily to him.

'No, as a matter of fact it isn't. I'm as sure of Peter as one can be about another person, but I suppose it would be more sensible to say I'm keeping an open mind.'

'As any sane person should do,' said Cyril. He also seemed in a quiet mood that evening.

'Well, I say it's not good enough.' John Bull's voice rose to almost a shout on the words so that a sudden silence fell over the room. 'I say there's only one person could have done it and he hasn't got an alibi, not likely. Your sister-in-law brought him here, Mr Anstey, sold him the Gillespies' cottage which she didn't ought to have done. Now see what's happened!'

Stephen looked a little taken aback at this sudden attack, but he hadn't time to reply. 'If police won't act,' a voice from the crowd near the bar took up the cry, 'we will!'

'Not that he'll show his face in t' village in daylight again in a hurry.'

It was Stephen who put the question. 'What on earth can you mean?' he asked, though both Antony and Jenny had a nasty feeling they knew already.

'Kids were throwing stones at him. They've got more sense than their elders and betters,' the same voice sneered.

'Where were the police?'

'Joe Kitchener was asleep, him being on duty at night just now. Sergeant Gilbey broke it up, but not before that Wainwright got a nasty gash on his head. And serve him right.'

'And that,' said John Bull triumphantly, 'is nothing to what's going to happen to him before we're through. If police won't take action we will, law or no law. Won't we, lads?'

A babble of consent broke out, definitely menacing. Suddenly Jenny was on her feet. 'Well, I think it's terrible!' She felt Antony's hand on her arm but he must have realised that it was no use expostulating at that moment, uncharacteristically she was far too angry. 'Just because he's a stranger that doesn't make him a murderer.' Then, turning to her husband with something like a sob, 'I want to go, Antony, I can't stay and listen to all this.'

Both Stephen and Antony remembered to say a brief Good Night to Cyril and Roland, but Jenny was out in the street before them.

'It isn't fair,' she said as soon as they joined her. 'Just because he's a stranger,' she repeated.

'Are you so concerned about Philip Wainwright?' Antony asked, and it was quite obvious to her that he was deliberately keeping his voice even in the hope of calming her. But she wasn't quite ready for that yet.

'I've lived with you and Uncle Nick long enough to be concerned about justice,' she said. 'And I'm concerned to see all the people here, who I thought we were beginning to know, turning into mindless monsters.'

'Come now, love, isn't that a little exaggeration? Not all of them.'

'No, of course not all of them.' She was quieter now but still obviously upset. 'But I've always thought . . . I've always liked Burton Cecil so much.'

'You will again, you know, when all this blows over,' Maitland assured her.

'Never!'

'Oh yes you will.' He sounded quite positive. 'Everybody has a more brutal side, and you must admit the events here have been enough to encourage it. But it isn't only that.'

'What then?' asked Jenny, and she sounded now more like herself.

'They're frightened. Not for themselves, of course, but for their womenfolk. You know that we agreed about taking Emma to Burton Crook without a word said between us. And I wouldn't let you out of my sight for a minute, except when I was sure that there were people about.'

Either what he said or the even tone of his voice had the effect of calming Jenny still further. 'I know that, Antony,' she said, 'and I wouldn't want you to. But what's to become of poor Mr Wainwright?'

'Have you considered that he may be guilty?'

'If he is the police will find out and he'll be tried and convicted in court. But not this way, Antony, not this way!'

'Take it easy, love, nothing has happened yet.'

'I shouldn't have thought Mr Bull was a man like that.'

'I'm not quite sure what you mean. This evening he was just a member of the mob, and anybody may do anything when fear enters into it.'

'I suppose you're right.' She had simmered down a little by now, though she still sounded doubtful, and not surprisingly her thoughts turned apologetically in another direction. 'I didn't have a single sip of my drink, Stephen, and I don't suppose you did either. I'm really sorry.'

'That can be remedied when we get home,' Stephen assured her. 'I'm glad enough you decided to leave, you might have been lynched for a tirade like that.' That was said lightly, as though not intended to be taken too seriously, but Jenny had a feeling it contained a warning too.

So they took Stephen back to Burton Crook, arriving much earlier than they had expected. A few words of explanation sufficed and Hugh quickly made up for their lack of refreshment at the Mortal Man. 'Tell me, Jenny,' he said, putting a glass down beside her, 'what makes you so certain of Philip Wainwright's innocence?'

'I don't know that I am. I mean, I'm beginning to agree with Antony when he says that the villagers' point of view is understandable, to a certain extent. But when I met him that day with you, Emma, I got the feeling . . . I couldn't believe he'd have hurt Dilys Jones.'

'He's been disliked ever since he came here,' said Emma, 'just because he wouldn't mix. But that isn't a reason for believing the man is a murderer.'

'I didn't say it was,' said Hugh equably. 'All the same, if Peter is innocent, as I think we all believe, who would you cast for the role of first murderer?'

'It could be anyone, anyone at all,' said Stephen. 'I suppose you realise the village is blaming you for selling Lane's End to Philip Wainwright, Caroline.'

'They might just as well blame me for Mabel's murder because I sold the Hawthornes their house,' Caroline pointed out. 'And as for who might be guilty . . . any man in the village who hasn't an alibi, I suppose.'

'It's only the police who have the facilities for finding out that sort of thing,' Stephen pointed out. 'We didn't get very far tonight.'

'Haven't you any ideas, Antony?' Hugh asked.

'Not one,' Maitland told him. He seemed strangely disinclined for conversation that evening.

'I suppose we shall just have to rely on Joe Kitchener and his companion,' said Hugh. 'And I quite agree' (though the suggestion had not been made out loud) 'that it's no use sitting here playing guessing games. We haven't got round to asking you, Emma, how are you getting on with the book?'

'I'm worried about Maltravers,' said Emma, rising to the bait as he had known she would.

'Oh, he's arrived has he?' said Hugh. 'I suppose Sir Jasper called him in, and at first he was unwilling to take the matter on.'

'Well ... yes,' said Emma. 'He's really a very inquisitive man, as I think you all know, but I always have to pretend that he isn't because it doesn't sound too well. Not a sympathetic trait. So when Sir Jasper telephoned him he asked him if he'd taken all the routine precautions—'

'Lock the door, look up the chimney, inquire if any dark-skinned gentlemen in turbans have been seen in the neighbourhood,' suggested Hugh irrepressibly. 'But I'm sure Sir Jasper was able to give him an affirmative reply.'

'Nothing of the sort,' said Emma with dignity. 'Ghosts, yes, but dark-skinned gentlemen in turbans would be going a little too far. But you know as well as I do – at least Antony and Stephen certainly know – that in these cases nothing must be touched.'

'Were the police in possession by the time Mr Maltravers arrived at – what was its name, Hanging Bailey?' asked Caroline.

'There was an inspector there—'

'I know,' said Stephen. 'He was rather muddy, from splashing about among the bogs, and he limped slightly because one of the dogs had got loose and bitten him in the leg.'

'Besides all this,' said Caroline, 'his hair had turned snow white—'

'–but he was gibbering so badly that no one could tell whether this was due to an encounter with the ghouls near the family vault, with the faceless horror, or even (though in this latter case the reaction seemed excessive) with the Grey Monk.' That was Hugh's contribution.

Antony glanced at Jenny and saw that she was relaxed now, not joining in the conversation but quietly sipping her drink and listening with interest, and he mentally called down blessings, both singly and collectively, on the Anstey family for distracting her attention – quite deliberately he was sure – from the earlier unpleasantness. 'I suppose,' he said, feeling it was time he took a hand, 'that he then asked for the full story, omitting no detail, however slight.'

'Of course he wanted to know,' said Emma, 'that isn't what's worrying me. It's that girl, he's fallen in love with her.'

'Isn't that a good thing?' said Caroline.

'No, of course it isn't my dear, you know he has to have a new girlfriend in every book. But he's getting really serious about this one, and suppose he marries her!'

'A happy ending,' said Stephen. 'I thought that was essential.'

'Yes, but he can't stay in England. You know his adventures are always in some far-off place,' Emma explained, 'and now I'm beginning to be sorry I made an exception this time. What would he do with her while he was abroad?'

'People are very broad-minded nowadays,' Hugh suggested.

'I don't write that sort of book,' said Emma, dignified again. 'There'd always be somebody to take offence if he had a really serious affair with someone else while he was married.'

'Have you no control over him at all?' Antony demanded.

'Not a scrap,' said Emma simply. 'I should never have allowed him to return to England, but having done so—'

'You could always make the girl the murderer,' Caroline suggested.

'Oh no, I don't think that would do at all.'

'Quite right,' Hugh approved. 'You can't have Maltravers moping all over the place with a broken heart. Never mind,

147

Emma, I'm sure between us we can solve the problem. Where have we got to?'

'He'd just arrived,' said Stephen, 'and asked for some information.'

'Six hours later,' said Caroline, 'as Sir Jasper ceased speaking, Maltravers looked across at him with the whimsical smile the baronet knew so well. He leaned forward to knock out his pipe in the huge open fireplace. "Call the household together," he said, and the other man looked at him in astonishment. "You . . . you know," he gasped. "I know," said Maltravers gently.'

'Well of course he does . . . eventually.' Emma sounded impatient. 'But not just yet, my dear, otherwise the story would be far too short.'

'Of course it would, and we shouldn't tease you,' said Caroline. 'Couldn't you give this girl, whatever her name is, a few really unpleasant characteristics?'

'Oh no, not possibly. She's the heroine,' Emma explained. 'That means she's got to be perfect, and if I changed her – even supposing I could – there'd just have to be someone else equally wonderful to take her place.'

'It seems an insoluble dilemma,' said Antony.

'As insoluble as our latest series of murders,' said Hugh, bringing the subject back to the point they'd all been trying to avoid. It was inevitable that there should be some further discussion, and he thought Jenny was ready now to take part in it calmly. But nothing helpful emerged, and the rest of the evening until the visitors left was spent in fruitless speculation.

It was getting late when Jenny parked the car again outside the shop, and later still when they crossed the footbridge over Farthing Gill and approached the cottage. There was a small garden in front and as they neared the gate a tall figure loomed up out of the darkness. Jenny and Emma, one on each side of him, clutched at Antony, so that Jenny – on his right – was later convinced she must have hurt him. 'Miss Anstey?' said a voice that both the women recognised.

Emma had enjoyed her evening and nothing could have exceeded her placid acceptance of this sudden appearance. 'Yes, Mr Wainwright?' she said, as though it was the most natural thing in the world to find him standing there.

'May I speak to you? And to your guests, of course. I suppose this is Mr Maitland?'

'Yes, it is Mr Wainwright, Antony,' Emma explained.

'Well, as you have him with you, you can't possibly be afraid of me,' Wainwright added sardonically.

'I'm not,' Emma said. 'But if it's about what's happening in the village I should tell you that Mr Maitland has a client already.'

'Yes, I know. Somebody was talking about it when I was in the shop. I wish I could say I should like to consult you as a friend, but I'm afraid I can't claim that privilege. But perhaps as a neighbour, a newcomer to the village—' He left it there and Jenny glanced quickly at Antony, but for once his face was a closed book to her.

'If you want to make a statement, Mr Wainwright,' he said, 'you ought to go to the police.'

'I'm not going to confess to the murders, if that's what you mean.' Oddly enough his voice sounded almost amused. 'I can't tell you anything about them that you don't know, nothing that would either help or hinder your client. But there's a situation developing—'

'I'm quite aware of that,' said Antony with feeling. He turned to Emma. 'I think we should hear what Mr Wainwright has to say if you've no objection,' he told her.

And Emma said, as placidly as ever, 'Won't you come in, Mr Wainwright?'

The delay that used to be occasioned by the lighting of oil lamps was no longer necessary, but even with the newly installed electricity it took a moment or two to get the party settled comfortably round the empty fireplace. 'I should be apologising to you, Miss Anstey, and to you, Mrs Maitland, for intruding like this,' Wainwright said, apparently unconscious

149

that this made it fairly obvious that his main object was to talk to Antony. 'But to me at least the matter is urgent.'

In spite of having spoken to him before Jenny hadn't realised – as she supposed Emma must have done – that notwithstanding his dishevelled appearance his voice was cultivated and his manner courteous. She said on an impulse. 'If we can do anything to help you—' But she faltered there and after a moment went on more slowly. 'I mean, of course—'

'Anything consistent with your husband's duty to his client,' said Philip Wainwright, almost as though he was laughing. 'I did tell you, you know, that I haven't come to confess.'

'Yes, I remember.'

'Have you heard the latest theories about the murder?' Wainwright asked, but it was obvious that he had no intention of changing the subject by the remark.

'It isn't everybody,' said Jenny quietly. 'At least not quite. Antony says that—' Again she broke off, thinking that she seemed unable to finish a single sentence that evening.

'I was wondering, Miss Anstey, if perhaps you could explain it to me. You're a native of the village.'

'Not exactly, but I've lived here for a long time. I think you must realise, Mr Wainwright, that in any country place a stranger finds it hard to be accepted, unless he or she makes an effort towards establishing friendly relations with his neighbours.'

'Which I haven't done?'

'You must admit—'

'Yes, I admit it. I'm not a gregarious soul. But heaven's above, those poor girls!' He sounded as if he really meant what he said. 'Why should they think I had anything to do with it?'

Maitland counted off the reasons on his fingers. 'Nothing like this happened before you came here,' he said, and his tone made it obvious that he was quoting. 'They don't want to believe that any of their friends – anyone that they know in fact – could have done a thing like this. And they're frightened, people aren't rational when they're frightened.'

150

'I suppose you mean that my enemies are the more simple-minded of my neighbours,' said Wainwright thoughtfully. 'I mean that in the old sense of the word, not at all in a derogatory way. I've come to have a great respect for the countryman's acumen about his own concerns.'

'Yes, that's very true. But there were one or two, even among the better educated, who felt that Dilys Jones's murder was only the beginning. The matter would go on from there.'

'You're saying that these people too accuse me?'

'No, I've no idea at all about their opinion now. I gather there was an unpleasant incident today.' Maitland seemed to be taking control of the conversation now, having come to the conclusion that nothing very coherent was to be expected from either of his companions.

'It was unpleasant, although there were only children involved. Stones can be sharp, whoever throws them. Sergeant Gilbey came to my rescue, or I might be in even worse condition now.'

None of them had commented before on the gash on his forehead but Emma did so now. 'Did you ask Dr Oaksley to look at your head?' she inquired.

'No, I didn't bother him. A little disinfectant took care of it' – again there was something about his tone that suggested amusement, though he didn't actually smile – 'at the expense of a little pain. But what I wanted to know, Mr Maitland, was: is there any action I can take to put a stop to all this?'

'If you could pin down who started the rumours you could bring an action for slander,' said Antony. 'I wouldn't advise it though.'

'That's the furthest thing from my thoughts,' said Wainwright, with unexpected vehemence. 'But I wondered if it would do any good if I issued a statement.'

'What would you propose to say?' It was a novel idea and Antony couldn't think of any possible wording that would be helpful.

'Just a declaration of innocence, I suppose, and an appeal for fair play. As you know I'm a solitary soul, I couldn't prove I had an alibi in either case.'

'I don't think, to be blunt with you, Mr Wainwright, that that would do much good. Are you worried that the matter will go any further, that there may be more violence I mean?'

'The possibility has crossed my mind, and I don't think I'm any braver than the next man.'

'Then you could ask for police protection,' said Maitland.

'That's the last thing I'd do!' And then, when he saw that they were looking at him curiously he added, 'It might give them ideas about me that perhaps they haven't got already.'

'The police are inclined to want evidence,' Maitland pointed out. 'They're not likely to be influenced by what the villagers think.'

'I wonder. Do you by any chance know if there were any fingerprints at the scene of the crimes?'

'As there's been no arrest I've no access to confidential information about the police inquiries,' said Antony. No need to mention Mrs Kitchener's confidences to Jenny. 'But I shouldn't think—'

'Besides, anyone would know enough to wear gloves,' said Emma, perhaps thinking of Maltravers again.

'So I'm afraid it wouldn't be any use trying to prove your innocence by offering your fingerprints for comparison, Mr Wainwright,' Maitland told him.

'I should have realised that for myself. Then you can't suggest anything useful that I *can* do?' He let his eyes roam from one to the other.

'If you don't like the idea of asking for police protection,' said Antony, 'I'm afraid I can't. Nothing direct, that is. If you'd care to give us some sort of an account of yourself, of your past life, I think we could undertake to circulate it in the village, but I have to tell you I doubt if it would have much effect. It might be something though, at least they couldn't call you a mystery man any longer.'

At that Philip Wainwright came to his feet again. 'I dislike

152

above all things talking about myself,' he said.

'Antony wasn't prying,' said Jenny quickly.

'No, I realise that. I believe – though I can't imagine why – that all of you have my interests at heart.' He turned with a jerky movement and went across to where Emma was sitting. 'At least, Miss Anstey,' he said, taking her hands in both of his in an awkward gesture that was obviously unfamiliar to him, 'I promise if I do confide in anybody it will be in you.' He released her, raised a hand in salute to Antony and Jenny, and was gone.

'Well, that was short and sweet,' said Antony as soon as the front door was closed and they had heard his footsteps going down the short path to the gate. 'I wonder what on earth possessed him to come here.'

'He's a very unhappy man,' said Emma slowly, thinking it out. 'And now I come to think of it, Antony, you ought to have asked him if he's seen anything on these nocturnal walks of his. He of all people might have done so.'

'I think he was frightened enough to have told us if there was anything like that.' He sat down beside Jenny on the sofa, took her hand in his, and began to play with her fingers. 'And why, my dear and most illogical wife, did you swallow his story that he was innocent hook, line and sinker?'

'*You* don't think he's guilty,' she flashed back.

'I don't think there's any proof that he is,' he corrected her.

'And neither does Emma,' said Jenny, as if that clinched matters.

'Doesn't she?' He looked at Miss Anstey inquiringly.

'I think I like him,' she said, 'and I think he has a genuine pity for Dilys and Mabel.'

'That needn't necessarily preclude him from being their killer.'

'No, I know that. I'm not such an innocent.'

'But I do think he was telling the truth, Antony,' said Jenny, 'and even if I didn't I can't stand people jumping to conclusions.'

'I hope that isn't aimed at me,' said Antony, amused.

153

'Because if it is I don't know how you've put up with me all these years.'

'You know that isn't what I meant. It's a pity about the fingerprints but I think we're right about that.'

'Of course we are. If there had been any the police would be fingerprinting people instead of just asking for alibis.'

'I'm sorry we had to disappoint Mr Wainwright all the same.'

'Disappoint him? Don't you realise, love, he was relieved at what we told him?'

'Are you sure about that?'

'Quite, quite sure. And if you weren't so single-mindedly intent on proving him innocent you'd have seen it too.'

'But that must mean—' said Emma.

'Not necessarily what you're thinking. But if not that, it means there's something in his past life he wants to keep to himself.'

'Something criminal where fingerprints are involved,' said Emma.

Jenny found the thought unpleasant and tried to shake it off. 'Do you think anything more will happen, Antony? In the way of violence against Mr Wainwright?'

'Not tonight anyway, they're all settled down in the Mortal Man and won't stir from there until closing time. Though come to think of it' – he glanced at his watch – 'it must be far beyond that now. Still, by the look of things when we left they'd most of them be pretty far gone by the time they got out of the pub.'

'Fighting mad?' Jenny suggested uneasily.

'Not tonight,' said Antony again, more positively this time.

'I'm surprised Cyril stayed.'

'Cyril is a philosopher, and so, in his way, is Roland. Stop worrying, love, and try to persuade Emma to offer us a nightcap. But not cocoa,' he stipulated. 'We may as well drown our sorrows.'

So they had their drink and Emma registered a vow to replenish their supplies tomorrow, a remark which drew some argument from Maitland, who said he would see to it himself.

While they argued amicably about that Jenny remembered that the Mortal Man must have been closed even before they came through the village, and as all was still and quiet Antony was probably right about there being no further trouble that evening.

And that was exactly how it was, in the way she was regarding the matter at least. They stayed up until almost midnight, and it was only the next day when Mrs Kitchener, against all precedent, arrived early and offered to make their breakfast, that they learned that young Ethel Bull had been killed in the village street the night before in exactly the same way as the other two girls. Strangled with a cord and the utmost efficiency.

TUESDAY, 31st August

I

Apparently Emma's first reaction, before horror or sympathy or anything else, was one of sheer incredulity. 'But where were the police?' she demanded. 'I know the village is being patrolled because I saw your husband and another man when we were coming home from Burton Crook last night.'

'They can't be everywhere at once,' said Mrs Kitchener, a little offended at this implied criticism of her Joe. 'Even if they're at t' other end of main street ... there's track up to Lane's End too, think on.'

'Yes, of course,' Emma agreed. 'But that still leaves all sorts of questions. How and where and when?'

'I just told you how,' said Mrs Kitchener, and for a horrible moment it sounded to Emma as though she felt a certain satisfaction in delivering the grim news. 'Cord round the neck, just like t' others. As for when, Joe found her at about ten past ten. He'd passed the same spot half an hour before or thereabouts and she wasn't there then.'

Antony came downstairs at that moment, still in his dressing-gown, and there was a pause while the three women told him in chorus what had happened. 'It still leaves one question ... where was she found, Mrs Kitchener?' he said when they had finished.

'Almost outside Dr Oaksley's house.'

'But what was she doing there? Surely she knew better than to go out alone with things as they are?'

'I only know what I hear,' said Mrs Kitchener. Her good

156

humour had returned again, and there was no doubt about it, she was enjoying being the centre of attention. 'But you'll have heard Nancy Bull has been ailing – at least Missemma will – and she was taken worse apparently, and that's why Ethel went to tell doctor. He's nobbut across t' road from them, two or three minutes' walk.'

'I thought she worked for Lily Shaw,' said Emma.

'So she did, and a good little worker I'll say that for her. But only in t' morning when pub's closed, Lily wouldn't have her around any other time. "Not fitting," she said, "a young girl like that. . ." '

'Surely Mrs Bull would have known better than to let her go, however ill she felt?' Emma protested.

'You don't know Nancy when she's ailing, thinks of no one but herself.'

'You're forgetting the telephone, Emma,' Antony put in. 'Why didn't she use the telephone?'

'Because it was out of order, that's why, and that's no wonder either these days.'

'Oh dear!' That was Emma with her favourite exclamation. 'And her father was in the pub almost opposite. Poor man!'

'Yes, it's a bad business. Inspector Wentworth's having his breakfast now,' she said, so that Jenny thought for a moment that she was changing the subject, 'but he told Joe to let you know he wanted to see you this morning, Mr Maitland, and if you'd get in touch with Mr Stephen Anstey to come down here he'd call on you as soon as he's finished. Joe being fair wore out,' she took care to add, 'which is only natural after working all night, I took it on myself to come along instead.'

'That was very kind of you,' said Maitland gravely.

'Then I'll just put coffee on and make some toast,' she offered, and went through into the kitchen.

The telephone rang as Antony reached it, and it was Stephen who had already heard the news. When told that his presence was needed he sounded a little flustered, because the inquest on Dilys Jones was to be held that morning in Rothershaw. But after some discussion it was arranged that his elderly partner, having not yet completely retired, should take care of that matter for him and he promised to be at Farthing Lee as soon as possible. 'I ought to have been there because of Peter,' he said, 'but they won't do anything but adjourn it. With all that's happened since they're bound to want to wait a while.'

'I suppose this is still part of the detectives checking up on everybody,' Emma said as Antony turned from the telephone. 'Otherwise I can't think why Mr Wentworth wants to see you again particularly, and Stephen too.'

'I'm afraid there's a rather obvious answer to that,' said Maitland abruptly, but to his relief Mrs Kitchener bustled in at that moment and they were all of them glad of the good strong coffee she had made and perhaps even more grateful that her presence prevented any more conversation for the moment. They had none of them much emotion left to spare for anything but the three young girls who were dead.

Inspector Wentworth and the inevitable Constable Tankard arrived at the same time as Stephen did, having met him at Rowan Corner. Antony let them in and found that, contrary to his expectations, contrary in fact to everyone's prevailing mood, Wentworth at least seemed in a comparatively amiable frame of mind that morning. He had the air of a man who, after groping in the darkness, suddenly sees his way clear before him. 'Well, Mr Maitland,' he said, 'we meet again.' And added, as Antony backed away from the door, 'Good morning, Mrs Maitland, Miss Anstey.'

'I could wish it were under happier circumstances,' Antony told him. 'Hello Stephen, I see you were able to arrange for your partner to cover the inquest. Which reminds me, Inspector, shouldn't you be in Rothershaw? I should have thought you'd be needed.'

'No dereliction of duty,' said Wentworth. 'Don't you worry your head about that. The chief constable himself said he'd attend and ask for an adjournment *sine die*. In all the circumstances that seems the best thing, because quite

158

obviously I'm needed here.'

'Yes, that's quite true.'

Mrs Kitchener had retired to the kitchen and there was a short pause while Emma got the visitors seated. The room seemed a little crowded; of the four men present Stephen was the shortest, and he wasn't exactly a midget. 'And you're wondering why we're starting with you,' said Wentworth, still with the note in his voice that might almost have been called jovial. 'We're wondering, you see, why that fellow Wainwright came here last night. At least I suppose this was where he was going. Constable Kitchener saw him coming towards the Gill at nearly half-past ten.'

'Are you turning your attention to Mr Wainwright?' Emma asked.

'Questions have arisen about him in the village, you must have heard that. This is just a matter of clearing things away, no more, no less.' His tone didn't give the faintest clue as to whether what he was saying was the truth or not. 'Anyway, Miss Anstey, the question remains. Did he come here?'

'Yes, he was waiting for us when we got back from Burton Crook.'

'What time would that be?'

'I didn't notice exactly, but I should think about eleven. Do you remember, Antony?'

'My impression is the same as yours, but I'm not sure either.'

'Then the question follows, why did he come here? And was it you he was wanting to see, Miss Anstey, or Mr Maitland perhaps?'

'Both of us, I suppose. At least, we're slightly acquainted and I think he felt I might be sympathetic, but what he really wanted was advice.'

'Advice about what?'

'He spoke of the situation in the village,' said Antony, seeing that the question made Emma uncomfortable. 'I wonder if you realise how ugly it is.'

'I've had the benefit of Sergeant Gilbey's opinion, not to

mention Constable Kitchener's. I think they've put me pretty well in the picture.'

'Then you won't be surprised that Wainwright was worried about it,' said Antony. 'He wanted to know why they felt like that about him for one thing, and between us we explained it as well as we understood it ourselves. And he wanted to know if there was anything he could do to stop it.'

'Could you suggest anything, Mr Maitland?'

'Nothing except the threat of an action for slander, which I told him quite frankly I didn't advise.'

'What was his reaction to that?'

'He wouldn't hear of it at any price. He seemed to think that issuing a statement might do some good, but of course that would have been worse than useless. So I suggested police protection.'

'And he wouldn't hear of that either?'

'No. In fact he left here quite soon after.'

'That brings us to the next question. You mentioned you came back from Burton Crook, but I believe you were at the Mortal Man earlier. Why did you leave there so suddenly?'

'That was my fault,' said Jenny. 'I couldn't stand the talk that was going on, it made me simply furious.' She seemed to be getting angry all over again at the recollection. 'I think it was because they were all so positive.... Antony told you the situation was ugly, Inspector.'

'So you had made up your mind about Wainwright's innocence already, Mrs Maitland?' said Wentworth pensively. 'Would that be because you believe in someone else's guilt?'

'In the circumstances Inspector, that's an extremely improper question,' Antony intervened caustically. 'However, I'm quite willing to answer it, which I expect is what you really want. I've seen nothing to convince me of anyone else's guilt' – that was literally true, in spite of certain doubts that crept in from time to time – 'but a good deal to convince me of Peter Dutton's innocence.'

Wentworth smiled at that, as though he felt he had surprised the other man into an indiscretion and was well satisfied with the fact. 'So at the time of the murder—?'

'What time was that, Inspector?'

'Around ten o'clock. That's judging by the time she left home and the time she was found. The medical evidence – which I've no doubt would be vague on the point – doesn't have to come into it.'

'Then I'll answer the question I think you were about to ask me. At that time we were still at Burton Crook, as Mr Anstey here will confirm, with his brother and sister-in-law. So I'm afraid we have no information to give you, but I'd be obliged if you'd answer one more question for me.'

'If I can, Mr Maitland.'

'About Ethel Bull's movements.' He was carefully not revealing the fact that Mrs Kitchener had already given them some sketchy information on the subject, but obviously it required clarification.

'The telephone in the shop was out of order and her mother seemed to be growing worse. I understand Mrs Bull has been ailing for some time. So Ethel very naturally decided to run down the road and fetch Dr Oaksley herself. I've already told you what time she is presumed to have died.'

'She hadn't given her message to the doctor then?'

'No, she never reached him, he knew nothing at all about her until the constable hammered on his door when he discovered the body.'

For some reason this readiness on his part to answer questions made Maitland vaguely uneasy. However he ventured a further comment. 'No one could have known about Ethel's movements beforehand, as somebody may have known Mabel Hawthorne's.'

'Somebody might not have cared,' Wentworth pointed out. 'If the murderer was on the look-out for another victim anyone would do. And I suppose he was monitoring the patrol's comings and goings very closely.'

'I see. That's perfectly logical, of course.'

161

Perhaps he looked a little bewildered for Wentworth said with no diminution of the good humour he had been displaying that morning, 'The real reason I wanted to see you and Mr Anstey is because I want to interview Peter Dutton again, and this time I'm sure that Mr Anstey, at least, will wish to be present.'

So that was it. Antony had been clear enough in his own mind already that this was the reason behind the inspector's desire for a meeting. He was about to make an arrest and he was answering questions about Ethel Bull's murder quite readily because he knew that the defence would be entitled to all the information at his disposal very shortly. But it was Stephen who protested, though possibly it would have been more discreet to make some pretence at least of misunderstanding what was meant. 'Surely after all that's happened, Inspector, you can't still think Peter's guilty. Are you saying he's a homicidal maniac?'

'I'm saying nothing of the kind, Mr Anstey. I think the motive for Dilys Jones's murder is obvious. As I remember it we've already discussed that.'

'But the others?'

'A cold-blooded attempt to disguise the motive,' said Wentworth, and now his voice was very cold. 'I think perhaps it would be as well if you came with us to the Duttons' house immediately, Mr Anstey, and I've no objection to Mr Maitland accompanying you if he wishes. I sent a message already to say that Peter should stay home from work this morning.'

'That wasn't necessary as a matter of fact, they suspended him after you were there asking questions,' Stephen told him. 'But I'll come, of course. What about you, Antony?'

'I should like to come, as the inspector says he has no objection.' It wouldn't do to get on the wrong side of Wentworth if that could be avoided. He'd had enough experience of the difficulties that could arise when the police looked askance at his activities not to risk alienating the inspector. 'Will you two stay here?' he asked, looking from

Jenny to Emma. 'I know I said nothing would happen when people were around during the day time, but on the whole I'd be happier if you'd do that.'

They agreed willingly enough, and the four men set out on their errand without any further delay.

As Parson's Row was only just past Rowan Corner it took them no more than ten minutes to reach the Duttons' cottage. Mary and Michael Dutton came into the hall together to meet them and their anxious faces were evidence enough, to Maitland at any rate, that they already suspected that the worst was about to happen. Peter was waiting for them in the tiny living-room; he was much calmer than his parents, though his uncomfortable look told its own story. He thanked Stephen and Antony rather formally for coming. 'Not that I'm at all afraid of answering questions,' he added defiantly.

Wentworth glanced rather pointedly at the clock. 'I think you all know what's happened,' he said.

'We'd have to be deaf and blind not to,' Peter retorted. 'The news came with the milk this morning. But—'

'Just a minute, Peter,' Stephen put in. 'I think before you say anything else Inspector Wentworth has something to say to you.'

'Indeed we have,' said Wentworth and glanced at his subordinate. Constable Tankard went into the usual rigmarole of warning, but it occurred to Maitland as he spoke how ominous the words must sound to someone hearing them for the first time.

Peter glanced again at Stephen when the familiar recital ended. 'Does it mean they're going to arrest me?' he asked.

There was clearly no reassurance that anyone could give him. 'It just means, Peter, that you must think very carefully before answering the inspector's questions,' Stephen told him. 'If there's anything you're at all doubtful about you'd better keep silent.'

'If they only want to know where I was last night—'

'That will do for the moment,' said Wentworth non-committally.

'—it's better to tell them, isn't it? I was here. Roland asked me to go to the pub with him, but I wasn't very keen. I didn't enjoy it much the other night, they did nothing but talk about that chap Wainwright and I think I know what it feels like to be suspected.'

'Can you offer any confirmation of that?' Stephen insisted. Obviously he was keen to keep the matter out of Wentworth's hands for as long as possible.

'We know that Peter never went out,' said Michael Dutton suddenly. His wife murmured her agreement.

There was no silencing Wentworth any longer. 'He was sitting in here with you, then?' he asked.

'No, I wasn't,' said Peter, before either of his parents could speak. 'I don't care for television, I'd rather read a book and the noise distracts me. So I was upstairs in my room.'

'As on the previous occasions?' said Wentworth. The inflection of sarcasm in his voice was unpleasant. 'It's a stone staircase, isn't it? No boards to creak. I'm quite sure you could have come down in complete silence without either Mr or Mrs Dutton being aware of the fact.'

'I could, but I didn't. And if I'd wanted to kill her, how could I have known that Ethel would be such a little fool as to go out by herself?'

'I've already discussed that point with your solicitor,' said Wentworth formally. 'He hasn't said so, but I'm sure he agrees with me that Miss Bull might have been a random choice made by somebody determined on murder if the occasion should arise. There was also an attempt to persuade me that you could have had no possible motive, but you're going to have to forgive me, Mr Dutton, I don't agree.'

That was to bring things out into the open with a vengeance. 'I think perhaps, Inspector, we've gone far enough,' Stephen said. 'Mr Dutton has been very frank with you—'

'Do you think so? Well, perhaps I agree with you, Mr Anstey, as far as what you say about this conversation having gone on long enough. I'm sorry to inform you, Mr Dutton, and sorrier still to do so in the presence of your parents, that Constable Tankard has in his possession a warrant for your arrest.'

Maitland felt it was time he took a hand. 'On what charge, Inspector?' he asked, with no appearance of haste but getting the question in pretty quickly all the same. Wentworth looked at him as though he thought he'd gone mad.

'Murder, Mr Maitland, what else?' he said with emphasis.

'I realise that, of course, but in view of the line of your questioning just now I think you must make it clear to us with which of the three murders that have been committed in the village Mr Dutton is being charged.'

'For the moment, with that of Dilys Jones. Further charges may follow,' Wentworth replied.

Peter waited quietly until Constable Tankard had finished speaking, then he turned, looking from Antony to Stephen so that his question might have been intended for either of them. 'What do I now?' he asked, and his voice was commendably steady.

Again it was Maitland who replied. 'I'm afraid you'll have to go with Inspector Wentworth and Constable Tankard,' he said. 'There will, of course, be no further questions except those Mr Anstey or your counsel put to you in preparing your defence.'

'I thought. . . . Won't you be acting for me?'

'Perhaps. But I have suggested to Stephen that it may be possible to interest my uncle, who has more experience than either of us, in appearing for you in court.'

'Sir Nicholas Harding?' said Wentworth in an incredulous tone.

'Certainly, if his other engagements permit. Your car's at the shop, isn't it, Stephen? Why don't you go into Rothershaw right away and see Peter through the formalities?'

That seemed a good idea and Stephen agreed readily enough. 'When shall I see you?' he asked.

'This evening, though I'll be in touch with you by telephone if anything happens in the meantime that you should know about.

I'm sure Emma will forgive me if I ask you to have dinner with us at Farthing Lee. Phone Caroline and tell her you won't be home.'

'All right, I'll do that. Meanwhile—'

'I thought it might be best if I stayed with Mr and Mrs Dutton for a few minutes at least.'

Comparing notes afterwards they both had to admit to an admiration for the old couple. Stephen at least had never seen anyone more thoroughly shocked or bewildered, but they did their best as long as Peter was in the house to behave as though what was happening was the most natural thing in the world. Mrs Dutton even went upstairs and packed a bag for him, and when the police party and Stephen had gone she assured Antony that Michael would look after her now, she would be quite all right. 'Peter trusts you and Mr Anstey, Mr Maitland,' said Michael Dutton, 'so we must do so too. I know you'll do everything you can to see he's cleared, even if you think your uncle could handle the matter better in court.'

'You can be sure of that.'

'Will you be here in Burton Cecil for long?'

'We only meant to stay for a few days, but we're on holiday, you know, so that can be extended if it seems a good idea.' Antony was finding it very difficult to know what best to say. 'Don't worry too much, but don't count on any miracles either. Your neighbours at least are solidly behind Peter, and I think you should find some consolation in that.'

'Yes, they know him better than that man Wentworth does,' said Mary Dutton, incomprehensibly cheered by the thought. Antony left them amid further expressions of gratitude, which he would very much have preferred to remain unuttered.

As he reached the street Roland Beaufort was coming out of his cottage two doors away. 'Just a minute, Antony,' he called, 'I want to talk to you.'

Maitland stopped obligingly and waited for him. 'I saw them taking Peter away,' Roland said abruptly.

Not much good trying to keep quiet about what had

happened. Whether he admitted it or not Peter's arrest would be all over the village in an hour. 'Yes, that's right, Roland,' Antony said.

'But they can't think he did all three murders,' Roland protested.

'I'm afraid they do.' Funnily enough, considering what a chatterbox Roland could be on occasion, Antony found himself trusting him, and after his session with the Duttons he badly needed someone to talk to. 'They think he had a motive to murder Dilys—'

'Because she wouldn't consent to him.' Roland nodded.

'—and that the other two murders were committed in cold blood, just to cover up the fact that he had a motive for the first.'

'I don't like the sound of that. Are you going to defend him?'

'I don't like it either, but I've agreed to come back for the trial, and if I can I shall persuade Uncle Nick to lead the defence.'

Like the inspector, Roland was surprised. 'That's flying high, isn't it?'

'A counsel of despair. He's far more eloquent than I am. But that's between the two of us.'

'Naturally.'

'In the meantime Stephen will look after everything. Unless, of course, there's anything I can usefully do before we leave Burton Cecil . . . but at the moment I can't see what that could be.'

'Well, it's about representing Peter that I wanted to talk to you. Neither you nor Stephen need worry about the legal costs, I'll pay them.'

Maitland stared at him for a moment. 'That's extraordinarily good of you, Roland,' he said. 'Have you any idea how much that's going to cost?'

'Quite a considerable sum, I think, but I can probably afford to pay it better than Stephen at least can afford to work for nothing.'

'Well, don't worry about counsel's fees, I feel I owe Peter something for doubting him for so long.'

'Sir Nicholas may not see it quite like that,' said Roland dryly.

'He will by the time I've finished with him.' Maitland sounded confident. 'But will you go and see Mr and Mrs Dutton and tell them you'll cover all necessary expenses . . . no need to go into details. The thing is they haven't thought of that aspect yet, but it's bound to occur to them sooner or later and they've really got enough worries without that.'

'I'm not much of a one for visits of condolence,' said Roland, 'but I'll do it if you think I should. You realise this is just going to make things worse, don't you? The feeling in the village about Philip Wainwright I mean.'

'Yes, I suppose that's bound to be the outcome. If there was another murder of course—'

'That would more or less prove Peter's innocence,' said Roland, and then smiled. 'Don't worry, I didn't really think you meant you hoped for one. Besides, I don't know if you agree with her but Jenny at least seems to be on Wainwright's side, and that certainly wouldn't help *him*.'

'No, it wouldn't.' But an idea was forming in his mind as he spoke, and perhaps his companion sensed something of this.

'Then I won't keep you.' Roland's hand was on the Duttons' gate by now. 'I'll perform my errand of mercy,' he said with self-mockery in his tone, 'and hope someone or other is making a note of it because I don't do all that many.' He paused again after he had taken a couple of steps and looked back over his shoulder. 'The pub was pretty crowded last night, as you saw,' he added, 'and I don't remember too many people except you and Jenny and Stephen leaving before closing time. So an awful lot of people will have alibis.'

II

As for Maitland, he turned towards the village, passed the churchyard, and then went up the steep path that had the church on one side and the vicarage on the other about half way up, to the cottage known appropriately enough as Lane's End. He had a feeling that some further talk with Philip Wainwright might prove, to say the least, illuminating.

It occurred to him as he went that perhaps Wainwright, a lover of solitude, might not let him in. But after all it had been he who made the first approaches last night.

In the event his fears were groundless. When he reached the cottage there was no sign of life, but Wainwright opened the door almost before he had time to knock. Perhaps he had been watching from the window. In any case, his reaction seemed to be one of pleasure rather than anything else. 'Have you some other suggestion for me after all, Mr Maitland?' he asked.

'Have you heard what's happened?' said Antony, following him in.

'Something else?' The question came sharply. 'Whatever it is I'm afraid I've heard nothing, the village grapevine seems to stop short at my garden gate.'

'To be precise two things have happened since we talked to you,' Antony told him. 'A girl called Ethel Bull has been murdered—'

'Not another!'

'—and Peter Dutton has been arrested.'

'Was it for all three murders?'

'For the moment only for that of Dilys Jones. But Wentworth made it perfectly clear there might be other charges later.'

'You're acting for young Dutton you told me.'

'Yes.' No need to add anything about Uncle Nick's possible participation.

'And so I suppose you're looking for an alternative suspect.'

'Not at the moment, as it happens. I mean, not here.' There

was a pause while he endured a rather searching look from his companion. 'You can believe me about that as a matter of fact,' he said.

'I believe I can. What is it you want then, Mr Maitland?'

'The trouble is your neighbours aren't going to like either of those things. I think you ought to get out of the village for the time being until things have quietened down, or preferably been cleared up altogether.'

'I don't know,' said Wainwright uncertainly. 'Where could I go? And wouldn't that seem like a confession of guilt, perhaps even give the police ideas about me?'

'I suppose that's true, but you can avoid it by telling them why you're going, and where. You can say it was on my advice if you like, I'll back you up, but in any case you don't need to worry too much, they have their own theory about this and you don't enter into it.'

There was a pause after that, too long for comfort. Wainwright was looking at his visitor with a rather sombre expression. 'Shall I tell you what makes it so difficult?' he said.

'Not unless you want to.' Whatever it was he had to say Maitland wasn't at all sure he wanted to hear it.

'I do want to.'

'If it's money—' said Maitland. Wainwright shook his head.

'It isn't money. Well I suppose that enters into it, but I've got enough for my needs and can even pay a modest rent if I have to. What I'm going to tell you may make you think twice about trusting me, that's why I feel you ought to know. It would also certainly convince the village that they're absolutely right about me, and might even make the police pause in the course of action they're following.'

'If that's so—' Maitland began, but Wainwright answered the question without allowing him to finish.

'I'm absolving you in advance, Mr Maitland. If you want to make use of what I'm about to tell you in your client's interests that's all right with me. Does that make you feel any better?'

'I only want to make it clear I've a duty to the court as well as to my client, and if what you're going to tell me conflicts with either of those obligations I can't possibly respect your confidence. Besides,' he added, with a glimmer of humour, 'you promised that if you told anybody about your past it would be Miss Anstey.'

'Then consider yourself her proxy. I'm grateful for the warning of course but . . . let's just put it I happened to believe you when you said you weren't casting me for the role of scapegoat.' To Antony's surprise there was an answering tinge of amusement in his voice.

'So long as you understand the position,' he said.

'You've explained it very clearly. To begin with, I can't blame the villagers for calling me the mysterious stranger, I've gone out of my way to keep to myself, but I wasn't being altogether accurate when I told you I'm naturally of a solitary disposition. I may as well start by telling you my name isn't Wainwright.'

'You've a perfect right to call yourself what you like, so long as it isn't for an illegal purpose.'

This time he laughed aloud. 'A very appropriate legal comment,' he said. 'Do you remember reading about a man called Philip Underhill, who killed his wife and her lover back in nineteen sixty-eight. It happened in Birmingham and may not have made the London papers.'

'No, I don't remember. Are you trying to tell me that was you?'

'I am. I'd been out of prison a couple of months when I bought this cottage through Mrs Anstey. I have a small independent income, and it had accumulated sufficiently while I was inside for me to do that. But you can see why I don't want to bring myself under police scrutiny unless it's absolutely necessary.'

Antony took a moment to think that out. 'I know very little of the circumstances so far,' he said, 'but surely it was suggested to you that a lesser plea might be accepted?'

'Yes, but you see I couldn't possibly claim temporary

insanity. I caught them together and I killed them, that was true enough, but it wasn't a shock to me at the time. I'd told my wife I was going away.... I can assure you there was plenty of evidence of premeditation.'

'How did you kill them?'

'With a shotgun which I obtained specifically for the purpose. It wasn't easy and involved deceiving a friend, but that's beside the point. It was a messy business,' he added thoughtfully, 'and something I assure you I've regretted ever since. But the police might say that my disillusionment with my wife had made me hate all women, and certainly that's what the village will think. I couldn't explain to them that I'm the one person in the district who couldn't possibly have done these murders because I know all about the remorse that tears you to pieces afterwards.' He paused there and his look at his companion was a challenging one. 'Well, Mr Maitland? Doesn't that make you doubt me?'

Antony didn't answer that directly. 'Did you love your wife very much?' he asked instead.

'As a matter of fact I did. That's why nothing mattered after I found out ... not the trial or going to prison or anything else. All I could think about when I came out was getting away from everything that reminded me, and I saw an advertisement in the paper and answered it, and here I am. Only you can understand now why I live rather a solitary existence.'

'Not unless you're doing it as a sort of penance,' said Antony, 'and there's no need for that; you should be making a new life for yourself now. I shan't tell anybody about this, you know.'

'I've already told you I expect you to tell Miss Anstey, and your wife, of course. And I'm sure they'll be as discreet as you will, but my own conscience might not allow me to keep silent. If people give you their friendship they have a right to the truth in return.'

'That may be so,' said Antony doubtfully, 'but why did you tell *me* all this?'

'Partly because it seemed only fair, and partly to explain the difficulties of my position. But perhaps I should have kept up the pretence,' he added with a certain diffidence. 'I'm no fonder than the next man of having people think badly of me.'

'I've no right to judge you,' said Antony abruptly. 'What I'd have done in your case ... but you see I'm one of the lucky ones. I can trust Jenny absolutely. But one can't blame someone else for committing a sin one isn't likely to be tempted to.'

'That's an original point of view.' But Wainwright sounded more startled than anything else.

Antony smiled at him, the sudden smile that had made him so many friends. 'I'm not condoning murder, but it's only too obvious you've condemned yourself more harshly than anyone else is likely to do. In any case, what you did was quite different from killing those three young girls. And I think, you know – and I don't believe I'm particularly credulous – that you're right when you say that, having once given way to your emotions and seen where that led you, you could never again do anything violent.'

'Thank you.' The astonishment was still in Wainwright's voice. 'I realise I'd no right to expect—'

Maitland was following his own train of thought. 'I wish I could say as much for the village. Which brings us back to the real purpose of my visit. Will you go away, for a night or two at least?'

'Yes, I ... if you really think that's what I ought to do. But there's no guarantee, is there, that it'll be safe to come back even then?'

'No guarantee,' Antony admitted. 'We'll just have to hope for the best. If you'll pack a bag, enough for a few nights, I'll go and fetch Jenny. She's the driver in our family' (he was grateful that Wainwright was preoccupied enough not even to look surprised at this) 'and we'll take you into Rothershaw. Come to think of it, I'll have to persuade Emma away from her typewriter too, because I don't think it's a good time for any woman to be alone, and Mrs Kitchener always goes home at lunch time.'

'And the police?'

'I think on consideration our best plan would be to try to find Sergeant Gilbey, or failing him Joe Kitchener. Either of them will know all about the talk in the village, and won't be as surprised at your decision as Inspector Wentworth might be.'

'Just as you say,' said Wainwright compliantly, and led the way to the door.

When Maitland got back to Farthing Lee there was a little delay while he explained the events of the morning so far. Fortunately Mrs Kitchener was cleaning the bath, or at least so they supposed because the taps were running full tilt, and there wasn't a chance of her overhearing them. Both Emma and Jenny were looking thoughtful when he had finished telling them of Wainwright's disclosures, and Jenny at least gave voice to her disquiet. 'If the police hear about that Antony—'

'Does it mean so much to you, love?'

'It's different when you know people,' said Jenny.

'My dear and only love, I'm desperately sorry. But if ever we know the truth—'

'You're telling me that it will be someone we know too?'

'I don't see any way of avoiding that conclusion,' said Antony rather sadly. 'It's only too obviously a local crime and by now—'

'Anything would be better than having innocent people suffer,' said Emma briskly. 'Do you think. . . . You know you must stay here as long as you like, Antony.'

'Jenny would tell you I always have ideas, but this time I'm completely in the dark,' Maitland confessed. 'If anything occurs to me . . . you know we both love being here, Emma.'

'Well, there's just one snag about Stephen coming to dinner this evening,' said Emma. 'We're invited to the vicarage for drinks first and I promised we'd go. That might make us a bit late.'

'It doesn't matter terribly, I'll give him a call and warn him.' But when he did so it was to find that the information had reached Stephen already.

'Caroline told me when I phoned her,' he said. 'We're all going, so she suggested that you should come back to Burton Crook with us. After all she was a journalist once, though Hugh likes to forget it,' (Hugh Anstey had some very old-fashioned ideas) 'so I expect she's anxious to know all the gory details.'

'She shall have them,' said Antony. 'See you tonight then.' But he realised as he spoke, that what he promised wasn't altogether true: Philip Wainwright's secret would go no further than this room. By now he could trust Emma, for all her scatterbrained ways, as confidently as he could Jenny.

The taps were still running and above their noise the strains of 'Abide With Me' – sung rather flat – had been added to the general pandemonium when Emma went upstairs to tell Mrs Kitchener that they were going out. 'You may as well come along, with us,' she added. 'I've just learned we shan't be in to dinner, and the nearest house is so far away I don't really like leaving you alone here.'

'That's all right, Missemma,' said Mrs Kitchener. 'Not but what there aren't things I could be getting on with at home,' she added, thoughtfully, so when they set out a few minutes later she had decided to join the party.

She left them at Rowan Corner to go up to the stone cottage that also served as the police station, and which was situated half way up Burton Bank. There were a fair number of people around in the village streets and they encountered Sergeant Gilbey, standing outside the Mortal Man, so that Antony was able to tell him of Wainwright's intentions, explain the reasons for the move, and ask if he had any suggestions as to where the fugitive might put up. Gilbey greeted this last question with a broad grin, as though aware that some unspoken motive lay behind it, but he answered readily enough. 'Mrs Dalby will give him a bed and say nowt to anyone. She's a pretty good cook, and she won't charge too much if that's any consideration.'

'I've an idea it may be a big one. You'll find him there, Sergeant, if you need him, but I hope all this talk will die down enough for him to return in a couple of days.'

'Aye, I do an' all.' It wasn't until he was walking away to catch up with Jenny and Emma that it occurred to Antony that Police Sergeant Gilbey might know a good deal more about Philip Wainwright's affairs than appeared on the surface. Well, the story would be safe enough with him. A countryman through and through he was a man who would stand no nonsense, but ever since their first meeting Maitland had come to have an increasing respect for his judgement ... and his compassion.

When he reached the square outside the shop Jenny was already in the car and Emma was standing talking to the old lady he recognised as Miss Murgatroyd. She looked as witchlike as ever, but this time was not accompanied by her cat. From what he could hear as he came up to them they were discussing the weather, but Miss Murgatroyd broke off, fixed him with a penetrating eye, and said in her deep voice, '*I am distressed for thee my brother Jonathan: very pleasant hast thou been unto me: thy love to me was wonderful, passing the love of women.*'

Maitland, completely taken aback, could think of no other response than Good Morning.

Emma laid a hand on his arm as though he might be in need of reassurance. 'I'm afraid we can't stay any longer, Miss Murgatroyd,' she said, 'Mrs Maitland will be waiting for us.'

'Go, and the Lord be with thee,' said Miss Murgatroyd. Antony, for once in his life speechless, sketched a sort of bow in her direction and followed Emma thankfully into the car.

They picked up Wainwright at Lane's End, and after the first exchange of greetings the drive into Rothershaw was made in a rather constrained silence. Mrs Dalby agreed to take him in, without seeming at all surprised at the request for a room for a few days. He declined their invitation to lunch with them, so they left him to his new landlady's tender mercies, and repaired to the Boar's Head to refresh themselves. It was still very warm, so when they got back to Burton Cecil Antony and Jenny spent the afternoon by Farthing Gill, ostensibly reading, until the clatter of the typewriter stopped and Emma called them in to prepare for their various evening engagements.

They were due at the vicarage at about six o'clock, and it was probably five to the hour when they reached the bottom of the lane. There was something different about the village tonight. For one thing all the children were at home, whether of their own volition or in obedience to their parents' command. But there were a good many groups of men gathered around the Mortal Man as though they were waiting for opening time. Most of them Antony recognised by now, though some of the faces were unfamiliar, and a man he didn't know but who seemed to know him gesticulated violently, so that they all stopped until he joined them. 'What's the matter Tom-Willie?' asked Emma.

'Just wanted to know Missemma,' said the man. 'Is Mr Maitland going to look after our Peter for us then?'

Emma turned an inquiring look on Antony who answered rather vaguely, 'As well as I can.'

This seemed to be the right answer and a ragged cheer went up from the group behind Tom-Willie. The party from Farthing Lee turned into the lane. 'I don't like the look of it,' said Emma as they went.

'But surely—' Jenny began, and broke off there, reframing her thoughts. 'Last night, Antony, you said there'd be no trouble because they'd been in the pub all the evening. That's what they're waiting for, isn't it? For the Mortal Man to open?'

'You may be right, love, but I think I understand what Emma means. Nobody ever stands in the streets here waiting for opening time, Adam isn't likely to run out of beer or anything else for that matter and that lot ... they normally have their supper – high tea or whatever – and then come back to spend the evening with their mates.'

'They look as if they're holding a meeting,' said Emma uneasily. 'Do you agree with what I'm thinking, Antony?'

'Yes, I'm afraid I do. I'm afraid it means they're going to take concerted action of some sort. It's likely they'll go in for a quick one to get up their courage, and then the fireworks will begin.

I'm only thankful that Wainwright is safely out of the way, and I think I'll ask Mrs Jerrold if I can use the phone when we get to the vicarage and have a word with Sergeant Gilbey.'

'He lives in Manningbridge, but there'd be no harm in his coming along to the Mortal Man himself for his evening pint to keep an eye on what's going on,' Emma agreed.

Maitland put this plan into operation when they arrived at the vicarage, explaining the position in as few words as he could. 'You probably know the feeling about Peter Dutton's arrest even better than I do, Mr Jerrold, and also the talk that's been going on about your neighbour at Lane's End. I've got a nasty feeling that some of your flock are going to get out of hand tonight.'

'Oh dear, and it's normally such a peaceful place,' said Mrs Jerrold. 'Would it do any good, Tom, if you went down and had a word with them?'

'If Mr Maitland's right I should rather think not,' said the vicar. 'But I'll go, of course, if you think it would do any good,' he added, looking inquiringly at Antony.

'To put it bluntly, I think it would be very unwise,' Antony told him. 'But if I may, I'll use your telephone to call Sergeant Gilbey, he may have some ideas as to how to calm things down.'

'By all means. You'll find his number written down in the little book by the telephone in my study. Through here,' he added, gesticulating. 'And meanwhile, the rest of us will go into the drawing-room, I don't suppose it will be long before your nephews and niece arrive, Emma.'

The drawing-room was large, with a high ceiling and long windows that looked out across the bright garden to the fields that sloped steeply upwards towards the moor. 'You can see Mr Wainwright's cottage from here,' Maisie Jerrold told Jenny, leading the way to one of them. 'I'm afraid since the Gillespies died the garden has gone to rack and ruin, but you can't really see it because of the wall. And when the lilac's out, and the laburnum, it still looks very beautiful.'

Just then the contingent from Burton Crook arrived, and the

position was explained to them. 'Antony's quite right,' said Hugh. 'They were still milling around when we came past and I didn't like the look of things at all.'

Antony came back into the room while he was speaking, and Jenny saw that it was one of the rare occasions when he had lost his temper. 'As far as they're c-concerned everything is back to n-normal,' he said. 'No need for any further patrolling, no need to expect any t-trouble at all.'

'That's surprising,' said Hugh, frowning. 'Inspector Went-worth might not know, being a stranger from Rothershaw, but surely Sergeant Gilbey can see what's under his nose.'

'He sees it well enough. I oughtn't to be blaming him,' said Maitland, calming down a little. 'Apparently they've had orders from on high. Everything is under control and there's no need for the villagers to feel any animosity towards anybody. The whole thing has been cleared up with Peter Dutton's arrest.'

'That doesn't sound to me like the sergeant,' said Hugh.

'That's what he told me. But he also said,' Antony admitted, 'that he'd phone Joe Kitchener to meet him at the Mortal Man for a quick one. Only it'll take him a little while to get over from Manningbridge on his motorbike. It's a winding road and we don't want him to break his neck.'

'He won't do that,' said Hugh comfortably. 'All the same, I'm happier to know he's coming.'

After that they all settled down and the vicarage sherry was dispensed. The Jerrolds were too polite to ask questions about Peter Dutton's arrest, his solicitor being among the company, so the talk turned to neutral matters. They were discussing Willie Barnes's latest misdeeds when the noise started.

On thinking about it afterwards Antony would have found it very difficult to describe. His first thought was that it was like a tidal wave surging ever nearer up the lane, but that may have been a wrong impression because as far as he could remember he'd neither seen nor heard a tidal wave in his life. All he could say for certain was that it started with a low murmur, gradually increasing in intensity, and that Jenny's hand shook as she put her glass down so that some of the sherry was spilled. 'It's more terrifying than anything I've ever heard,' she said rather shakily.

Antony's eyes narrowed a little as he listened, but he made no move. The vicar on the other hand jumped to his feet and made a rather violent gesture with his hand which might have meant, 'Stay where you are,' and went out into the hall, closely followed by Hugh and Stephen. 'There's glass in the top half of the front door,' said Maisie Jerrold quietly to the others. 'They'll be able to tell us what's happening.'

Caroline glanced at her watch. 'They've had a whole hour since opening time,' she said. 'Time enough to imbibe a little pot valour.'

Meanwhile the noise outside grew louder. They could hear individual voices now, though it was difficult to distinguish what they were saying. Presently the din seemed to stabilise and the three men came back into the room.

'I hope Wainwright's cottage is insured,' said the vicar looking worried.

'If he took my advice when he bought it, it is,' Caroline assured him. 'But what's happening outside?'

'It's difficult to judge how many men there are, anything between thirty and fifty, quite enough to be unpleasant. The one in the lead – I couldn't see who it was – has a Tilley lamp hooked onto a pitchfork. I can't think what he needs that for. They're obviously making for Lane's End.'

With one accord the party moved towards the window. Antony, pulling Jenny close to him, felt her shiver and put a comforting arm round her shoulders. It was Hugh who announced what they could all see for themselves. 'They're in a circle more or less in front of the cottage, and I think they're calling for Wainwright to come out.'

'Do you think I should try to reason with them?' said Mr Jerrold in a worried way.

'Tom, no!' said his wife.

'But—'

'Mrs Jerrold is quite right,' Maitland assured him. He didn't turn as he spoke, his eyes were still fixed on the scene outside. 'It could be dangerous, but what's more to the point it wouldn't do a scrap of good. They're a long way past listening to reason.' And as he spoke the hubbub seemed to intensify and they heard the sound of splintering glass.

'There go the windows,' said Stephen, stating the obvious. 'I hope—'

'What are we going to do?' Caroline asked with something like desperation in her tone. 'We can't just sit here and do nothing.' Jenny thought, a little fancifully, that perhaps since she had taken up dealing in real estate a house had become something more to their friend than it was to the rest of them . . . something with a personality and a life of its own.

'We can't do anything either, short of inviting martyrdom,' Stephen retorted, 'as Antony has already pointed out. Not against so many. But I'll telephone Joe Kitchener if you like, it's much too late to try Gilbey again.'

'We don't want him to be murdered either,' Caroline pointed out.

'I'll tell him to send for reinforcements, and not to move out of his own cottage until they arrive,' Stephen told her.

'In that case I suppose it couldn't do any harm.'

Like Maitland before him he went to the telephone in the study, and there was a silence while he was gone. Antony, still with a protective arm round his wife, was wishing devoutly that the rest of the party, the residents of Burton Cecil, weren't being forced to watch these people, their neighbours for many years, behaving in a way that could only be described as bestial. For himself it wasn't too difficult to make allowance for the shock and horror that had engulfed the whole community during the past week, but it might have been different if he had been a permanent resident of the village.

After a few minutes Stephen came back. 'The line's dead,' he reported. 'I can't even get the dialling tone and if they've bothered to cut your wires, Vicar, I'd be willing to bet

181

somebody must have nipped across and done the same thing to the police station.'

'That sounds as though they mean business,' said Hugh. 'I could go across the fields and give Joe a message though.'

'You'd have to cross the lane first,' Caroline pointed out. 'I don't think,' she added rather shakily, 'that would be a good idea at all.'

'This time I must agree,' said Mr Jerrold, with as much authority as he could put into his voice. 'As Mr Wainwright is safely in Rothershaw—' He broke off, staring with the rest of them at the scene outside.

In front of Lane's End was the bobbing light of the Tilley lamp and a crowd – Maitland couldn't even go so far as Hugh had done in estimating its number – of dark figures milling around it. The shouting had become a dull roar, continuous, infinitely menacing. One of the men raised an arm, a stone flew, and again there was the sound of breaking glass. And then there were four men, somehow more purposeful than the others, who went forward into the neglected garden. They had something between them, he had to strain his eyes to see what it was . . . a bundle of straw. He wondered vaguely whose barn it came from, but almost before he had time to formulate the thought it had been thrown by a strong arm and with deadly precision through the shattered window of the room to the right of the front door. A moment later the Tilley lamp, unhooked from the pitchfork, had followed it. For a moment nothing seemed to be happening and then with terrifying speed flames leaped up and began to spread. Maitland wondered inconsequently whether perhaps both things had been thrown by a member of the village cricket team. The aim must have been extraordinarily accurate.

Emma gave a long sigh. 'So that's that!' she said. 'Do you suppose they really want poor Mr Wainwright to be burned to death?'

'I think it's more a manoeuvre to get him out into the open,' said Stephen, and gave her arm a reassuring pat.

'And do you think he'd fare much better outside?'

Stephen hesitated, and it was Hugh who said, 'I'm afraid he wouldn't. But as he's safely in Rothershaw that's one less thing to worry about.'

A few minutes later their vigil was interrupted by a hammering on the front door. Maisie Jerrold made a move to go out into the hall, but her husband was before her. Antony had time to wonder whether it had occurred to the raiders that their quarry might have sought sanctuary either in the church or the vicarage, but to his relief it was Joe Kitchener who followed Tom Jerrold back into the drawing-room. 'Saw the flames,' he gasped. He had obviously been running, and frankly he hadn't the figure for it. 'Phone's out of order, been down t' Mortal Man, though. Fire engine's coming and a squad of men,' he added with a quiet satisfaction. 'Meanwhile they told me to stay put, no place for one man alone.'

'If I could help, Constable—' said Hugh. Caroline said afterwards that she could have killed him for the offer, though probably the words were spoken automatically. It was only too obvious that there was nothing that even five men could do.

'No thank you, Mr Anstey. Vicar tells me Mr Wainwright's over to Rothershaw. Good thing that.'

'Very fortunate,' said Mr Jerrold. He moved back to the window and glanced again at the scene outside. 'It's well away now,' he said. 'It was a good thought to call the fire brigade, Constable, but I don't think there's a hope of saving the cottage.'

So they waited. Whatever the others were thinking Antony was conscious mainly of sympathy for the men outside and the blind instinct that had led them into actions that – surely – they must later regret. It would be, of course, the uniformed branch of police who answered the constable's summons, but he found himself fervently hoping that perhaps the fire engine would arrive first. And for once things turned out as he wished. It was only by a moment or two, but the first thing that happened was that Manningbridge's fire engine swept into view its bell clanging wildly. And just as abruptly the crowd melted. They didn't stop to consult together or reach any unanimous decision as to what should be done, they just disappeared into the darkness. By the time the first of the police cars arrived there wasn't a soul in sight but Joe Kitchener, come out of cover, strutting across the road.

Mr Jerrold turned again from his vantage point. 'In the circumstances I don't think there's any need for us to go out just now,' he said. 'Later, I suppose, they'll want to know what we saw. I didn't recognise anybody.' It was obvious that he was definitely relieved to be able to say that. 'I wonder if any of you did?'

It was Antony who responded first. 'I should imagine it was quite impossible at that distance with everyone milling around.' There was a murmur of agreement, and most of them turned from the windows, though Stephen lingered for a little while watching the fire-fighters at work.

The vicar was making the rounds with the sherry decanter. 'It occurs to me, my dear,' he said, 'that as the only eye witnesses the police will have some questions to ask of us before long. It would be more convenient for them if they find us all together here. What can you do, Maisie, about feeding the multitude?'

After coping with parish emergencies this mild request left Maisie Jerrold unshaken. 'Soup and sandwiches,' she said promptly. 'Will you give me a hand, Caroline? No, stay where you are, Emma. It wasn't a nice experience and it probably left us all a bit shaken.'

The modest repast was more than adequate, the police interview brief, but it was only too obvious that everyone concerned was glad to be able to deny having recognised any of the crowd. As they were walking down the lane later Stephen reminded Antony that the Magistrates' Court hearing that must follow Peter Dutton's arrest would be held the following morning. 'Will you be coming with me?' he asked.

'There's nothing to do but to reserve our defence,' said Antony. 'I think it would be best if I had a word with Philip

Wainwright. He's safe and sound, thank goodness, but this business is bound to be a blow to him. So unless you want me particularly—'

'No, I can manage,' said Stephen. 'You don't think this business will – will give the police's thoughts another direction?'

'I don't see why it should,' Maitland told him, thinking as he spoke that things might be different if the detective branch knew about Wainwright's past. Sergeant Gilbey, who had always viewed his plainclothes colleagues' activities with an indulgent eye, was a different matter. A shrewd man, not one to be easily deceived, but quite capable of keeping his own counsel when he felt it was the right thing to do.

WEDNESDAY, 1st September
I

The following morning Jenny drove Antony to Rothershaw, and he extracted a promise from Mrs Kitchener not to leave Farthing Lee until they got back. It was about ten o'clock when they arrived and Mrs Dalby, who seemed to have taken a fancy to her new lodger, put her front room at their disposal. Philip Wainwright joined them a moment later. 'It was good of you to come,' he said, 'but at least you won't have the unpleasant task of breaking the news to me. The police have been here already.'

'What had they to say?'

'Nothing much.' His tone was commendably casual. 'Just, had I any particular enemies among the neighbours? Things like that. But I'd be awfully glad if you'd give me a few more details.'

Antony obliged, rather more fully than Jenny would have thought necessary until she realised later that he had his own reasons for going into so much detail. Wainwright interrupted occasionally with a query, so that it was obvious that he wanted to know everything there was to know about the event. 'And you both had ringside seats for all this,' he said when the story was finished. 'That can't have been very pleasant for you, Mrs Maitland.'

'It wasn't,' said Jenny, 'but we were all so relieved knowing you were here.' She looked at him for a moment and then said impulsively, 'You seem different this morning, Mr Wainwright.'

'They say confession is good for the soul,' he answered lightly. 'Now don't look so startled, Mrs Maitland, I'm not about to add any further sins to the catalogue I gave your husband yesterday. But neither of you rushed away from me screaming when you knew about my past, and you're taking so much trouble on my behalf it seems obvious you trust me.'

'I never believed the village was right about you,' said Jenny. 'As for – as for what happened years ago, I think it's best forgotten.'

'I don't know about that,' said Wainwright thoughtfully.

It was obvious that Jenny would have questioned this statement, but Antony put in rather quickly, 'What will you do now? Apart from collecting your insurance, I mean. Caroline said she was pretty sure you'd looked after that side of things.'

'Yes, I did. I shall rebuild,' said Wainwright laconically.

'I'm glad to hear that. I thought all this might have given you a distaste for Burton Cecil.'

'To understand all is to forgive all,' said Philip Wainwright. 'I don't know if I can explain this very well, but this morning after the police had been is the first time that I've ever really understood the meaning of that saying.'

'If I don't ask you what you mean by that Jenny will certainly do so,' said Antony, smiling.

'Merely that – you may both think this is very silly – in hearing about the blind fury of the men whose actions you observed last night and have just described so graphically, and trying to see the reasons behind the way they felt, I've come for the first time to realise that perhaps there might be forgiveness for me too, even from myself. Or if you think forgive is too generous a word, perhaps I should do a little forgetting. Enough to allow myself to make a new life as you advised me to, Mr Maitland.'

Jenny was momentarily speechless, but Antony said quietly, 'That's the best bit of news that's come of this unpleasant business.'

'There is a proviso, of course,' Philip Wainwright went on.

'If you mean you want us to keep quiet about what you've told me—'

'Nothing like that. I'm quite satisfied you won't say anything, unless of course you'll need my evidence for that poor boy, Peter Dutton, in which case I suppose you'd have to tell Stephen Anstey.'

'I haven't told him and I don't intend to. As for your evidence, I wouldn't even think of using it. Even if we did call you, what could you tell the court that would be the slightest use?'

'I might confuse the issue,' said Wainwright seriously. 'Reasonable doubt ... isn't that all that's needed for an acquittal?'

'At your own expense. That's not a trick I'd stoop to, or Stephen either if he knew as much as we do. We'll get Peter off fairly or not at all.'

'Even yesterday I think I'd have said I didn't care. Today ... as I told you, that wasn't what I meant when I spoke of a proviso. But if this affair is never cleared up to the satisfaction of the villagers I can hardly stay there, can I?'

There seemed to be no answer to that, and the meeting broke up after a little more talk about the events of the last few days. When they got back to Farthing Lee in time to release Mrs Kitchener to get Joe's dinner, Emma was still at her typewriter. She always preferred to work regularly but she sought the solace of Maltravers's company particularly when things were bad. So Jenny, with a little help from her husband, went through into the kitchen to get some lunch ready and inspect Mrs Kitchener's offering for their dinner that evening. 'I suppose you realise,' said Antony, as she washed the lettuce, 'that Wainwright's provided us with an additional reason for finding out who really killed all those poor girls.'

'Yes, of course I realise it,' said Jenny. 'Talk about being between the devil and the deep blue sea. What with the police arresting Peter Dutton on the one hand and the villagers ready to murder poor Mr Wainwright on the other. But neither of those is the most compelling reason.'

'I know, what if there's another murder?'

'That's too awful to contemplate, though it would at least clear Peter. There'd still be Mr Wainwright's problem though and I must admit, Antony, I'd like to see him re-establish himself here and live a normal life again.'

'I know, love, I feel the same way. But I don't know what I can do about it, I haven't the police's facilities for questioning the whole village.'

'An awful lot of people were in the pub at the time Ethel Bull was killed,' Jenny pointed out. 'Roland and Cyril could probably tell us—'

'Roland says very few people left until closing time.'

'Well, he's out of it anyway. His statement certainly implied that he was there himself, but I doubt if he was trying to mislead me, it could be too easily checked. And of all the people who have any connection with the girls who were killed,' Maitland said, following his train of thought single-mindedly, 'there's only Ivor Lewis who wasn't at the Mortal Man last night. And Peter of course.'

'Yes, but I don't really think—'

'Neither do I,' said Antony. 'I was going to say that I don't think Ivor Lewis has an alibi for either of the other murders, if that means anything. But if we're looking for a homicidal maniac it may not be anybody in the village at all. And even if it was, and even eliminating the people who were in the pub last night, the list of possibilities is far too long.'

'Yes, but you were thinking – weren't you, Antony? – that perhaps the police are so far right . . . one of the murders was inspired by a motive, and the others were done to conceal what it was.'

'To make them look like sex killings in other words,' Maitland agreed. 'The trouble is, love, that's probably just what they were.'

'Yes, but . . . oh, I suppose you're right. Only it did occur to me that someone who found himself in great difficulties – I don't know what, and I haven't the faintest idea about that – might have known about what happened in the village before

189

and decided that murder was the best way out.'

That led to a moment's complete silence. 'Heaven and earth!' said Antony softly after a moment. 'What a bloody fool I am!'

'Does that mean you agree with me?' asked Jenny rather suspiciously.

'It means it rings a bell loud and clear,' said Antony emphatically, 'and I must say I'd like to know whether that wretched old woman knew something, or whether she was just talking at random.'

'What wretched old woman?'

'Miss Murgatroyd. You were in the car so you didn't hear her. Give me a minute to think about it, love.'

'You've had an idea,' said Jenny. 'You've thought of a motive.'

'It needs a bit of thinking out and it isn't watertight by any means. Look here, love, if you've finished that salad let's call Emma to lunch and we'll go into the whole thing afterwards, when she's gone back to work.'

Jenny agreed. As she had, in any case, a nasty feeling that she wasn't too keen on finding out the truth, or wouldn't have been if it hadn't been so important for so many people's happiness, she was glad enough to put off the moment of revelation. She knew her husband well enough to be sure already that whatever idea had come to him would prove to be the right one; but she also knew that he had far less confidence in his own instincts than she had.

Emma, summoned to the table, wanted to know, of course, exactly how that poor Mr Wainwright was, and the subject carried them pretty well over the interval while they had their lunch. Afterwards she went back to work again, and Antony and Jenny went down to their favourite spot near Farthing Gill. It was hotter than ever, and Jenny took off her sandals and dabbled her feet in the water as she was so fond of doing. She made no attempt to break the silence. When Antony was ready he would tell her what was on his mind, and she knew his ways well enough to be content to wait.

After a while, 'Patient, aren't you, love?' he said teasingly.

Her attention was caught immediately. 'Are you ready to tell me what Miss Murgatroyd said to you?' she asked.

'It wasn't only what she said, it was because you reminded me . . . it did cross my mind once when I was talking to Stephen, but then I didn't think of it again, perhaps because it seemed like too much of a coincidence.'

'I don't know what you mean.'

'Only last year, Jenny. The man who killed those babies had a motive for wanting just one of them dead. And this time it was staring me in the face. You don't think,' he added, suddenly conscience-stricken, 'that I dismissed the idea because I don't much care for Inspector Wentworth and it was he who first propounded it?'

'Antony! You haven't changed your mind about Peter Dutton?'

'Nothing like that, love. I'd better explain, hadn't I?'

'I'm not at all sure that I want to know the answer to this puzzle,' said Jenny uncertainly.

'My dearest love, I understand. It isn't the first time you've said it to me . . . it's different when it's someone you know.'

'And it is?'

'I'm very much afraid so, though as I said I've nothing like proof of what I suspect.'

'Can you find any? You see,' she explained carefully, 'I may seem to be a bit of a coward about this, but I realise as well as you do that anything's better than having the wrong person get the blame.'

Antony put out a hand as though absent-mindedly to cover hers. 'As for proof . . . I just don't know. Things may seem a little clearer when we've talked it out. So let's go at it systematically, love, from the beginning. Who were the most likely suspects when Dilys Jones was killed?'

'Well, the most likely one of all was Peter Dutton, of course, and I know at first you thought he'd done it. Roland did suggest that a man of Ivor's age might have found it a strain living in the same house as a young and attractive girl, but I don't know how serious he was about that. And Mabel Hawthorne was a newcomer here, she hardly knew anybody except the vicar and his wife, and I don't suppose you're suggesting that Mr Jerrold is the murderer.'

Antony had a smile for that. 'As far as I know he hasn't an alibi for any of relevant times,' he said, 'but no, I'm not suggesting that.'

'Well then, poor little Ethel Bull. Did you know, Antony, she was only seventeen?'

'How did you come by that bit of information?'

'From Mrs Kitchener. Anyway, I was going to say she also told me that Ethel hadn't a regular boyfriend, though she added that she was just the sort of girl that someone or other might take advantage of.'

'A useful source of information, our Mrs Kitchener.'

'And it wasn't the only thing she told me. If you're wondering if there was any reason within her family for wanting her dead, there's only herself and her mother and father, and we know where John Bull was the night she was killed, wherever he was the other evenings.'

'You're forgetting, Jenny, Roland said only a few people left the Mortal Man, but he hasn't yet told us who they were.'

'You don't think—?'

'Not really. If I'm right we've taken our speculations a little too far. Go back to Mabel Hawthorne, love, and think about her husband.'

Jenny stared at him uncomprehendingly for a moment. 'Samuel Hawthorne?' she said. 'They've been married six months, no time at all really, and he was so proud of her, so happy, so distressed when we saw him after her death.'

'*Was* he? Think about it.'

'I . . . I was sure—'

'Don't ever grow up, Jenny,' her husband implored her. 'It would be almost as bad as if you suddenly became logical.'

'I don't know what you mean.'

'It never occurred to you, I suppose, that Samuel Hawthorne is a homosexual.'

That silenced her again for almost a full minute, but he made no attempt to break the silence. Oddly enough, it never occurred to her to question the accuracy of the statement, even though it surprised her. 'Then why did he marry her?' she said at last, putting her finger on the point that really bewildered her.

'That's something I can't answer. But don't you think that, having done so, he might well find the situation intolerable? And when he came to Burton Cecil and heard – as you pointed out – all the talk about what went on here seven years ago, don't you think that might have put the idea of getting rid of her into his head?'

'And he concocted a plan . . . Antony, it would be absolutely diabolical, too horrible to contemplate.'

'There have been three murders of very young girls,' he reminded her. 'If you want my opinion, nothing can make that fact much worse.'

'No, you're right of course,' Jenny agreed. 'But you never said a word about this to me before,' she added reproachfully.

'About Samuel's sexual preferences? I thought the least said the better. And I never dreamed of course . . . I wasn't thinking of cold-blooded murder, not even when Dilys was killed.'

'Antony, have you really thought this out? The thing that worries me is—'

'Why he should have married her at all,' Antony finished for her. 'You said that before and I couldn't answer you then any more than I can now. But while we're thinking about it, love, let me tell you two other things that struck me without really registering at the time. When we visited Samuel after Mabel's murder he never said a single word to indicate that he was at all curious about who might have killed her. And the little speech he made when we left, which I think you took at face value, sounded stilted and insincere to me.'

'I suppose you're right and there's another thing, Antony. If

193

something was said on that occasion that alarmed him, it would account for Ethel's murder following so very quickly on the other.'

'That's right, love. What did we talk about?'

'I don't really remember, except that he said he was going to leave Burton Cecil and didn't care whether the house was sold or not; and one of us asked if he was going back to Manchester.'

'That's it, love! What do we know about his life before he came here?'

'Only what he told us himself. He lived with his mother until he married Mabel about six months ago. His mother died about a month after that. And he seems to have plenty of money, didn't Caroline say he bought the house outright? Besides, he doesn't seem to have to work.'

'That may be it. Did he always have money, or did he inherit from his mother?'

'We've no means of knowing that,' Jenny pointed out.

'No, but let's suppose for a moment that it was the latter. He lived with old Mrs Hawthorne, she must have known about his homosexuality. She wasn't a young woman and it would be a miracle if she was broad-minded about it.'

'This is all guesswork, Antony.' But in her heart she had no doubt about his main premise at least.

'I know it is, but Uncle Nick's hundreds of miles away, too far to start an argument. And it would explain things, Jenny, why he married Mabel I mean. If the money was his mother's he might have done it to appease her, to make her feel he was about to mend his ways. That would go some way towards accounting for it, wouldn't it?'

'Yes it would, and I've been feeling so sorry for him,' said Jenny, suddenly indignant. 'I could have sympathised with Peter Dutton if he'd killed Dilys in a moment of frenzy, though of course I'd still have been even sorrier for Dilys. But that sort of cold, calculating plotting . . . it's altogether too much!'

'I quite agree with you, love.' For all the seriousness of the moment there was an underlying current of amusement in his voice. 'But let's suppose for a moment that this idea of mine is right – and we don't know yet that it is – how do we set about proving it?'

'Of course it's right, you're always right about people, Antony.'

'Jenny love, you know better than that. Think of—'

'I know, what Uncle Nick always calls your lack of cynicism,' said Jenny. 'But this time ... it is a problem, isn't it? And the police could look into it so easily.'

'Yes, but they won't. Inspector Wentworth,' said Antony judiciously, 'is a pigheaded bastard. We'll get no help from him.'

'You might if you can take it just a few more steps forward. Oughtn't you to be talking to Stephen about this, Antony?'

'Yes of course, I must do that as soon as possible. And I'd like Hugh and Caroline in on the discussion as well because they know so much more about the neighbourhood and Caroline was the first person to be in touch with the Hawthornes.'

'And Emma knows more than either of them,' said Jenny. 'We don't want to disturb her, Antony, so why don't you walk down to the telephone box by the Mortal Man and give Stephen a ring, and the others too to make sure they're free. Tell them we'll have dinner early and be all ready for them if they come round at about eight o'clock.'

'You're very decisive this afternoon, love,' said Antony, scrambling to his feet and holding out a hand to pull her up. 'I'll follow your suggestions as long as you perform your watching act in the house, not out here. Your safety is even more valuable to me than Emma's is, you know.'

'Nothing will happen now that Peter's under arrest.'

'All the same I'd rather not risk it. There's just a chance he's got a taste for killing. The appetite grows by what it feeds on, whatever that means. So stay in the house, love.'

'Of course I will and bolt the door too if you'd like me to,' Jenny offered generously. 'But I haven't quite finished—'

195

'More instructions!'

'Yes, because we never seem to have had the chance to replenish Emma's supplies at the Mortal Man. I expect they'll be closed by the time you get there but if you go round to the side door Adam will let you in.'

'And if I take that rather hefty shopping bag of Emma's it will conceal the evidence nicely,' Antony agreed. 'I expect there'll still be a good many police around in the village.'

II

The party from Burton Crook arrived at almost exactly eight o'clock, by which time Antony had broken to Emma the theory he had formed. By now the doubts that always plagued him had come to the fore and he sounded tentative, but if he expected her to be either surprised or shocked he was the more mistaken. 'I admit I never thought of it as a motive for murder,' she said thoughtfully, 'though I can see now you're probably right about that. But of course I realised from the first that it wasn't quite a normal marriage.'

'That's a nice way of putting it,' said Antony, smiling at her. 'I must remember it for future use.'

The typewriter had been pushed to the far corner of the desk and its place was taken by an unusually large array of bottles, together with a motley collection of glasses among which whoever played bar-tender might expect to find something of the sort he wanted to answer each request. Hugh took it upon himself to do the honours, and knowing by now pretty well what everyone would want there was no doubt about it that his attention was more on what Maitland was telling Stephen than on what he was doing. Caroline cast an occasional uneasy glance at Emma, but seeming eventually to be reassured by the older woman's placid manner gave her attention wholeheartedly to the discussion. 'It's awfully difficult to believe,' she said doubtfully when Antony had finished.

'Like to bet on it?' said Hugh, turning with a glass in each hand which he brought across the room and placed carefully, one beside Emma and the second beside Jenny. 'I've seen him at work, you know, and you haven't.'

'No, but you've told me about it often enough,' Caroline retorted. 'I'm quite ready to – to grant your premise, Antony, but if two murders were committed to hide the motive for the third it doesn't really make Mr Hawthorne any more likely a suspect than Peter Dutton. From the police's point of view, I mean, you know I believe in Peter's innocence.'

'You're not quite right there, Caroline,' said Antony rather apologetically. 'If Peter had committed the first murder out of frustration because Dilys was a good girl and wouldn't have anything to do with him before they were married, it wouldn't necessarily make him the kind of man who'd go out afterwards and kill two other girls just as a cover-up. But somebody desperate to get out of an intolerable situation would have been – at least to my mind – more capable of making such a cold-blooded plan.'

Stephen had been silent since Antony had finished speaking, apparently lost in thought, but now he looked up and asked, 'Are you proposing to present these conjectures of yours in court when Peter's trial comes on?'

'They wouldn't amount to proof you know,' Maitland told him. 'And as for what Uncle Nick would say if I suggested such a course—'

'They'd provide a case as circumstantial as the one against Peter.'

Emma spoke up there. 'I don't think you're quite right about that, Stephen dear,' she said, 'because Peter was known to have an appointment with Dilys that evening. Doesn't that make all the difference?'

'I know you haven't seen Samuel since Mabel was killed,' said Antony. 'What about the rest of you?'

'Hugh and I went round for a brief visit,' said Caroline.

'Well, perhaps he didn't tell you what he told us. He'd meant to go and meet Mabel after the evening service on Sunday but got interested in a book and forgot the time. Suppose he went. It was completely safe, he was on a perfectly innocent errand and needn't take any action unless he was quite sure that nobody had seen him. And Mabel staying behind the others for a few minutes gave him all the opportunity he needed. Doesn't that put the two cases almost exactly on a par, with perhaps the scales dipping a little in Samuel's favour.'

'Yes, I suppose it does,' said Emma.

'In any case that wasn't what I meant,' Antony explained. 'I've never yet accused anyone of a crime in court unless I was sure they were guilty, though I admit that on some occasions my certainty has fallen a good way short of legal proof. But in this case such a drastic – and, I admit, dangerous – course of action may not be necessary. Jenny pointed out that if we could just get a little more information Stephen and I could go to Inspector Wentworth with it, and even he might listen to us, at least so far as to put some additional inquiries in hand. I have my own reasons for wanting to get things cleared up quickly,' he added, and nobody but Jenny and Emma could have realised that he was thinking of Philip Wainwright as well as of his own client.

'Peter being in custody is the best guarantee that there won't be another murder,' Hugh pointed out. 'If you're right that is, and the killings were cold-blooded and didn't have the usual kind of sexual motive. And as I think I made clear I agree with you about that.'

'Unless Samuel has got a taste for killing,' Emma put in.

'Antony thought that was a possibility,' said Jenny, and shivered.

'We were talking,' said Stephen, 'about whether we could put a case together sufficiently watertight to take to Inspector Wentworth.'

'I think we must try to do so, and do it quickly. Another thing Samuel told us,' said Antony, 'was that he intended to go away as soon as the funeral was over ... Mabel's funeral I mean, of course.'

'The police would want him for the trial if they make the additional charges against Peter that they spoke of,' Stephen said.

'Yes, so they would but I don't think that's any guarantee that he'd stay around. And if Emma is right – and as Jenny says the idea had already occurred to me – he just might go and do the same thing all over again somewhere else. If being married seemed so terrible to him it might have brought out a latent hatred of all women.'

'That's a nasty thought,' said Stephen. 'Anyway, this slightly more circumstantial story we're going to Wentworth with. . . . How are we going to set about constructing it?'

'I wonder, Caroline,' said Antony, 'whether you remember who acted for Hawthorne when he bought the house.'

'Stephen acted for the vendor,' said Caroline. 'It was practically his first job after he came here.'

'And I remember my opposite number quite well,' said Stephen promptly. 'James, James, James *and* James. I couldn't forget a name like that.'

'Yes, but I don't suppose you know any of them personally?'

'They're mostly dead.'

'Any of the present partners then?'

'No, I'm afraid not.'

'Then I'll have to get in touch with Geoffrey Horton. He's a solicitor friend of mine in London, and can look up old Mrs Hawthorne's will at Somerset House.'

There was a short silence while they all seemed to ponder that. Hugh was the first to speak. 'Do you think that, if you can prove that most of Hawthorne's money came from his mother, that would make it more likely that he married to oblige her and so provide some confirmation for this idea of yours?'

'Thank you for not saying this wild idea. But that's it exactly.'

'I've already said several times that I think you're right, but as far as the rest of the world's concerned it'll still be pretty thin.'

'Of course it will, and I'm not particularly enamoured of the prospect of trying to put it over to Inspector Wentworth. Even so, I think it's got to be done. And while Geoffrey's hunting up the information we can all be thinking about our first move. Come to think of it,' he added, 'I'll phone Geoffrey now if I may, Emma, then he can put someone on to the search first thing in the morning.'

The gathering broke up by ten o'clock, Hugh having to be up at some ungodly hour for the milking, and none of them having much taste that evening for casual chatter.

THURSDAY, 2nd SEPTEMBER
I

It was four o'clock the following afternoon when Geoffrey's call came through, inevitably disturbing Emma's train of thought; though as she told the Maitlands afterwards, 'It didn't matter a bit, my dears, I'm not at all temperamental.' Antony put down the receiver, only to pick it up again immediately and put through a call to Stephen. 'Call in on your way home, there's a good chap,' he said. 'It won't take very long but I've something to tell you.'

Unless Stephen had broken all records on the road from Rothershaw he must have left the office within a few minutes of Antony's call. Emma hadn't gone back to work, so they were all together when he arrived. 'You've got the information?' he asked eagerly, almost before he was in the room.

'I certainly have. It was a quite straightforward will, Geoffrey said, and as Samuel Hawthorne was the sole heir and had complied with the provisions of the will there were no complications and probate was granted quite quickly.'

'Provisions?' said Stephen.

'Yes, this is the interesting part. He would benefit only on condition that he was married before his mother died.'

'Good Lord!' That was Stephen again, with something more than astonishment in his voice.

'You may well say so. I think – don't you? – that we can deduce a little more about the circumstances from what we now know. For instance, the solicitor who drew it up must certainly have pleaded with her not to make that condition, and if he

201

knew about Samuel's tendency he may well have seen where it might lead. I don't mean to what's happened, but the unhappiness to both Hawthorne and his bride. I think we may assume, too, that there was a good deal of discussion in the office, Geoffrey says there always is when there are any unusual provisions to a will. And one other thing strikes me, old Mrs Hawthorne may or may not have been terminally ill, and her son may or may not have known about it, but it would be pretty much of a coincidence if he chose exactly one month before her death to marry . . . unless he knew.'

'But that's more, far more than we expected,' said Stephen excitedly.

'In any case it must be put to Wentworth so that the police can inquire into it.'

'Do you think they will?' asked Emma. 'You know Inspector Wentworth, when he's made up his mind to a thing, that's it!'

'I think you're underestimating him, Emma,' Antony told her firmly. 'I've said this and that about him from time to time, but he won't want to see a miscarriage of justice any more than the rest of us. I think the real question we have to face is whether Samuel will stand up under police interrogation or not. I've more or less made up my mind about his guilt, and you three are all kind enough to believe me . . . at least, I think you do. But as I pointed out before the evidence is still circumstantial.'

'His motive is far stronger than Peter's anyway,' said Stephen. 'What do you suggest we do now, Antony? I don't think even Inspector Wentworth would expect us to tackle him about all this tonight, though if we wait till morning he'll probably accuse us of suppressing evidence.'

'That's the problem,' said Antony. 'What do you think about it, Emma?' he asked, turning to her quickly.

'Wait until he's had time to have his dinner and then go and see him at home,' said Emma promptly. 'Any woman will tell you that the way to a man's heart is through his stomach. And I'm sorry if that's a *cliché*, but it happens to be true.'

'It's his mind we're talking about, not his heart,' Antony

objected. But when the time came both he and Stephen followed her advice to the letter.

II

To Maitland's eye Detective Inspector Wentworth was looking sleek and well fed when they reached his home that evening, so he mentally awarded Emma full marks for her suggestion. Mrs Wentworth had seemed in a little doubt as to whether her husband would see them, but eventually agreed to convey a message to him. It was impossible to tell how this was received, but at least he agreed that they should be let in, and seemed to be in one of his moods of unexpected congeniality when they joined him. Mrs Wentworth, obviously well trained, disappeared discreetly and closed the door carefully behind her.

'Still here, Mr Maitland?' said Wentworth when greetings had been exchanged. 'I suppose you've come to put me right about the murders in Burton Cecil.'

'Why did you think we wanted to see you?' asked Antony, interested.

'My wife only said it was Mr Anstey, and he might have wanted me for any one of a thousand reasons. To find out the dates of the other inquests, for instance. Now that everything's cleared up there's no reason why we shouldn't proceed with the inquest on Miss Jones either.'

'I'm not particularly interested in the inquests, Inspector,' said Stephen. 'And would you say everything's cleared up?'

'I knew it!' He slammed his fist down on the arm of his chair as he spoke to give emphasis to his words. 'You're going to tell me this riot – or whatever you like to call it – in Burton Cecil two nights ago ought to make a difference, that perhaps the vendetta the villagers have against Philip Wainwright has some basis in fact.'

'I wasn't going to tell anything of the sort,' Stephen retorted. He seemed in a faintly belligerent mood this evening. 'It's the last thing that was in my mind. And I think riot is quite a good word for it. The poor man's house was burned down, you know.'

'So I heard. Inquiries are being made, of course, though they haven't got very far as I understand it.'

Maitland broke in there, it seemed safest to take the initiative out of Stephen's hands. 'I may as well make it clear to you right away, Inspector, that far from suspecting Philip Wainwright both Mr Anstey and I are quite convinced of his innocence. As you know, he was staying in Rothershaw at the time of the fire, but it was my wife and I who took him there, after some persuasion.'

'The devil you did!'

'There's nothing secret about it. Staying in the village, it was only too obvious that the feeling locally might lead to trouble. No, what we want to outline for you, Inspector, is an alternative theory that I think you may feel should be investigated. I'll admit right away it's no stronger than the case against Peter Dutton, except in the matter of motive. But in common justice—'

'I don't need a lecture from you on that subject, Mr Maitland,' said Wentworth in a very snubbing way. When Antony thought about it afterwards he decided that though he'd been doing his best to be tactful the inspector was probably justified. 'We'd better have Constable Tankard in' – he glanced at Stephen as though he expected some argument – 'if you're quite determined to go through with this.'

So there was an uncomfortable interval while Constable Tankard and his notebook were sent for and then Maitland began his story. He was lucid, as might have been expected, and also did his best not to irritate Wentworth any further, making a parallel between the police theory about Peter Dutton's motive in committing three murders instead of one and his own theory concerning Samuel Hawthorne's. He also stressed the fact that he and his wife had met the Hawthornes socially, which naturally gave them a certain advantage. Constable Tankard, that silent man – Antony wondered briefly whether he would be quite so silent when he became an inspector too – was visibly impressed, but there was no telling what Wentworth was thinking. His face was completely inscrutable, and for all either of the visitors could tell he might have been about to throw them out of the house!

Instead, to their complete surprise, he said slowly after a pause that they found almost unendurable, 'You may be right. Oh God, you may be right!' It was the first sign of emotion – other than a faint animosity – that Antony had ever seen in him.

'I think we are,' he said quietly. And suddenly his mind was filled with all the difficulties of the situation, all the doubts that he had been doing his best to keep at bay.

'So what you believe is that Samuel Hawthorne, knowing his mother to be dying, married to please her and to ensure his inheritance.'

'The part about the will can be proved, Inspector,' Stephen put in eagerly. Perhaps he sensed that his companion would be grateful for the intervention. 'And if inquiries don't reveal that he was a known homosexual, which I think they will, the wording of that clause creates a strong presumption—'

'And the source of your information?'

'Somerset House. I live in London, Inspector . . . remember?' said Antony, rousing himself, 'and have plenty of friends glad enough to oblige me in a thing like that. But of course you'll want to confirm it for yourself.'

'Very well, we'll leave it there.' It was an odd thing that he didn't sound altogether unwilling to do so. 'So Hawthorne chose a young bride, almost from the schoolroom you might say, not knowledgeable enough to go running to her best friend or perhaps to his mother with any tales of his inadequacy. Though I have to point out to you that many known homosexuals have married and raised families.'

'Yes, and I daresay that's what Samuel thought he could do too. I think that's why—'

Again the detective didn't let Antony finish. 'Why he moved

away as soon as he could after his mother's death to a place where he wasn't known.'

'And he heard about the murders that were committed in Burton Cecil before,' Stephen added.

'I wasn't forgetting that. Your argument is that he found marriage increasingly distasteful, that he was driven almost mad by the effort to maintain an apparently normal relationship with his young wife.'

'I suppose some people would say, quite mad,' Antony said softly. 'Poor devil.' But again the thought was there to plague him . . . if I'm right.

'Have it your own way.' Wentworth was anxious now to get on with his interpretation of the story. 'So the gossip he heard about the previous murders put ideas into his head. Merely to murder his wife would have been to bring himself into undue prominence; the first and last murders may have been to cover up the motive, and the fact that Mabel Hawthorne was the intended victim. But have you also considered the possibility that he may have obtained some satisfaction from getting back at women for the torment he was suffering in his unwelcome marriage?'

'Yes, that had occurred to us, and also the possibility that when he left this neighbourhood he might continue in the path he'd been following . . . unless he's stopped.'

'Well, at least,' said Wentworth, looking from one of them to the other, 'we can be thankful for one thing, that you didn't go off yourselves to have a confrontation with him. From what I've heard of Mr Maitland—'

There was something in his tone that was not very far from amusement, and though his remarks annoyed Antony he took some heart from that.

'What are you going to do?' he demanded.

'You're quite right in saying there's a case for investigation,' the inspector admitted cautiously. 'We shall put inquiries in train in Manchester, of course, of these solicitors you mentioned, Mr Anstey. It was a good thing you remembered their names. But meanwhile I think it might be a good idea, Constable, if we went along and had a talk with this Hawthorne first thing in the morning.' He glanced at his watch. 'Too late tonight.'

And with that they had to be content. 'More than I expected,' said Stephen when they were safely outside in the street again.

'No, I don't think so. He can see the validity of what we've told him as well as we can, and he certainly doesn't want to see the wrong man convicted, even if at one point I did think he was rather keen on getting an arrest made quickly. Now I'm pretty sure that was only from fear that the series of murders might continue.'

'Well, we've done what we can,' said Stephen. 'We shall just have to wait and see.'

FRIDAY, 3rd September

I

The next morning neither Antony nor Jenny could settle to anything, though Emma took prompt refuge after breakfast with Mr Maltravers. So they walked up and down beside the Gill, knowing that with the window open they would hear the telephone if it rang. 'When do you think we might hear something?' asked Jenny.

'It may take some time, love,' Antony told her. 'There are a number of things Wentworth can put to Hawthorne, starting with his mother's will, the precise reason for that particular clause, and the coincidence of the fact that he married one month before old Mrs Hawthorne's death. Samuel will know perfectly well that the true answers are there in Manchester for the seeking. It may take some time but I think he'll admit the truth in the end. And when Wentworth presses his questions – as he will do – do you think Hawthorne will be able to hide his distaste for the female sex?'

'You're right, of course, but I do wish it was all over,' said Jenny. 'Do you think he'll try to take the matter any further than that today?'

'If either Stephen or I had asked him that question last night I don't think he could have told us the answer himself. He'll use his judgement.'

'People always do in – in any interrogation,' said Jenny. 'At least, that's what I understand from hearing you and Vera and Uncle Nick talking. But I was wondering, and this is where you're much more likely to be right than I am, Antony, if he presses on beyond the points you've mentioned, how will Mr Hawthorne stand up to it?'

Maitland gave that some consideration. 'Obviously I don't know him well,' he said at last, 'but I know his type, though I'm not saying it's one that covers all men with his sexual preferences. I'd put him down as essentially a weak man, but that isn't to say he won't have a strong sense of self-preservation.'

'Well, we shall just have to wait and see,' said Jenny, unconsciously echoing Stephen's words of the evening before, and not at all reconciled to the situation.

'In any case, if things get to that stage, Wentworth will have to warn him, at which point he may very well scream for a solicitor. We're talking as if the whole thing's a foregone conclusion,' he went on, 'as though we had no doubts at all. But what if I'm wrong?'

'You're not,' said Jenny positively. 'You're only saying that because you don't trust yourself.'

'I'm not infallible, love, and if I've put the poor chap through all this for nothing—'

'You're beginning to have doubts about Peter Dutton again,' she said accusingly.

'No. No, I'm not, or about Wainwright either. But still I've . . . oh, I suppose I've got a sneaking sort of sympathy for Hawthorne if he was caught in the kind of trap we're envisaging.'

'I'd save my sympathy for Dilys and Mabel and Ethel if I were you,' said Jenny, quite forgetting, in her anxiety to calm his fears, the feelings on the subject that she had expressed the day before. But there was really nothing else to be said, they had discussed the subject exhaustively, so they resigned themselves to waiting.

II

In the event it was Stephen who brought the news. 'Inspector Wentworth telephoned me just as I was ready to leave the office,' he said, 'so I thought it would be almost as quick to let you know in person.'

Maitland said nothing but his eyes were fixed thoughtfully on the other man's face. It was Jenny who demanded, 'What did he say?' and Stephen turned to her smiling.

'The message was that he was going home to get his dinner, because thanks to us he'd had no lunch,' he said precisely.

'Don't tell us he's been with Mr Hawthorne all this time?'

'It seems he has, or most of it. And Constable Tankard too, of course, but I don't think *he* feels in a position to complain. The other part of the message was that I can start proceedings immediately to get Peter Dutton released.'

Jenny made no reply to that. 'But what about Hawthorne?' Antony asked, when the silence had lengthened a little.

'He's been arrested,' said Stephen shortly.

'On what grounds?'

'He admitted to all the points we'd made, including your guesses, Antony, and also that he'd known his mother was very near death, I suppose he knew her doctor could confirm that. And late this afternoon, about an hour and a half ago, I think, he confessed to having committed all three murders.'

'Stephen, you're not telling us everything!'

He turned his eyes to Antony for a moment as though asking for understanding. 'No, Jenny, and I don't intend to,' he said. 'Let's just leave it that it was a – painful scene, nothing you'd want to hear about, and leave it at that.'

'Something better left to the imagination, I suppose,' said Jenny. The slight bitterness in her tone was lost on Stephen, but Antony had the grace to look abashed. He had learned painfully, of long experience, that the one thing Jenny hated above all others was to be kept in the dark.

To distract her he said, 'There's one thing you'll have to tell us, Stephen. I think that in each case except Mabel's he'd determined on murder, but any girl would have done.'

'Wentworth didn't mention that point, but it must have been like that. Hawthorne had no way of knowing their movements.'

'That still leaves one question, the one that's been nagging at me from the beginning. Dilys may have met him, but couldn't have known him well. How did he persuade her – a good girl, as everyone's agreed – to go into the wood with him?'

'The inspector must have been curious about that too, because it's one of the questions he was able to answer. Besides being a nice girl Dilys was gullible. I think you mentioned one of the Lewises telling you that. Hawthorne just told her that Peter had taken a stroll under the trees while he was waiting for her and slipped and hurt his leg. He wasn't sure, it might be broken. Almost before he'd finished, she was off into the wood as though the devil was after her.'

'As in a sense I suppose he was,' said Antony. 'Poor silly girl,' he added sadly. And that, come to think of it, was as good an epitaph as any for the three of them.

'We may as well go in and tell Emma then,' said Jenny. The typewriter had ceased its clatter some time since. 'I expect you'll be letting the Duttons know that Peter's all right,' he added.

'I did that before I came here,' Stephen told her. 'Funnily enough they didn't ask me any questions, for which I was grateful. The fact was enough for them.'

There was a silence after Stephen left them but after a while, 'I'll tell Emma if you like,' said Jenny with real nobility.

Antony turned his head then and smiled at her. 'That I should like to hear,' he said. Jenny's explanations were notoriously complicated. 'She'd be very little the wiser when you'd finished.'

'Yes, I know.' Jenny was not noticeably cast down by this criticism, to which she was well accustomed. 'It's just that I thought—'

'I know what you thought, love, but you feel just as deeply about this affair as I do. In any case, there's really very little to tell except the bare facts of Hawthorne's confession, and Emma, bless her, isn't likely to insist on spending the whole evening rehashing the subject.'

In which he was perfectly right. They spent one more day at Burton Cecil, mainly occupied in saying goodbye to their various friends there, and then set off back to Bill Cleveland's farm, which was their base of operations when they were holidaying in that part of the world. It was a fair way round by car, though as Antony pointed out if they weren't burdened with suitcases it would have been very little more than ten miles' walk, southwards across the moors into the next dale.

EPILOGUE

Just before they headed back to town at the end of the long vacation Antony and Jenny paid a flying visit to Farthing Lee. It was late afternoon on the Sunday when they arrived, and as Emma came to the door with her usual warm greetings they were able to see over her shoulder that Caroline, Hugh and Stephen Anstey had already arrived.

'I thought you'd want all the latest news,' said Emma, momentarily darkening Antony's mood, though he couldn't deny there were things he was curious to know. Emma was even more brightly attired than usual today, in a long dress at least ten years out of date which was festooned with flowers of such a gaudy hue as to put nature herself to shame. The shawl with the humming-birds which seemed to be her constant companion both summer and winter, clashed with them horribly, but now that September was drawing to a close there was a little more excuse for her wearing it.

When greetings had been exchanged and they were all settled down, except for Hugh who had taken over his usual role as barman, Stephen looked from Jenny to Antony inquiringly. 'I've got a feeling,' he said, 'that neither of you are too keen on raking up memories.'

Jenny took it upon herself to answer. 'Tell us what happened about the great Burton Cecil riot,' she said, thinking that that at least was a fairly safe topic. 'When we left the police were baffled.'

Stephen grinned. 'Nobody was ever arrested,' he said, 'not

213

even for creating a disturbance, let alone for arson.'

'When Peter Dutton came home and the news of Haw-thorne's arrest got about' – Hugh spoke over his shoulder without turning around – 'there were some shamefaced looks from some of the men, and a rather blustering attitude from others, according to their nature.'

'That doesn't altogether surprise me,' said Maitland rather dryly.

'It was quite natural,' Caroline agreed, 'but it was a long time before the talk died down. Hugh swears he was telling the truth when he said he couldn't identify anyone among the crowd—'

'I was,' Hugh interpolated.

'—but I'm sure he has a pretty good idea who was there.'

'Of course I have, but it isn't evidence,' her husband agreed. 'And I'm afraid you've got to face the fact, Antony, that you've got most of the credit for saving Peter, and for stopping them all from making fools of themselves by lynching Philip Wainwright when they saw him again.'

'But Stephen—'

'It wasn't my fault,' Stephen protested. 'I kept my promise not to say a word to anyone about your part in the business, but you know how it is, once an idea gets about in a place like this there's no stopping it.'

'I'll forgive you,' said Antony, secure in the knowledge that by tomorrow evening he'd be back in London. 'What about your client?'

'Peter? He's got his job back, and Roland is doing his best to keep him amused. He's changed though, more subdued than he used to be. I think it will take him a while to get over Dilys's death.'

'It will pass,' said Antony. 'They used to meet – what was it? – two or three times a week. There hadn't been time for her to become – well, to become a part of him. Do you agree, Emma?'

'Yes, I do,' said Emma, and Antony was suddenly convinced that she was looking at something long past. 'In some ways it's dreadful to be young,' she went on, 'but in time ... I don't

214

suppose he'll forget, but to use Stephen's phrase, he will get over it.'

'Did Wainwright come back to the village after all?'

'He certainly did. He's staying at the Ings with Sarah Benson. He asked me to suggest somewhere suitable so I put him on to Caroline for advice.'

'Sarah doesn't usually let rooms,' Caroline said, 'but I know she was glad of the money. He told me he wanted to oversee the rebuilding of Lane's End, which seems a good idea.'

'And Maisie Jerrold is happy too because he's been to see her to ask her advice about the garden,' said Emma. 'Of course, nothing can be done until the builders go, but it seems he wants to put it back into order and you know what she is about flowers.'

'That isn't the best of the story,' said Hugh. He had finished his task by now and joined the rest of them. 'Two nights ago he turned up at the Mortal Man! Caroline was showing some chap the Hawthornes' house, so Stephen and I had gone in for a quick one.'

'What on earth happened?' Antony asked.

'Nothing very spectacular,' Hugh told him. 'There was a moment of stunned silence and then a positive clamour of voices demanding to be allowed to buy him a drink. Which gave the game away pretty thoroughly if any of them had stopped to think about it, but Wainwright merely smiled and accepted a glass of bitter from the man nearest him.'

'After that everything returned to normal,' said Stephen. 'I think he'd been rather clever in allowing just the right amount of time to elapse before putting in an appearance ... not too little, not too much.'

'That sounds as if he's decided to join the community,' said Antony. 'He'll need friends.'

'No difficulty about that, he seems a nice enough chap,' said Hugh. 'Caroline asked him to dinner when he first moved in. He declined then politely enough, but now she's renewed the invitation and he's accepted it. And as Emma says, Mrs Jerrold seems inclined to approve of him. He's even tidied up his appearance, by the way, and bought some clothes more suitable for country wear.' He subjected Antony for a moment to rather a close scrutiny. 'I don't think you need worry about him,' he added.

'I don't. Why should I?' said Maitland rather quickly.

'I haven't the faintest idea,' said Hugh blandly. 'Because it's your nature, I suppose. And to finish the story, after which the whole subject can be swept under the carpet, I understand from Stephen that Samuel Hawthorne is still undergoing psychiatric tests.'

'From what I hear he's more or less gone to pieces,' said Stephen. 'It seems very doubtful that he'll be found fit to plead. And that's enough of that, except that Caroline tells us she asked Wainwright whether the insurance money had come through and he said, "Handsomely". It seems to me that that, perhaps, is the most extraordinary thing about the whole affair.'

'I've been wondering, Emma,' said Jenny, picking up her cue, 'how you got on with your story. You said you were in difficulties when we left.'

'I had allowed myself to be distracted by events,' said Emma, rather grandly.

'Well, I've been thinking about it,' said Caroline, 'and I've got it all worked out. May I tell you?'

'Of course, my dear,' said Emma, who had a very soft spot for her niece by marriage. Fortunately she never minded teasing about her own work, and at the back of her mind there was a vague hope that some day Caroline – who had been a journalist before she married – might do something in that line herself.

'We'd got to the place where Mr Maltravers said he knew who the murderer was. No, not you, Emma, this was our story when Antony and Jenny were here before and you all came to Burton Crook. After that the whole cast of characters would assemble, white-faced in the great hall.'

'Remind us, Caroline, who was there,' Stephen prompted.

'Well, Mr Maltravers of course, and the man Emma was having such trouble with because he sometimes seemed about to speak but actually never did so.'

'And the other character who was worrying Emma,' said Antony, entering into the spirit of the thing. 'That fair-haired girl, who screamed now only occasionally.'

'That's right,' said Caroline, 'I was coming to her. Then there was Parker, the butler, an oddly dignified figure; Sir Jasper himself; the knife and boot boy ... I'm sure he comes into the story somewhere, Emma; and, of course, the cook.'

'A stout woman called Perkins,' Emma agreed. 'But she isn't actually present at the *dénouement*.'

'That can't be all,' Antony protested, 'not in a place like Hanging Bailey.'

'It's enough for my scenario,' said Caroline firmly.

'You're forgetting the sleek brown and white cow called Blossom, and three pigs who had missed their way and were sitting in a dark corner wondering where their supper was,' Antony told her.

'I'll go along with the pigs if you like,' said Caroline, 'but I think the cow is going a bit too far. Shall I go on?'

'Of course you must,' said Hugh, 'after arousing our curiosity like this. Maltravers looked round the circle of anxious faces – if I know pigs they were looking anxious too – and began to speak.'

'I wrote the rest of it down,' said Caroline, picking up her handbag and beginning to rummage in it. 'Because it's the answer to the whole mystery and therefore important and I didn't want to forget anything.'

'Go ahead,' Stephen urged her. 'I'm sure Emma will be grateful to you.'

'I wonder,' said Caroline, smiling affectionately at her hostess. 'However, here goes. "In a case like this," said Maltravers, "there are many factors to take into consideration. The latest occupant of the library I am told, is unknown to all of you, so I can only conclude that he is the long lost heir. This

217

brings each one of you into the list of suspects." '

'You're wrong Caroline,' said Antony suddenly, 'you should have let me keep the cow. You could then have put in parenthesis, "He encountered the cow's eye and added, 'Except you, Madam,' with a courteous bow in her direction."'

Caroline ignored this. ' "Brings each one of you into the list of suspects," ' she repeated. ' "Sir Jasper as a usurper; you" – did you tell me once that the strong silent man was called Durant, Emma? – "because you knew the dead man abroad and left him to die in a camp on the shores of the Amazon." For a moment the man addressed seemed about to speak but nothing came of it. Maltravers went on remorselessly, "This innocent-looking girl because she planned on becoming the mistress of Hanging Bailey; Mrs Perkins, with whose affections the dead man trifled years ago before he left England; even this boy," he added, eyeing the knife and boot boy with distaste, "the fruit – I must assume – of their intrigue." '

'That's all very fine,' said Hugh, 'but how did he decide which one of them was guilty?'

Caroline read again: ' "If you'll pardon me for saying so, sir," said Mrs Perkins, "the heir left home these twenty years ago; and young Bert here he's nobbut fourteen." "Exactly," said Maltravers, unable to hide the triumph in his tone, "that proves it. The guilty party was Parker the butler." And as they turned to look in perplexity and horror the fact of his guilt was clearly written on the manservant's distorted face. "You fiend!" he cried, "I was the heir, not he!" And with a last maniacal laugh he plunged through the window behind him.'

Antony couldn't resist it. ' "A pity perhaps," said Maltravers reflectively, "that it was a ground-floor window." '

'What do you think, Emma?' asked Caroline. 'Doesn't that solve all your problems?'

Emma smiled back at her. 'I'm sorry to disappoint you, my dear, a fortnight, even a week ago, I might have found some suggestions there, but I finished the story on Friday.' There was a chorus of congratulations. 'So I was able to devote yesterday and part of this afternoon, to concocting something special for dinner in Jenny and Antony's honour.'

'That's all very well,' said Antony, 'what about the girl who was being such a nuisance? Maltravers had fallen for her, and you said you couldn't persuade him out of it.'

'I couldn't. And I know I rejected the suggestion when it was made at the time,' said Emma, 'but I decided to make her the villain. Or should I say villainess? Anyway, that means Maltravers will go into the next story with a broken heart, which I can exploit to make him more interesting. Besides, it gives him a reason for going abroad again, and I cannot, I really cannot, struggle any longer with the prosaicness of life in England.'

Antony exchanged a rather awed look with the rest of his fellow guests. 'In view of everything,' he said, 'I call that pretty rich!'

Only one further reference was made to what had happened in Burton Cecil a month ago, and that only indirectly. The party from Burton Crook had left, but Emma and Jenny and Antony were sitting round what Emma said was the first fire of the season, unwilling to bring their evening to a close because the Maitlands would have to make an early start next morning. 'Caroline thinks she's sold Samuel Hawthorne's house,' said Emma.

'That's going to be good practice for Stephen, isn't it?' Antony commented. 'If he's employed in the matter, of course. I mean,' he added, seeing Emma's puzzled look, 'arranging the completion when the vendor's in prison.' To Jenny's relief the reminder of the part he had played in Hawthorne's downfall seemed to be weighing less on his mind now, perhaps because it was accompanied by the realisation that Peter Dutton's future was secure and that Philip Wainwright was in a fair way to leading a normal life again.

'I hadn't thought of that,' said Emma.

'I should have thought that whoever's considering buying might rather have had the house next door,' said Jenny.

'Apparently they're quite different in design and he preferred the one the Hawthornes had bought.'

'Isn't he superstitious?'

'If you mean that poor Mabel's ghost might be still hanging about, she wasn't killed in the cottage, you know.'

'Of course I know,' said Jenny. 'I just thought—'

'If anyone's ghost is haunting the place I imagine it would be Samuel's,' said Antony.

'Perhaps,' said Emma doubtfully. 'But that wouldn't be a proper ghost.'

'I'm sorry if it wouldn't meet your standards,' Antony apologised. 'All the same you didn't really answer Jenny's question.'

'Whether the prospective purchaser is superstitious? I suppose I don't really know the answer to that, but Caroline said he's a writer and she got the impression that if he met a ghost he'd ask it to have a drink and proceed to question it within an inch of its life. Of course that isn't really an appropriate thing to say about a disembodied spirit,' she added thoughtfully, 'but from what Caroline said it seems to have been his attitude.'

'I'd rather him than me,' said Jenny with a slight shudder.

'Oh no, my dear, I don't agree with you at all,' Emma insisted. 'Empty houses are a far worse reminder of unpleasant things than occupied ones. Where are you going, Antony?'

'No further than the desk,' he assured her. 'I was going to freshen our drinks. We've known you long enough now, Emma, to poke your fire if we want to, so I don't see why the same thing shouldn't apply to liquid refreshment.'

'Of course not, you know I've always told you to make yourselves at home,' said Emma.

'I want to give you a toast,' said Antony, when he had finished and replaced the decanter on the tray. He came back to the fireplace and picked up his glass but remained on his feet. 'To you, dear Emma, and Maltravers,' he said, 'and may his

220

broken heart inspire him to even greater deeds of valour in the future. And if you'll forgive me for introducing a more sombre note, to Burton Cecil, and may there be no further murders here for at least another two hundred years.'